DANGEROUS PASSAGE

Shadow was standing on the perching wall with no safety belt visible, keeping his balance by leaning a hand against the silver eagle's wing. He looked tiny in comparison; she towered over him. But he was showing no sign of fear, in spite of the terrible danger of his position.

Even if the bird did not bite his head off, she could topple him off that high wall with the slightest movement.

Then the duke moved as fast as an eagle. His bow was drawn and the feather at his eye before anyone knew what was happening.

But Shadow had moved also. He spun around and leaped out into space and was gone as the arrow passed where he had been.

Women and men screamed.

By Dave Duncan
Published by Ballantine Books:

A ROSE-RED CITY

SHADOW

SHADOW

DAVE DUNCAN

A Del Rey Book

BALLANTINE BOOKS • NEW YORK

A Del Rey Book
Published by Ballantine Books

Copyright © 1987 by David J. Duncan

Library of Congress Catalog Card Number: 87-91478

ISBN 0-345-34274-7

Manufactured in the United States of America

First Edition: November 1987

Cover Art by Darrell K. Sweet

For NICK
who liked it best

TABLE OF CONTENTS

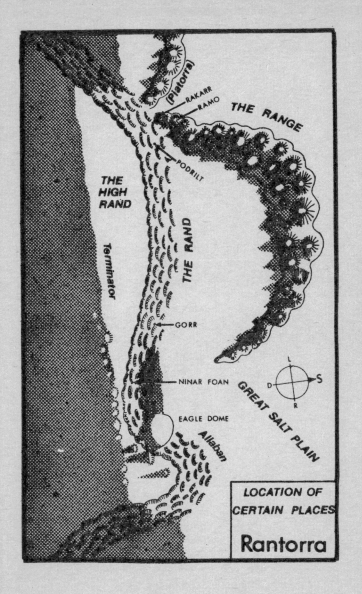

(Piatorra)

RAKARR
RAMO

THE RANGE

THE
HIGH
RAND

PODRILT

THE RAND

Terminator

GORR

NINAR FOAN

EAGLE DOME

Allaban

GREAT SALT PLAIN

L
D — S
R

LOCATION OF
CERTAIN PLACES

Rantorra

PART ONE

CRIME

1

> "He who ever trusts a bird,
> Never speaks another word."
> —*Skyman proverb*

SALD HARL was running, running as hard as he had ever run in his life. He clutched a bulky bundle in both arms and pounded along the ornate pavement with the low sun at his back. His long, spindly shadow jigged endlessly before him, running just as hard as he.

Running in the palace grounds was forbidden. Wearing a flying suit in the palace grounds was forbidden also, but he had already broken so many regulations that a few more would not matter, and if he was going to be late for a royal summons, then perhaps nothing would matter much anymore.

If he twisted an ankle . . . The roadway was paved in squares of white alabaster and black basalt, but generations of feet and hooves had worn the softer alabaster into toe-catching hollows, and the carriages and landaus jolting past him set up a continuous clamorous rattle over them.

He had no time to admire the sculptures ornamenting the marble balustrades which flanked the avenue or the swans swimming on their reflections in the ornamental lake on his right. To his left the gilded pheasants strutted unseen on silk-smooth grass amid the blazons of the rose garden. Sald had not visited the palace since he was a child. Contrary to his expectations, it did not seem

3

smaller than he remembered; it seemed much, much larger, and he was very, very late.

Splendid ladies and elegant gentlemen strolled along, pouting in haughty disapproval, as he zigzagged between them, dodged the wheeled traffic, and ran, ran, ran...

A flying suit was not designed for running. It was a great garment for keeping off the cold at the top of a thermal, up in the nose-bleeding roof of the sky. Down in the murderous heat of the rice level, swooping above taro fields or date palms, he could unfasten it down to his crotch, but not here, and it was cooking him.

Then he caught his toe against one of the basalt edges and fell flat on his face.

The bundle cushioned his fall, except for his elbows. He winced, took a couple of deep breaths, started to rise, and then saw that he was lying before a pair of very shiny boots. Military boots. His eyes flicked from side to side, and he saw more boots. He scrambled to his feet and saluted.

Oh, God! Of all the officers in the entire Royal Guard, this one had to be Colonel Lord Pontly, Commandant of Training School—Pork Eyes himself.

Sald Harl was much better at making friends than enemies. There were not many people in the world who disliked him and few whom he disliked, but Lord Pontly qualified on both counts. On the occasion of Sald's class graduation, for example, there had been the episode of the pig in the bed...

Colonel Lord Pontly was a short man, no taller than Sald himself, but twice the width and thrice the depth. His uniform gleamed and sparkled impeccably, and his puffy face bore a very thin mustache, capable of registering extreme disapproval at times. This was one of those times.

"Harl?" he murmured. "Harl, isn't it?"

"Sir!"

"And an ensign now, I see? When did that accident occur?"

"About a hectoday ago, my lord," Sald said between puffs. He blinked as sweat trickled into his eyes.

"I think we can correct the error." Lord Pontly glanced at the commander beside him, who smiled obediently.

"Disorderly conduct, my lord," he said. "Improper dress."

"Oh, surely we can find a few more atrocities?" his lordship muttered. "Stealing washing, from the look of it. What exactly are you carrying, Ensign?"

Sald was trembling with the effort of standing still when every nerve was screaming frantically at him to hurry.

"Court dress, my lord."

Pontly's eyebrows were as linear as his mustache, and they rose in graceful astonishment. "Whose court dress?"

"Mine, sir."

The colonel looked at the commander, and the surrounding troopers looked at one another.

"And why would you be needing court dress, Ensign?"

"Sir, I am summoned to the Investiture," Sald said, trying not to moan the words.

Pontly's globular face flushed slightly. "If I recall correctly, Ensign, you are not of noble birth?"

"Sir, my father is a baronet."

Sald could sense their disbelief. A commoner never received a royal summons. He groped in his pocket and produced the royal writ. He tried desperately not to fidget as Pontly read it through from start to finish.

Pontly turned very red. "You are going to be late, Ensign!"

"Sir, that was why I was running."

Pork Eyes went redder still. Running within the palace grounds was a trivial indiscretion compared to insulting the king. "You will disgrace the entire Guard! Explain!"

Sald gulped. "The courier sought me at my posting—at Jaur, my lord. I was on furlough at my parents' house, Hiando Keep. I did not receive the writ until yesterday."

At that news, colonel and commander exchanged

thoughtful glances. There was little love misplaced between the royal couriers and the Guard. Sald could see
the temptation fermenting in their minds. If Ensign Harl
was late for the start of the Investiture, then he would
not be admitted at all. There would be a court-martial.
The fault could be laid to the courier.

That would not save Ensign Harl, of course—nothing
would—but it might muddy the royal couriers a trifle.

"Hiando Keep is on Rakarr, is it not?" the commander said. "Eight hours' flight from Rakarr to Ramo,
more or less?"

"What time exactly yesterday did the courier arrive?"
Pontly demanded, a predatory expression on his rotund
face.

"Just before two bells, my lord," Sald said. *Get on
with it!* For a moment he considered an appeal to Pork
Eyes's better nature: Let Sald go about his business now
and report back to him later. But he knew it would not
work. The sun would move first.

Pontly frowned. "And when did you leave Rakarr
Peak?"

Sald could lie, of course, but if there was going to be a
trial, then there would be witnesses called. "A little after
three bells, my lord."

Pork Eyes's eyes widened; the charge sheet was filling up. Sald had flown from Rakarr to Ramo faster than
even the couriers did, perhaps faster than it had ever
been done, but time like that could be made only by
detouring out over the plains, riding the giant thermals of
the desert, risking immense changes in altitude, which
could bring on sky sickness, crippling or even killing.
The desert was very much against Guard regulations.
The desert was death.

"Six hours?" the commander muttered. The surrounding troopers were pursing lips and exchanging
looks.

"Well?" Pontly barked. "Why did you delay so long
after you received the writ?"

"Court dress, my lord," Sald said desperately. He
tried to explain quickly that he did not own court dress.

Only the nobility ever needed it. Boots, hose, breeches, doublet, cloak, plumed hat—some of those he had scrounged from neighbors in a hasty flight around the local manors and castles, and the rest his father had rummaged out of the attics. But the coat of arms—his mother and sisters had worked all through third watch, while the rest of the world was abed, sewing, embroidering, cutting, and stitching.

"Why would His Majesty summon a—a mere ensign in the Guard to an Investiture?" the commander asked softly.

That was a very good question, and Sald would dearly have loved to know the answer. He could not expect an honor or a title or an award, certainly; therefore he must have been called for an appointment of some sort. The courier had told Sald all he knew. The Investiture had been a surprise to the whole court, but Prince Shadow was dead, killed by a wild in the line of duty. His most probable replacement was Count Moarien. That would leave a vacancy in the king's bodyguard...and so on. Obviously the required shuffle had turned out to be large enough to justify a General Investiture, and when everyone had rolled one place up the bed, there was going to be a gap at the bottom, some very humble slot into which Ensign Sald Harl would apparently fit. Assistant Bearer of the Royal Chamber Pot, perhaps?

Pontly looked at the commander. The commander looked at Pontly.

"I think he might just make it, my lord, on wheels."

His lordship's mustache curled in anger. Reluctantly he nodded: His prey was going to escape him. The couriers were evidently not at fault, and if there was a court-martial, then he might be asked why he had delayed the accused.

"Get him there!" he barked.

The next passing landau was halted, and its protesting occupant summarily evicted. Sald Harl went roaring off along the avenue, wheels drumming on the paving, hooves clattering, coachman's whip snapping, and pedestrians bounding to safety. Sald leaned back, clutching his bouncing bundle, sweat still running down his ribs. He looked at the commander, who had boarded beside him.

"Thank you, sir," he said.

He knew the commander also. An elderly man, close to retirement, he lectured on pathfinding in Training School; Sald had flown with him a few times. He was studying Sald now with a quizzical expression. "How many hops?" he demanded.

"About twelve, sir," Sald said uneasily.

"And who chose the thermals—you or your mount?"

"I did, sir."

The commander hung on tight as the landau went around a corner. He looked thoroughly disbelieving. "Six hours from Rakarr?"

Sald hoped that his face was already red enough that a blush would not show. "Er . . . I did let him give me a few hints, sir."

The commander shook his head angrily. "I warned you about that a dozen times, Harl! And just because he didn't kill you this time, don't think he won't try in future!" He scowled. Then he smiled admiringly. "Six hours, huh?"

"More or less, sir," Sald said.

It had been much closer to five.

He made it with minutes to spare, reeling into the robing room with his bundle, heart thundering and the inside of his head hammering like a smithy.

The room was packed with nobility being groomed and preened in front of mirrors by teams of valets. The only space he could find was next to an elderly and obese duke, whose cloak was being arranged by his attendant as though it were a priceless and timeless masterpiece of sculpture. Sald started to strip, ignoring both amusement and disapproval among the onlookers. Full court dress was not designed to be put on without assistance; tight hose would not pull over sweaty legs. He grabbed a passing page, a spotty youth a full head taller than himself, and ordered him to fasten the buttons on the back of his coat.

Then he crumpled his flying suit into a bundle and stuffed it behind the mirror and looked at himself.

It was even worse than he had imagined, from antique boots and wrinkled hose all the way up to tousled curls and a hat which fortunately he need only carry, as it fell over his ears if he tried to wear it. And the coat of arms —not all the red in his face was from hurry. The workmanship would probably pass, but the heraldry it displayed was ludicrous in this company: He had only two quarterings. The fat duke next to him had at least thirty, his coat a kaleidoscope of minute armorial symbols, an ancestry stretching from the Holy Ark itself.

Two quarterings! He was a molehill among mountains. His left side was just passable, four quarterings. His mother had once been a lady-in-waiting to the queen herself, qualified by that breeding, but on the right, his father's side, there were only two. Sald Harl was privately convinced that this whole horrible experience must be the result of some error by a palace scribe who had somehow put the wrong name on the writ. Even Lady Harl had admitted that she had never heard of a man with only two quarterings being presented at a formal court function.

He was apparently the youngest man summoned to the dubbings, which could be a source of pride if the summons were not an error. He was also the shortest, which was equally gratifying. But he was by far the most lowly.

Mirrors did not normally bother him. He was young, slim, and fit—and short. But what he could see in this mirror was going to create a scandal if it were allowed into the Great Courtyard. He had not even thought to bring a comb.

The valet beside him had a portable table littered with all sorts of equipment, including at least three combs. Sald braced himself to address a senior peer, and at that moment the duke decided that he was perfect. He turned from the mirror in Sald's direction, and Sald bowed.

It was as if he were not there. The noble eyes passed right through him as their owner continued his turn and then moved off toward the center of the room. The mirror showed Sald's face turning even more furiously red than before.

The valet was an elderly, wasted, and elongated man, but he had noticed. Watery old eyes gleaming with amusement, he produced a damp cloth and silently wiped the goggle marks from Sald's face; Sald had not seen those. Then he splashed some liquid into his hands and applied it to Sald's hair, briskly and efficiently.

A door opened, and the noisy hubbub died a lingering death. Out of the corner of his eye Sald saw that Feather King of Arms had entered with followers. God! They were ready, then. The valet started doing hasty things with a comb—evidently this ramshackle young trooper was an interesting challenge for him.

And all this for what? Ever since the courier had burst in on the Harls' dinner, Sald had wrestled with that problem, and he kept coming back to the same answer: He was about to be named equerry to some snot-nosed juvenile aristocrat, some duke's grandson who fancied himself as a skyman and wanted a private instructor on hand. Yes, my lord, no, my lord, may I kiss your arm, my lord. Royal appointments could not be refused.

Yet such a trivial indenture would normally rate only a line in the court gazette, not a dubbing at a General Investiture. It just did not make sense!

King of Arms was lining them up by rank.

The valet was struggling with the coat, pursing his lips and still not saying a word. Then he stepped back, his face inscrutable. Sald opened his mouth to speak, but stopped when he heard his own name spoken.

"Ensign Harl?" It was Feather King of Arms, supreme heraldic officer of Rantorra; with parchment face and glacier eyebrows, he was stooped and ancient and dignified as death itself. His livery outshone anything else in the room.

Sald bowed and received a barely visible nod.

King of Arms swept his eye over that despicable coat.

He could have recited every family represented after that glance, minor though they all were.

"Five, four, three, king, queen, prince, king again, one more; the reverse on the way out?" King of Arms said quietly.

"Certainly!" Sald was not that ignorant.

King of Arms motioned his monumental head toward the end of the line of nobles and was about to vanish into the crowd.

"A question, my lord," Sald said brashly, this man being a relatively safe target for his bitterness. "There has not, perhaps, been an error?"

The faded old eyes flamed. "Did you say *error*, Ensign?"

"Yes!" Sald snapped. "I always understood that presentation at court was reserved to persons of higher lineage than mine."

"So did I," King of Arms said icily, and walked away.

The valet had started to tidy his equipment. Sald reached for his money pouch, but of course it was in his flying suit, behind the mirror. "You have been most kind," he stuttered.

"It was an honor, Ensign," the old man said, beaming down at him.

The line had started to move. "No, it was a kindness," Sald insisted. "Hardly an honor, after a duke."

The valet's smile became cryptic. "An honor to help those who serve our beloved sovereign and his family."

With his mouth still open, Sald dashed to take his place at the end of the fast-vanishing line. What had that meant? His mother, he recalled, always said that the servants knew more than anyone else in the court.

He stepped out into sunlight—and the vastness of the Great Courtyard. Trumpets blared barbarically. Finely groomed ladies and elegant gentlemen, the high nobility of the realm, the elite of Rantorra glittering in splendor, rose with a hiss of silk and brocade as the noble appointees came into their midst. A matching line of ladies emerged to join the men, and together they paraded

down a center aisle toward the distant and empty
thrones.

All around the high walls, on tiered balconies, the
lesser nobility and some of the commonality stood in silence to study their betters. Even men with less than two
quarterings, perhaps.

There were more men than women in the procession,
so only the men near the front had partners. At the end
of the line came Ensign Harl: youngest, shortest, lone-
liest.

When the fat duke reached the open space before the
thrones, he stopped. The next man moved to his right,
and the next to his. When Sald arrived, he paraded along
the whole line of highborn hindquarters and found barely
space to squeeze between the last man and the wall,
turning to face the dais and the thrones. The fabrics
whispered again as the audience sat down.

The thrones faced the assembly and also faced sunward. High above, on top of the wall, a fixed mirror
jutted out at an angle so that the rays of the unchanging
sun were reflected downward and the thrones glowed,
brilliant in the shady courtyard.

There were a few minutes of expectant silence.

Unnoted in his edge position, Sald gaped around like
the hick country boy he was. The Great Courtyard was
the largest enclosed space he had ever seen. High above,
slowly circling in the azure sky, were four—no, six—
guards. What happened, he wondered, to a trooper
whose bird crapped on the court? A posting to the hot
pole to make ice cream, perhaps?

Far beyond the courtyard wall he could see the distant craggy top of Ramo Peak, but it could not compare
with the view he had had from the desert, a view few
men had ever seen: the Range in all its splendor. Even
his home peak of Rakarr he had never seen so well, set
off by the hazy backdrop of the Rand itself, a crumbled
rampart rising miles above the plain, glowing bright
against the midnight blue of the sky over Darkside, itself
glittering with the distant reflection of ice. But Rakarr
was a tiny peak, barely high enough to catch rain, and

hence poor for cultivation. Ramo Peak, as he had seen it from the desert, had been breathtaking—its immense vertical extent from airless, waterless rocky uplands, faint and remote, down through pastures and then all the crop levels, barley and wheat and the others, to the lowest habitable, rice; and below that the useless jungle, and then the barren foothills clothed in the dense and poisonous "red air" of the desert and the crucible plains.

The congregation rose again.

The royal fanfare was played.

The entourage entered: guards and priests and court functionaries.

The king and queen followed.

It had been a long time since Sald had been close to the king, but he could see little change. The famous flaxen hair might be turning to silver in parts, but when the king stepped into the carpet of sunlight around the thrones, his hair blazed as brightly as the gold circlet it bore. The fair-skinned face was the same, the darting, penetrating eyes. Diamond decorations sparkled on his royal-blue court dress. No quarterings there; the front of his coat bore the eagle symbol only. Aurolron XX, King of Rantorra, tiny and immensely regal.

But Queen Mayala! Sald was stunned. Where now was the legendary beauty which had once been the toast of the kingdom? Like a woodland sprite, Mayala had floated on the edges of his childhood, a fairy-tale queen with trailing honey hair and a smile for which men would cheerfully have died. She floated no more; eyes downcast, hunched, shrunken inside her royal-blue gown, no taller than the king himself, servile even, she shuffled along beside him. Her hair looked dyed, her face waxen. If this was the best they could do with her for an Investiture, how did she look in private? He had heard no rumors.

Side by side, the royal couple advanced toward the thrones. Immediately behind the king walked King Shadow, wearing identical clothes—minus decorations, plus a black baldric—a portly yet a somber man.

Then came Crown Prince Vindax.

He had not changed—the jet hair, the beak nose, the easy athlete's walk were just as Sald remembered. His eyebrows had grown perhaps even bushier. No quarterings for him, either—he wore sky-blue and the talon symbol of the heir apparent. Prince Shadow was dead, so Vindax's brother, Jarkadon, walked directly behind him, filling the post until Count Moarien's appointment became official. The king and queen settled on the thrones, and Vindax took his place at his father's side, Jarkadon still at his back. The senior officials moved smoothly to their appointed places.

Vindax's eyes scanned along the waiting line of hopefuls and found Sald. There was no change of expression, but the royal eyes noted the shabby boots, the baggy hose, the despicable coat. Then the study ended, and Vindax looked away.

But his interest had been observed, and necks craned to see who had been so honored.

There, thought Sald, was his problem. His mother had been a lady-in-waiting. As a child he had attended the palace school, and he was the same age as Vindax— few ensigns in the Guard had ever been on first-name terms with the crown prince. Later they had met again, when Vindax was learning flying from the Guard trainers. So when some young courtier had mentioned that he wanted an equerry who was a good skyman, the prince himself would have graciously mentioned the name of Harl. Amusing type, knows his manners, clean about the house . . .

The anthem was played, then the archbishop prayed, inaudibly to mortal ears.

Vindax looked no more at Sald, but Sald studied him. The prince was amazingly unlike the rest of his family. Could flax and honey produce jet? Certainly that thought must have been mulled over a million times by thousands of people since the prince's birth, but to speak even a hint of it would be treason. Jarkadon, by contrast, looked more like the king than the king did.

The lord chancellor read the proclamation, finally bidding all those etcetera draw nigh. Nobody moved.

A herald removed the scroll from the chancellor's hand and substituted another.

"... know therefore that it is our pleasure ..."

There must be forty dubbings to come. Three or four minutes had to be allowed for each to be called, to advance, to receive a few gracious words from the monarch ... it was going to be a long time until they got to Sald Harl.

And the chancellor reached the end of the first citation:

"... our right trusty Sald Harl, Esquire, ensign in our Royal Guard."

It was like hitting a sudden downdraft. He hardly registered the shocked bubbling of the court around him.

First? He had been planning to watch the others.

His feet moved by themselves, and he floated balloonlike above them, along the line to the center. Turn. Bow. Five paces. Bow. Four paces—make them longer. Bow again. He was within the hot circle of sunlight ...

Shadow? Had that proclamation said "Shadow"?

Oh, Great God Who Guided the Ark!

Bow to king, queen, prince, king again. Take one step. Then he stood at the edge of the dais, white-faced and sick to the roots of his soul.

Aurolron XX rose and paced forward, King Shadow at his back.

The penetrative power of the royal gaze was legendary. It was said that no man in the kingdom could face it. But that was not true when the kingdom had just crumbled into rubble and buried you up to your ears, when every muscle had frozen with shock. The twin sapphire flames burned above Sald, and he stared back into them with no trouble at all—an easy feat for one whose life had been totally ruined without warning. Chosen career, skymanship, private life, family, friendships—all had been snatched away in an instant.

For a lifetime the blue eyes and the black stayed locked, and the king's eyebrows rose in mild amusement.

"And how is NailBiter?" the king asked softly.

"Well, Your Majesty." They had researched him, of
course.

The royal brows frowned at the brevity. "Out of
DeathBeak by SkyHammer." The king's interest in his
bloodstock was famous, and his knowledge encyclope-
dic. "We had great hopes of that pairing—yet there has
been but one chick, and it seems that only one man in
our entire Guard is capable of handling him."

Five minutes ago, that royal compliment would have
sent Sald Harl into delirium.

"An exaggeration, Majesty. And I am teaching him
better manners."

The long eye contact ended as the king blinked. He
almost seemed to smile. He spoke even more softly.
"Perhaps you can do the same for our son?" But no answer was expected to that.

The king raised his hand, and a page paced forward
with a black baldric on a scarlet cushion. Sald's knees
found the edge of the dais. The king laid the baldric in
silence over Sald's head and across his chest—and by
that royal act turned a man into a shadow.

Sald rose. He moved one pace back and was about to
bow—

No! Up from his childhood, from classes in protocol
in the palace school, seeped a long-forgotten maxim:
Shadow bows to no one. He froze.

Should he play it safe and begin his new job with a
major display of ignorance before the entire court?
Never! But if he was wrong, then he would be guilty of
lese majesty at the very least. He looked to King
Shadow and got the merest hint of a head shake.

So the commoner awarded the king a barely perceptible nod, the sort of nod a fat duke might so easily have
given an ensign, and moved one pace to the side. Appointments took effect immediately. He looked to Vindax, and this time the signal was positive. Certain he was
dreaming, he stepped up on the royal dais and walked
toward the two princes. Jarkadon backed away for him,
smiling sardonically.

Sald moved into place behind Vindax: his place now.

The place from which nothing must remove him, save only death.

There were more appointments, honors and decorations and awards. The peacocks and the butterflies strutted and fluttered in the sunlight, but Sald saw almost none of it. Only once did he take notice, when his fat neighbor from the antechamber waddled forward to be inducted into the Order of the Golden Feather: His Grace, the duke of Aginna. It was a travesty! That great slob could not have ridden a bird in his life.

He thought of the news arriving at Hiando Keep. His father would swell with pride. His mother would be horror-struck, his sisters full of tears.

The court whirled in iridescent grandeur.

The end came. The royal party withdrew—and the fifth person in that party was Sald Harl.

No, it was Shadow. Prince Shadow, if he need be distinguished from King Shadow, but normally just Shadow.

He must adjust to life without a name.

The procession proceeded along corridors. Without warning, Vindax turned to a door, but Sald had been expecting that and did not miss a step. As he pushed the door shut behind them, he noted crystal and silver on carved sideboards, and one small window; this must be some sort of pantry. A cowering little man was waiting.

Vindax walked to the nearest wall and then swung around, black eyes glinting with amusement. "Welcome, Shadow!" he said.

"Highness..."

The prince's eyes said that he had made an error.

"I don't know this stuff!" Sald said angrily.

"Then you've forgotten it! Shadow is never presented, so you know nobody. Rank only, rarely title. Never formal address—not even names unless you must."

"Thank you, *Prince*."

Vindax raised a cynical eyebrow. "It isn't quite that bad."

Sald knew that his resentment was obvious, that he

was therefore showing ingratitude, and that he was being mocked because of it. He liked to remember Vindax as a childhood friend, back when they had both been too small to appreciate the chasm between a baronet's heir and a king's. He tried not to remember the adolescent Vindax of flying classes, when a commoner struggling to get by on ability alone must never upstage the heir apparent.

"Why me?" he demanded.

The prince shook his head and leaned back against the wall. Except in the security of the royal apartments he must always have a wall behind him—or Shadow. "Strip," he said. "We haven't much time."

The timid little man was fussing with clothes. Sald reached up to remove the damnable black baldric.

"We're the same size, more or less," Vindax said. "You'll wear my second best until we get some for you."

Cloak and coat . . . Shadow would wear the same garb as the prince, except for the decorations. He would taste his food, possibly sleep in the same room.

"But why me, Prince?"

"Many reasons, for many people. My father, for example?"

He hadn't changed a fraction—he was still all arrogance, mockery, charm. And wits.

The breeches went next, and the valet had produced underwear, to show that this was to be no half effort. Sald must start matching wits again. It had never been easy. "You would tell the king that I am nothing, so I am your creation and owe everything to you. You alone have my loyalty."

He had scored. "Close."

"You would have told the queen that I am an expert skyman."

The prince smiled. "Right reasons, wrong parents. Chief of protocol?"

"You told him that the appointment of a nobody would not disturb the balance of court factions." Obviously he was right again. "And the truth?"

"You're the best man, of course."

Sald could not believe that. "I heard Count Moarien—"

"Moarien sniffs. Sniff, sniff, all day long. Probably snores."

He was being mocked again.

The new breeches were silk, the softest material he had ever handled. "Many don't sniff. Why me?"

The dark eyes studied him carefully. "You're my second Shadow. You heard what happened to the first?"

"A wild struck him."

"It wasn't a wild. Idiot Farin Donnim had been feeding his bird batmeat. He lost control. It took Shadow in an instant."

Half into a coat which proclaimed him to be crown prince of Rantorra, Sald paused. "What happened to Donnim?"

"Nothing—his uncle's a duke. But you do it to me and they'll cut you into meatballs with blunt scissors."

NailBiter must learn his manners quickly, then. Every time he flew now, he would have a prince stretched out under his beak, a tempting royal breakfast within easy reach of a quick strike.

But they would take NailBiter from him. How much flying did Vindax do, anyway? A few state visits here and there, a bit of hunting. Sald Harl's sky days were apparently over.

The valet adjusted the black baldric with care.

Vindax was still studying him with sardonic amusement. "My father's on his fifth Shadow. One tried breathing through a hole in his back, the second was heard to remark that the soup tasted bitter, and two were mistaken for rabbits."

"You're trying to scare me."

"I want you scared." Vindax lacked the king's penetrating gaze; his eyes were a blunt instrument.

The valet bundled up the discarded clothes as though planning to burn them. He probably was. The trooper flying suit was back in the anteroom—it didn't matter. Sald's money was still in the pockets, his keys . . . None

of those mattered. His two quarterings did not matter.
He had no name and no rank.

The valet bowed and vanished, never having said a
word. Vindax straightened up.

"My duties?" Sald asked.

Vindax looked at him with fake astonishment. "My
life, of course. At the cost of your own, if necessary."

"I know that bit," Sald said.

The prince shrugged. "You are seen and silent, that's
all."

"Do I have any authority?"

Vindax smiled faintly. "Normally, no. But in any affair which pertains to my safety, you are paramount. You
can even give orders to the king, although I don't recom-
mend it. No limits at all."

So he could keep NailBiter, but he would have no
time for training. "King Shadow?"

"You outrank him."

If a choice must be made, the prince's life would take
precedence. The arrogance was understandable.

"The flying part I can handle," Sald said. That had
been the original purpose of Shadow. "It's the stiletto
and strychnine part."

"Today is the banquet," Vindax said irritably, anxious
to be off. "I've set aside tomorrow for learning. As
Shadow you're head of my bodyguard. You have a staff
—hire and fire as you please, but some of them have
been at this for kilodays. King Shadow will give you
pointers."

"That's still not the truth, Prince," Sald said. "You're
wearing exactly the expression NailBiter does when he's
snatched a mutebat and thinks I haven't noticed."

The prince flushed. "And what do you do then?" he
asked, dangerously.

"I make him as mad as I can. If he gets mad enough,
he spits it out."

The black eyes glared, and Vindax reddened further.
"Get insolent with me, fellow, and I'll have your head!"

"That's what NailBiter thinks."

The prince gasped audibly and then burst into a roar

of laughter, but laughter with a curious metallic ring to it. "All right! I'll spit. Back when we flew together, how would you rate me?"

Sald—Shadow, now—hesitated and then saw that flattery was certainly not part of his job. "Potentially good. You had the courage, the reflexes. Not patient enough. Inclined to be reckless. That's my fault also, so I can't judge it. But you never got enough practice."

"Of the twenty days before Shadow's unexpected resignation," Vindax said, "I flew nineteen. I expect to fly every day for the next thousand, with a few exceptions. Some days only a couple of hours, true, but some are going to be long, long hops."

Now it was Sald who gasped, and Vindax nodded with pleasure at the effect.

"I'm going to explore my inheritance, Shadow," he said. "From one end to the other, from salt to ice, Range and Rand. My father never did, but he agrees that it is a good idea. Far too much this court does nothing but gossip, and knows nothing. So I'm getting my practice in now, and the jaunts start soon. You were chosen because you're a damned good skyman, and I need one."

Sald sighed with relief. "Then I am truly grateful—and honored. And I swear that I will gladly serve as Prince Shadow, and to the limits of my ability."

When NailBiter had spat out the mutebat, he was rewarded with a tasty morsel. Vindax smiled in satisfaction at the speech. "And for a start," he said smugly, "we'll do the big one: the Rand. All the way!"

For a moment Sald did not comprehend. Leftward, the Rand led only to Piatorra, and relations between the two kingdoms were supposedly strained at the moment. Rightward lay wild, poorly settled country: frontier. He knew almost nothing about it, for Rantorrans normally thought only of the Range. But the Rand there was habitable, for it roughly paralleled the terminator. And "all the way" must mean all the hundreds of miles to where it swung abruptly darkward and vanished into the ice layer on Darkside.

He gasped. "To Allaban?"

A black glare barbecued him. "To Ninar Foan!"

Of course. The rebels still held Allaban—Sald had forgotten his history as well as his protocol. The siege of Allaban . . . the keeper of the Rand . . . Queen Mayala . . .

It was curious that Aurolron had never even attempted to recover Allaban. Was Vindax planning a war, now or when he came to the throne?

"Reconnaissance?" Sald asked cautiously.

"Partly." Then the prince grinned. "Also the duke of Foan is premier nobleman of the realm, and he has a daughter."

A long way to go for a date!

"And no son," Vindax added. "So if she has buck-teeth or one tit bigger than the other, then we'll marry her to my brother and he can be the next keeper at Ninar Foan. Don't tell him that! Politically she's the obvious match for me. We'll see if she's beddable. Now we must go mix with the rabble."

Sald needed to know what he was required to do— where to stand, when to sit, how much to drink when he tasted the wine—but his mind was still caught up in the thought of the Rand. "How long?"

"About a hectoday, there and back."

A hundred days in the air: new country and watch after watch of soaring, finding the thermals, analyzing the terrain—his heart began to pound at the thought. It would be the adventure of a lifetime and the best thing NailBiter could get. It would not give Sald back his freedom, but it would help.

Vindax had apparently misread his expression. "Don't worry—you cover me, but the others will cover you."

"Why?" Sald demanded, and his stupidity provoked royal impatience.

"Because otherwise you'll crack like an egg."

Sald bristled. Was his courage being questioned? Or his skill? He was as alert as any, and NailBiter would see danger long before he would. "NailBiter can dodge anything in the sky," he said—and stopped.

Shadow's job was to not dodge: a great honor and a very short life expectancy.

Vindax read his expression correctly this time and nodded in grim satisfaction. He headed for the door without another word.

The crown prince's enforced absence from public view was ended. He walked out to play his role in the life of the court, followed one pace behind, as always, by Shadow.

2

"It's an ill wind that changes direction."
—*Proverb*

"**E**LOSA? Elosa! Wake up!"

Elosa opened her eyes and blinked up at her mother. Jassina, on the cot in the corner, awoke with a scream.

"Quiet, you stupid girl!" the duchess snapped. "Leave us!"

Jassina scrambled to her feet and ran, stumbling, to the door. It thudded shut behind her.

"I don't believe I heard you knock," Elosa said.

"Very likely not," her mother agreed. "Put your wrap on and come with me. It's important."

There was only one important thing around Ninar Foan at the moment. "The prince? You've had word?"

"Yes. Hurry!"

Obviously the duchess was not about to explain. Elosa put on an expression of wounded dignity and took her time. The dingy pink lighting did nothing to improve her bleary-eyed feelings, nor did the gray stone walls and threadbare carpet. She had been evicted two days before from her own room, which was much larger and more fancy—and sunside. She found it hard to sleep without sunlight shining in her window; her father took the church's precepts seriously and required that all the castle drapes be closed during the third watch, but even as a

24

child, Elosa had sneaked out of bed when her parents had left and let the sun back in.

She slipped into her blue vicuña wrap, which was conveniently lying on the chair by her bed, then sat before the mirror and started to brush her hair. Normally Jassina did that for her. She was hoping that the delay would annoy her mother enough to make her say what all this was about, but the duchess had moved over to the window, a brooding, angular figure in moody brown colors. What her father had ever seen in the woman was a constant puzzle to Elosa—too tall, faceted in flat planes and sharp joints, her colorless hair pulled back in a bun, and a constant air of suppressed despair. Although perhaps that was worse lately?

Elosa herself had inherited not only her father's glossy black hair but also his trim skyman frame—she was deliciously tiny and proud of it. In her leather flying suit she looked like a boy, very fashionable among the aristocracy, and she came from the very highest levels in the aristocracy. Her mother, a mere earl's daughter, did not.

"There was an eagle in the sun today," the duchess muttered. "That always means bad news."

"I expect if you were feeling less liverish you would have seen an onion or a floor mop," Elosa retorted, tossing the brush away. Obviously the hair strategy was not going to work. "Now, do I get an explanation?"

Her mother strode to the door, tapped, and opened it. That tap gritted in Elosa's ears. She had not merely been evicted from her own room and forced into sharing with Jassina, but the anteroom which should have been her maid's was now occupied by a *man*, and she had to pass through it to enter or leave her own.

At least he was awake and dressed. Sir Ukarres rose with difficulty, leaning on his cane and bent sharply at the hips. One side of his wrinkled ocher face was permanently pulled down, giving him a quizzical expression; the eye on that side was blind. He was as ancient as the Ark, but also impossible to dislike for very long at a stretch. As well as being a distant relative, Ukarres was seneschal, and it was he, not the duchess, who was making arrangements for the crown prince's visit; that lady had no excuse at all for her bad temper and frayed nerves.

"Elosa!" he said in his whispery voice. "Please forgive this imposition. It distresses us greatly to disturb you like this, and before three bells, too."

"I had not noticed that so far," Elosa replied.

"Are you going to leave him stand there all day?" the duchess demanded, closing the door.

"I thought you were in charge," Elosa said. "Uncle, please sit. I shall be quite comfortable here." She perched on the bed.

The old man eased painfully back into his chair. The duchess stepped over to the window and stared out at nothing once more. Ukarres leaned both hands on his cane and studied the floor for a minute, as though uncertain how to begin. He did not even have a carpet over the flagstones, Elosa noticed.

"Elosa, my dear," he said at last. "You are very close now to your seventh kiloday, and therefore adulthood. I have regarded you as an adult for some time now, and I hope I have treated you as such? What I have to tell you is very much adult business. We are relying on you for discretion."

That was more like it. "Of course I shall respect your confidence, Uncle."

Ukarres nodded and gave her his scanty-tooth smile. "Good! We have just had word that the prince is making better time than expected. He has sent word that he will reach Vinok today. If the hunting is good, he will remain there a day or two. Otherwise he will be with us by first bell tomorrow."

Elosa's heart started a little solo dance in fast time. "That is good news."

Sir Ukarres hesitated. "Yes . . . and no. Of course the whole place is in a panic now—we were not ready."

He seemed to dry up, and Elosa felt a twinge of uneasiness. "What's wrong?"

The old man glanced at the duchess, who was still

looking out the window, and then back to Elosa. "Have you not noticed? You remember when the royal courier first brought the news that the prince was coming?"

Elosa would never forget that excitement, that moment. They had all been dining in the great hall when that scarlet figure had appeared in the doorway. She would never forget—he was the first royal courier she had ever seen. "Of course, Uncle."

"I don't think your father has smiled since."

What? But it was true that her father had seemed strangely preoccupied lately. And her mother was certainly bitchy.

Now it was Elosa who glanced at the duchess's back and found no help there. "You mean he doesn't welcome the prince's visit, Uncle?" she asked.

"It is a grave responsibility," he said. "And not only have we just had news that the prince is almost upon us, but there is also word of danger. Remember, this is in confidence." His voice dropped, although it was never much more than a whisper. "There will be an attempt made on his life when he is here—here at Ninar Foan."

Elosa gasped. "The rebels? They wouldn't dare! And how could they? The castle is impregnable! Uncle, you are joking."

He shook his head. "We have clear warnings of treachery, Elosa, within the castle itself."

"But..." The idea was too absurd, and yet surely he must be serious. "Then you must guard him!"

"Oh, he is always well guarded," Ukarres admitted. "I do not for a moment say it will succeed. But even the attempt would be a disaster for the honor of your father's house." He shuddered. "Think of the king's vengeance!"

"Vengeance?" Elosa snapped. "Uncle, you forget your history—the king owes Father an eternal debt."

"It is not history to me," Ukarres said sadly. "And debts, being orphans, die young."

"But..." she said again. "But the castle servantry are all father's thralls and have served us all their lives! Who?"

"We don't know. Your father does not know."

"Elosa," her mother said, wheeling around. "He is worried to death. You must have noticed how ill he looks? Or don't you even see—"

Ukarres held up a hand to silence her. "Your parents —and I—are extremely worried. We take this very seriously. Your father has decided that Vindax should be warned—advised not to come here."

Not come? It was unthinkable. All her life she had known that her destiny was to marry the crown prince. After all, she was the daughter of the premier noble, and there was a great dearth of eligible girls within Rantorra and even in the adjoining kingdom of Piatorra. She had all the qualifications: breeding, rank, age, beauty. When that royal courier had appeared, she had been certain that he was bringing the invitation to court which she had long dreamed of. And instead the prince himself had been coming to Ninar Foan. No crown prince had ever done that—nor any king of Rantorra, either, without an army. His reason was obvious. And now he was to be stopped?

"Obviously," Ukarres said, "such things cannot be said in public. Nor can they be written—the honor of your house is involved, my lady. It is a shameful thing, but less shameful than the alternative. Your father will take the message himself."

Just for a moment she was suspicious. The problem with Ukarres, Vak Vonimor said, was that he did not know a bowstring from a knot; but her mother would not engage in trickery, and she could think of no motive for the old man to make up such a story.

"When?" she demanded.

He looked surprised at the question. "After two bells, when everyone is asleep . . . and the meeting with the prince will be more private while most of his party are asleep also. Nobody else knows this, of course, my dear. The preparations are going ahead, but tomorrow there will be word of some crisis in Ramo which demands the prince's return."

"Why are you telling me this?" she demanded.

"Because I know how disappointed you will be," he

said. "I thought a day to prepare yourself..." His wrinkles deepened in an understanding smile; somehow the lopsidedness made his smiles irresistible. "I know it must be a blow for you, my dear. I am sure that the prince will send for you to come to court, afterward."

She was about to say that she would go to Vinok with her father, and then stopped in time. Her father would refuse. "Peddling my wares?" he would ask, and she could hear his scornful tone quite clearly. No, she had a much better idea.

"Thank you, Uncle," she said, rising.

He struggled to his feet. "My sorrow, to be the bearer of bad tidings. And now it is almost three bells. I shall be prompt for breakfast, for the first time in memory."

"I must go and see about the flowers," the duchess said.

"And I must get dressed," Elosa said.

She hurried toward her room, worried that her face might reveal her excitement. As the door closed behind her, Ukarres and the duchess glanced at each other and exchanged nods.

Elosa scrambled into her flying suit without even summoning Jassina to assist her. She, not her father, would warn the prince! Her father had rescued the queen; she would warn the queen's son! Poetic! Ironic! And she knew she looked best in a flying suit—first impressions were important.

She would soar in over the hills, lonely, heroic. She would kneel to him, her raven hair falling loose as she pulled off her helmet. If he was any sort of man at all, that would stun him.

How to stop her father, though? She could leave a note for Ukarres, but that might be discovered too soon, in time for pursuit. No, she would lay a false trail.

She headed for the aerie. Three bells had not yet rung, and she met no one; all were asleep, she assumed, until she neared the top of the stairs and heard the noise.

Normally the aerie was a peaceful place, four walls of stout bars supporting a high pyramid roof. A man could step between those bars; an eagle could not. Around the central stairwell, within the caged area, was the piled litter of generations—tables and bins and bales and discarded harnesses and helpful clutter which would always yield up a useful scrap or gadget when required.

Beyond the bars on all four sides lay the terrace, flanked by a low wall whose top provided perching for the birds. Always fifty or so of them stood there, still and silent giants, their backs to the room, staring out over the world like enormous silhouetted gargoyles. The wind blew gently from darkward, even and constant, stirring small motions in the birds' feathers, swirling tiny ripples in the mute dust which coated the floor and gave the aerie its distinctive musty, bitter smell.

Silent giants, the birds preened themselves, and they preened their neighbors' heads, but mostly they just stood. Once in a while a bird would shift from one foot to the other, clanking the rungs of its leash, or bend its head to snatch a pebble from the range pot, or feak its beak against the parapet; but mostly they just stood, staring out into the world as though thinking grave thoughts. Their eyes glared fixedly, but sometimes their heads turned to try another view. Much of the time they showed no movement except the eternal restless ripplings of their scarlet combs. As a child she had wondered greatly what they thought and what they watched. The castle and town were spread below them, so they could know everything that happened in the world of men—if they cared. Certainly no one moved within the aerie but the birds knew; nothing could creep up on an eagle. At times all the heads would line up, and it was likely then that goats or sheep were moving on the distant hills. A bird could see a smile farther than a man could see a man, so it was said.

Once in a while a mutebat would swoop down from the rafters to snatch up a pellet and whir back again. Once in a long while a bat would fly too close to a great waiting beak and then—*snap!*

There were browns and bronzes and silvers. The browns wore the livery of their country cousins, the wilds, the original stock. Bronzes were common, and she had heard tell of some that verged on gold. Silvers were very rare, and Ninar Foan had worked for generations on its silvers; her own IceFire was almost pure, the best silver in Rantorra, her father said. Only a few dark pinions marred her blue-white splendor, and the scarlet comb shone above it like a ruby. IceFire had been Elosa's sixth kiloday present. Breeding birds was a long-term task; they were likely to outlive their owners and their owners' grandchildren.

Her happiest childhood memories were of this aerie, playing in the litter, watching the birds. How excited she had been when one arrived, a vast spread of wings obscuring the sky! And even more excited when one departed, its gallant rider aboard, leaping off into space and suddenly not there. One of the first things she had been taught was that the bars were the limit; step through the bars onto the terrace and the birds would eat you. She had not really believed that then, although she did now, but within the cage she had played until that day when her father had first taken her into the sky. She had been barely past her second kilo, and yet she remembered every moment. That day the eagles had stolen her heart.

The aerie was not peaceful now. Elosa stopped at the top of the long stairs in astonishment. The place was total bedlam, men and boys running around with loads and getting in one another's way. A line of boys was sweeping up the dust, raising hideous, choking clouds of it, turning everything gray. The familiar junk pile had almost vanished, being systematically dragged over to darkside and hurled. Vak Vonimor, the eagler, was loud in argument with several helpers, apparently rehashing yet again the best method of ridding the aerie of mutebats, and tempers were rising. Men were tidying and stacking equipment: saddles and harnesses and hoods. As fast as one group formed a neat pile, it seemed, another would move it. The birds were twisting their heads back and forth, disturbed and fretting.

The prince was coming, and Ninar Foan's aerie was

getting its first real reorganization in a megaday. Typical
of men, she thought, to leave it until almost too late.

She surveyed the chaos for a few moments in silence
and then took the bird by the beak. She marched over to
Vak himself.

"Master Vonimor!"

He glanced around, rolled his eyes, and muttered
something which Elosa decided not to have heard.

"My lady?"

"Be so kind as to have IceFire dressed at once,"
Elosa said firmly.

"My lady..." Vak Vonimor was not a patient man,
and it was said that he feared only the keeper himself—
and his daughter. Today perhaps only the keeper. "His
Grace instructed us to move the birds, my lady. And to
make the place ready. He assured us that no birds would
be flown today." His round face was picket-fenced with
dust and sweat; it did not, however, look too convinced
of victory.

"I have decided—he has agreed that I may fly," Elosa
replied.

"IceFire is not due for a kill today," Vonimor muttered, yielding to the inevitable.

"I was not planning to hunt her, merely to get away
from all this...this mayhem."

He rolled his eyes again. "Very well, my lady.
Cover?" He glanced around. "Tuy! Dress IceFire and
take...take ThunderClaw."

The youth addressed broke into a wide grin and
dashed away before Vonimor could change his mind.
Elosa scowled, but it had no effect. Vonimor knew very
well what she thought about Tuy Rorin. He had been a
young hellion when she was a young hellion, only
slightly older than she and more hellionish, given to pulling hair and jumping out at girls from dark corners. Now
he was more inclined to pull girls into the dark corners,
scything a promiscuous swath through the chamber and
scullery maids. His mother was a cook, his official father
the gateman, but even as a child he had obviously belonged elsewhere, and he had announced his arrival at

puberty by developing the charm, the great hooked nose, and the bushy black brows that were unmistakably of the House of Foan. Her father had sown several such around the town and castle in his youth, and Elosa preferred not to be reminded. None of them resembled him as Tuy Rorin did, fortunately. A cook's son... half brother? Ugh!

ThunderClaw was a perfect choice for Elosa's purposes, though: very old. No match for IceFire.

"Where are you headed, my lady?" Vonimor asked. The duke had strict rules. In these wild hills, all fliers must report plans and destination before departing.

"Going to meet her princey," a voice muttered, and there were snickers. Elosa swung around furiously, but she could not tell who had spoken—and she got grinned at.

"To Koll Bleek," she snapped. She developed a convenient cough from the dust and beat a retreat to windward. The perching wall there was empty, so she went out and leaned on it, staring up at the Rose Mountains glimmering against black sky, half-concealed in equally ruddy clouds. Clouds and ice and no air, or not enough for humans. The birds could fly there, it was said, although why they should want to she could not guess. There was certainly nothing to eat on the High Rand.

Koll Bleek was rightward. She would head that way, lose Rorin, and double back alone. He would have to report her missing. The search would keep her father occupied. Dangerous, true. Not very kind, true; but she would not be a very convincing messenger if her father turned up a few hours later with the same message.

Or a different message? There was an interesting thought!

Then Tuy Rorin was back, wearing a battered old flying suit with more patches than IceFire had feathers. He was setting to work with a hooding pole. She marched back into the melee to watch. "Never trust a groom unless your eye is on him." So her father had told her a hundred times. One loose girth is enough.

Rorin, though, knew what he was doing. IceFire and

ThunderClaw happened to be neighbors, so he need hood only them and the two on either side, dropping the big bags on them from a safe distance. The birds turned their heads and glared angrily when the hoods appeared, but they froze like mountains as soon as the bags were on—only then could they be safely approached. He clipped a safety belt to the bars, scrambled nimbly onto the wall, and reached under the hoods to strap on the helmets. Her father said it was even safe to touch the great raptor beaks under the hood, as a hooded bird would not move. She did not intend to try, ever.

At first Tuy could not find Elosa's own saddle and offered her another, which she declined. She would be sore enough after a trip to Vinok and back.

When he had the birds saddled and unhooded, Rorin fetched two bows and quivers, grinning impudently. Her archery was notorious.

"Ready, my lady."

"Thank you, boy," she said graciously. The birds were blinkered and safe to approach. He gave her a hand to scramble onto the wall and then up into the saddle and stirrups—a hand too helpful to be respectful. Impertinent wretch! She heard the leashes clatter loose, and he swung up easily onto ThunderClaw at her side, ignoring the envious jeers from his dust-smeared comrades left behind. The bird settled slightly on her haunches under his weight. Elosa, stretched up as far as she could, was just able to reach IceFire's comb. She stroked it and felt the bird rumble with pleasure. She was suddenly very nervous at the start of this adventure, but Tuy was waiting, eyeing her expectantly.

"Ready!" She pulled back on the reins, and the blinkers flipped open. As always, IceFire instantly swung her head around to the left—it was an annoying trick of hers. Perhaps she merely wished to see who had mounted her. Perhaps her intent was more sinister, for a bird could easily bend its head far enough to bite its rider. Whatever IceFire's motive, it was always balked, for the left rein went slack at once and the blinker sprang back over the huge golden eye.

IceFire straightened and then launched, and Elosa felt once more the vast surge of excitement and dread as she fell into the void, the rush of cool air, the secret fear that perhaps this time the wings would not open—it was simultaneous terror and exhilaration, the sensation that made flying the greatest thing in the world. If love was greater, then she had yet to find out and would be much surprised at the discovery. With her free hand she signaled for wings and got them; a slight easing of the right rein swung her mount toward the left updraft. Rorin had expected the other and was already turning He shouted angrily and corrected. She'd show him!

She streaked down over a great darkness and felt the surge of cold wind, as familiar and constant as the castle corridors. She banked IceFire, glided across into the warm thermal, and began to circle. Where was Rorin? She looked around, puzzled, and saw that he had taken her air, was already above her, and close enough that she could see the grin under his goggles. That was his post, of course, but she was annoyed that he had managed to get there so easily.

In graceful stillness, the eagles soared upward above town and castle. The sun stood clear on the skyline now, a bloated red egg blotched with magenta dust clouds—if that was an eagle her mother had seen in it, then it was seriously diseased.

Elosa swooped without warning to catch the stronger thermal from Grassy Ridge. Rorin held formation as though he were tethered. ThunderClaw might be old, but she was experienced, and Rorin had inherited his real father's skill at flying. Even an old bird like Thunder-Claw could fly all day if need be. The birds' wings never seemed to tire, unless they had to beat them, and that was a sign of very bad guidance.

They rose higher and higher yet. Ninar Foan was a tiny scab of buildings on its spur, and even the spur was dwarfed now by the jagged hills around. The sun was clear of the horizon, almost white, smaller and much too bright to look at.

"That's high enough, my lady!" Rorin shouted. He was getting nervous, and truly the air was thin. Her chest was heaving with the strain. Obviously she would not be able to elude Rorin. So a future queen of Rantorra would have to meet her prince in the company of a cook's bantling. That thought burned.

They were almost into the cloud cap, and her head was about to burst. She crested IceFire and dived.

In a moment, the air felt better and her eyes cleared. She twisted around and saw that ThunderClaw was still in position. Damned good flying, she admitted grudgingly.

At this height the sun was fierce in a blue sky, the horizon below it blazing white beyond the shadowed edge of the Great Salt Plain which ran all the way to the hot pole. Ahead and below her lay the giant's jumble of jagged blocks and mountains that formed the Rand— browns and reds mostly, speckled here and there with welcome patches of green near springs and at the base of ice falls, tumbled down in divine chaos from High Rand to Salt Plain, a giant's staircase, the shadowed sides featureless pits of sterile blackness.

To her left the Rose Mountains glowed pink beyond the terminator, tips of ranges buried in the great petrified ocean that covered Darkside. Darkness and vacuum on one side, deadly heat and thick red air on the other, and the barely habitable harshness of the Rand between. Yet it was only the coincidence of middle elevations and terminator that made even Rantorra habitable at all.

Could she reach Split Rocks? She wasn't certain. If she fell short, then she would have to swing over to Gimaral, and that would be a wide detour. She toyed with the idea of asking Tuy's advice and rejected it. Go for it! She held her course, stretched prone along IceFire's back, glorying in the cool caress of the wind, watching the jagged peaks rising on her left and seeming to creep closer.

This was living.

* * *

Even the greatest thrill in the world can pall after
many hours, and Elosa was truly grateful to see Vinok
ahead. She had made good time, only once falling short
of the thermal she was aiming at, having to glide sunward and find another and then backtrack. But she was
stiff and cold and very thirsty, her canteen long emptied.
Rorin was puzzled by the unexpectedly long journey. At
first he had brought ThunderClaw in close and tried to
make conversation, but she had deliberately refused to
explain.

Always the great slope of the Rand lay ahead, climbing higher to bright peaks against dark vacuum on her
left, falling away on her right into black velvet, adorned
by the silver horizon under the sun. From time to time
she passed over areas with springs, green blessings in a
rock desert, most marked by solitary cottages of the
herdsmen who guarded livestock from the wilds. She
saw some of them at their lonely work; it took much
meat to feed the duke's eagles.

Then she saw Vinok, a minute tower, square and
pointed, standing on the lip of a cliff with a good thermal. Behind it rose a long, barren, rubbly slope leading
up to yet another great cliff. There was no sign of the
prince's party, and the tower was deserted, one tiny
work of mankind in a vast wilderness. A narrow green
gully nearby told of a small spring.

She glided down and guided IceFire in to the perching; she thought that the bird seemed grateful also. Tail
and wings spread to brake, then the talons rasped on the
wall and the wings folded. There was silence and peace
from the long, long rush of air.

"Well, turn around, silly!" she snapped, for there was
no one there to hear her. Birds were deaf and mute, and
to speak to them was a mark of a beginner.

IceFire moved her head slightly, scanning this new
place. Then she raised one foot and pivoted around.
Elosa released the reins and unstrapped her harness.

Gratefully she slid down to the terrace, staggering with stiffness. She picked up a chain and shackled the bird, then stepped through the bars.

Vinok was a smaller version of the castle aerie, one of the innumerable bird posts established generations ago by Vindax IV along the length of the Rand. In theory they were for the use of royal couriers and the Guard, but there were few couriers and the Guard never came. The more isolated tended to fall into ruin and neglect or were adopted by wilds, but many were maintained by local landowners for hunting lodges, as her father maintained this one. It had been recently tidied and made respectable, she noticed—undoubtedly for the royal visit.

A shadow flashed past the tower, wheeled, and flashed past again—then swooped off to regain air in the thermal for another attempt. Tuy Rorin was having trouble making ThunderClaw come to roost, and Elosa found that amusing. At the next attempt he succeeded, and the eagle settled down close to IceFire and turned at once.

"Everything all right, my lady?" he called, twisting around in the saddle.

"Seems so," she replied, wondering why he was not dismounting.

"Then . . ." He pushed up his goggles and regarded her hopefully, the clean patches around his eyes giving him a comical expression. "There are some goats on the hill, there, my lady. And ThunderClaw seems to think she's earned one."

Elosa was about to snap a refusal, then reconsidered. Rorin's opportunities to hunt wild game would be few— taking out the birds to pick up domesticated feed animals would be all the hunting he would know. She could be gracious and give him the chance. More important, it would be poor skymanship to fly ThunderClaw home right after a kill, and that would give her an excuse to remain longer at Vinok, perhaps even through third watch, for a return tomorrow. She knew that there were ladies in the prince's party, so it would be quite proper.

"Go ahead!" she said—and ThunderClaw was gone.

Then she stamped her foot in anger, realizing that she should have made him undress IceFire first. Suppose the prince arrived and her bird was still saddled, sitting on a perch? She would have to do it herself. It would be valuable experience, she decided nervously, with no one around to see if she made a mess of it. No one around to help if she lost a hand, either.

"Don't be morbid, Elosa," she could hear her mother saying.

The hooding poles were clearly visible, and hooding was no problem. She found the safety belts and put one on. The wall was high for her, but she managed to climb up, remembering how easy it always seemed to Rorin and the other men. There were disadvantages to being small.

Then the heart-stopping part: She must reach up under that black bag and unfasten the helmet. She had to climb back into the saddle to reach the front strap, the one near the beak. She was not sure which strap should be done first, or if it mattered. Her fingers brushed the underside of that steely beak, and she shivered; she fumbled quickly with the buckle. Done! The neck strap was easy. She pulled gently, and the helmet slid over the comb and fell loose. Well, that wasn't hard at all!

Aware that Rorin would have been finished long since, she set to work on the front saddle girth, then jumped down and did the thigh girths. The saddle slid to the floor with a satisfying flop. She picked up the equipment and slipped back through the bars with it—and was stopped short by her safety belt. There was no one there to see, but she felt herself blush at the laughter of those nonexistent watchers. Anything else? No! It was all done, and she could remove the hood.

"There you are, Icey," she said proudly. "Thought I couldn't do it, didn't you?" A real skywoman!

IceFire was probably wondering why it had taken so long.

No. IceFire was studying the cliff above the hillside. ThunderClaw was barely visible, but her shadow was flashing and leaping along the rocks as she stooped on her prey. The goats were hard to see at this distance, tiny bouncing dots fleeing in terror and yet somehow clinging to that nearly vertical surface in the way that only goats and flies could. Rorin would never do it, Elosa decided. She certainly would not attempt it, and she was fairly sure that Father would not either—the rock was too steep, and if a wing were to graze it, bird and rider would be instant raven meat.

ThunderClaw broke off her attack and swooped away, far below the escaping goats, gliding down the slope toward the tower, heading into the thermal to find altitude once more.

Lesson for you, Master Rorin! Would he try again? The herd had reached a vertical face and was cowering on a narrow ledge. He might try an arrow and hope to pick up the meat from the bottom of the cliff, but it was very difficult to make a bird strike at a motionless target —too difficult for Tuy Rorin, she thought.

Another shadow streaked across the cliff face, much faster. At that speed it must be a wild, and Rorin was now prey himself. Then she saw that this bird also had a rider and that he certainly knew what he was doing. An incredible stoop! One moment she had noted the shadow high above the goats, and the next instant bird and shadow and herd had merged and parted and the eagle was far below, spreading wings and curving out of its dive, clutching a goat that had surely died without ever seeing what was coming.

Unbelievable! Her father would not have attempted an attack at that speed, certainly not against a quarry on an almost-vertical cliff. She would have been impressed had it been done by a riderless wild. The men at Ninar Foan had been sneering about the palace fliers of the Royal Guard, but if that performance was typical, then it was the locals who had much to learn.

The royal party? She ran out to the terrace, safely far from IceFire, and peered aloft. There they were, eighteen or twenty of them, minute specks floating in the thermal. She could see no others, apart from the solitary hunter, and he now came rushing in on the tower, still gliding on the momentum of his dive: more fine judgment! Tail spread, talons reached—and an enormous bronze was sitting motionless on the parapet, the goat dangling from his beak, fierce gold gaze studying the aerie. It was a huge bird, bigger even than IceStriker, IceFire's father.

"Turn around, featherbrain!" a male voice roared. Elosa jumped and then laughed to herself. If an expert like this talked to his bird, then she certainly could—and would do so in future. The bronze did not turn at once; he started sidling along the parapet toward IceFire, the goat swinging limply.

"Oh, cut out the flirting!" the voice said laughingly. The blinkers snapped shut, and the bronze stopped—and then turned! The rider had made a blinkered bird turn with foot signals, and she had never seen that done. The rider unbuckled, jumped down, and shackled his bird. Then he reached up and tied the reins back to the saddle, opening the blinkers. That was a calculated risk, she supposed, for the bird had its beak full, but her father would not have allowed it, and she noticed that the newcomer moved swiftly to the safety of the bars.

It was the prince!

The prince himself!

Elosa's knees started to shake. He was very short, trim and moving easily, although he had probably spent a whole watch in the saddle. He pushed up his goggles and smiled across at her, but headed swiftly toward the staircase. What a wonderful smile! And what a skyman! She had heard that the prince could fly well—he would hardly have attempted this journey otherwise—but she had not been told that he was a master. She ought to be curtsying—no, dummy, bow in a flying suit—but he was obviously heading for the stairs.

Perhaps he needs a pee, she thought, and suppressed a giggle.

"Who are you?" he called.

"Er . . . I bring a message . . . Your . . ."

But the prince had vanished down through the floor, boots clattering on the steps.

Elosa's heart was trying to fight its way right out of her chest. To think of the crown prince in the abstract was one thing, but actually to see him was quite another, to see him as a flesh and blood human male. And what a male! For the first time she realized that she had been dreading this moment, fearing to have a real face superimposed forever on the ideal face she had conjured for her ideal prince, real bones and meat to replace her dream. There was only one crown prince, and she was quite prepared to accept whatever her destiny sent her— physical attraction was something she had not been counting on. That would be a bonus.

What a handsome couple they would be!

She pulled off her helmet and shook out her hair. She told herself firmly to calm down and stop trembling. With a smile like that, he was nothing to fear. Ladies of her station married for dynastic and political reasons; she should not allow sex to intrude.

Why had he come on ahead, leaving his entourage aloft? Perhaps, being prince, he got first shot at the game.

The prince came trotting up the stairs again, went over to the terrace, and looked up. He waved his arms in some sort of signal.

He wore a plain blue flying suit with no insignia except the talon that was his symbol and a black diagonal stripe. She ought to know what that was for—she would have to brush up on her heraldry before she got to court. Perhaps he was in mourning for some distant relative.

Now he came back through the bars and walked over toward her, studying her with surprise. He was carrying his helmet now, as she was, and his hair was dark and curly.

"A woman!" he exclaimed. Then he smiled. Oh, that smile! "I beg pardon...a lady." He did not bow—but then, he was royalty, so that must be correct. "A lady bearing a message?"

She dropped to one knee and bowed her head so that her hair fell over one shoulder.

"I . . . I am Elosa, daughter of the keeper, Your—"

"The devil you are!" the prince said.

She looked up in surprise. His eyes had narrowed in sudden wariness. "And what message can possibly require so highborn and so beautiful a courier?"

No, she was not going to tell him about Ukarres's stupid plot. He had plenty of guards with him; he could not possibly be in any more danger at Ninar Foan than he was always in at court. He was her destiny! She would not be cheated. Her father would not come—he would be too busy searching for her around Koll Bleek. The prince would not send her home alone; he would order her to stay here over third watch, and tomorrow he would see what a fine skywoman she was. If her father wanted to warn him away again afterward, well, at least he would have had a chance to get to know her properly.

"I just came to say that you are indeed welcome to Ninar Foan, Your Highness."

3

"Sow trust to reap loyalty."
—Proverb

THE crown prince was ten days ahead of his official
itinerary when he arrived at Vinok. He had been eight
days ahead of it at Gorr and five behind at Sastinon. His
progress, in short, had been unpredictable—and that
was Shadow's doing.

Flying in itself was dangerous. A flight along the
whole length of the Rand was especially perilous because of its duration and because much of the country
was poorly settled by men and well inhabited by wilds.
For a prince to attempt such a trip was very close to
folly; the inhabitants of savage lands tend to have long
memories for injustice, real or imaginary. Rebels might
plot political advantage; brigands might dream of ran-
som.

What was needed, Vindax had long since decided,
was something he had first met as a child in the palace
school. He had not then known what it was, only that a
few of the more humbly born seemed to have already
developed some different way of thinking. He ran into it
again when he went through the motions of enlisting in
the Guard in order to gain flight training. No one was
deceived into believing that he was an ordinary recruit,
but one benefit was that he came to know a few young
men from outside the aristocracy.

44

Once again he discovered this unfamiliar way of looking at the world, that he eventually analyzed as an ability
to see it as it really was and not as it should be, plus a
willingness to make it into what it might be, not what it
ought to be. Eventually he put a name to it: common
sense. And he discovered also that common sense did
not flourish among the rituals of courtiers or the rule
books of their bureaucrats.

Just knowing that it existed did not impart it, however. He was an aristocrat himself, and he could not
think that way. But when he conceived his journey to
Ninar Foan, he knew at once that he must include some
of that common sense among his baggage. It was for that
reason that he had scandalized the family, the council,
and eventually the whole court by insisting on appointing
a commoner as his new Shadow.

Tongues wagged and heads were shaken, but he had
his way. At the banquet that followed the dubbings, the
topic displaced even the queen's health.

And the very next day, that same commoner set the
court on its ear a second time.

Shadow had spent an entire exhausting watch absorb-
ing information under the restless eye of the crown
prince. He had greeted first bell with relief, expecting
that the worst part of his day must now be over, but it
was not to be. Now he was living the life of a public
personage, one which could not be divided as neatly as
that of lesser mortals into periods of work, play, and
sleep. The next item on the agenda, he learned with horror, was dinner with the king and queen.

The monarch lived a very public life, and such private
gatherings were rare. How the two Shadows fared at
them depended on the king's mood—they might be ex-
cluded, or ignored like furniture, or treated as family
members—but this occasion was designed to evaluate
the new appointee, and there were six places laid around
the table. It was an intimate affair, employing only six
footmen, two butlers, and enough gold plate to establish
a barony. The table stood on a secluded terrace, well

shielded by shrubbery and flowers, shaded by tinsel trees. It overlooked the palm garden but could not itself be overlooked by anyone. In Ramo, most events took place outdoors, in the constant gentle sunshine.

The king was being gracious, dressed in the plain white garb that he preferred. The queen was being even more gracious in a gold gown which did not suit her pith-hued complexion; she inquired politely after Shadow's dear mother, whom she had obviously confused with some other lady. She also tended to drop things and forget what she was saying in midsentence.

Jarkadon was a younger version of the king and an older version of the obnoxious child Shadow remembered, wielding a humor like a skinner's knife. His seventh kiloday was only six days off, and there was some discussion of the state ball, but the diners had barely reached the soup course when the king displayed his interest in birdflesh by remarking, "And what mount will you fly on your journeying, Vindax?"

The crown prince glanced sideways. "Shadow? Your advice?"

Shadow choked in the process of tasting Vindax's soup. "I think agility would not be advisable, Prince—it would merely make it harder for the rest of us to cover you. A flying rock—probably a mature female. Certainly nothing which could outfly NailBiter."

"NailBiter?" The king's frown chilled the air. "You do not propose to fly cover on our son with that terror?"

Awash with despair, Shadow faced that gaze of blue ice. "Yes, Your Ma—King. He and I are a good team. I should be less comfortable on a strange bird, and I can hardly practice now without neglecting my other duties." But he had just lost hope.

Vindax was amused. "Which is more important, Shadow?" he asked. "NailBiter or your lunch? I shall remain here. The palm garden is directly below us. If you think you can convince us?"

Shadow rose and left in silence.

By the time he had visited the prince's apartment and donned a flying suit, he had worked up a heady dose of

anger. *Show the bastards!* He stormed into the aerie, and
NailBiter, he thought, brightened at the sight of him,
turning his head to glare even more ferociously than
usual. His comb rippled and reddened, and he fluffed his
glassy bronze plumage, but he was not pleased at the
unusual tightness of the saddle girths.

Bird and rider plunged from the roost. The palace was
well located on a rocky plateau flanked by no less than
three updrafts, and Shadow had no problem gaining altitude, as he studied the royal palm garden far below and
planned his trajectories. Then a simple knee movement
folded NailBiter's wings, and they dived ... open wings
to level out ... skim between palms ... off into the far-
side thermal. A few such passes and he had the trees
well placed and could start being fancy, folding in the
bird's wings for narrower passes, until he was flashing at
full attack speed between trees which he could have
touched with outspread arms. It was simple insanity, and
yet he felt strangely unmoved by the danger. He had
already lost his life the day before, had he not? Word
was spreading, courtiers pouring into the palm garden to
watch this spectacular suicide.

On one pass he banked NailBiter and looped back the
way he had come, flying his eagle like a sparrow. Show
the bastards.

Then he tried a couple with his hands in the air, Nail-
Biter blinkered and blind, guided only by his rider's legs.
He was running out of ideas. Should he try to steal the
dinner off the royal table?

How many passes did they need? He had made his
tenth or twelfth and was climbing once more in a thermal
when a guard challenged him. Shadow recognized the
heraldry on the uniform—this was the Honorable Ja
Liofan, a cocky young bastard who couldn't put an
arrow in a barrel if he was leaning on it, and obviously
the only guard not smart enough to recognize Shadow or
ignorant enough to interfere.

Liofan was higher and behind and had his bow drawn,
but troopers were trained to escape from such predica-
ments, and NailBiter could identify the threat by in-

stinct. A swerve, a few beats of the bronze wings, a
bank—and the positions were reversed.

Shadow was unarmed, but his mount was not, and a
touch of boots against thighs was enough to bring down
the great talons and launch an attack. Liofan gaped in
horror and dived, NailBiter close behind. The two birds
hurtled over the palace, less than five lengths apart, Ja
Liofan probably measuring his life in seconds. He
twisted around to shoot—and the arrow went ludi-
crously wide. He swerved again...lost air...and the
deadly talons were closer still...back down across the
palace rose garden, barely skimming the trees...Any
guardsman who tried what Shadow was doing would be
instantly cashiered. If he lost control, then he was going
to commit a very fast murder.

Now Liofan was in full flight, his bow discarded, his
screams quite audible. NailBiter's comb was dark crimson with the rage of bloodlust, and Shadow no longer
needed to direct him, was rather fighting to hold him
back from closing, the bird throbbing in frustration, be-
wildered by the conflicting signals. Far out above the
city, Shadow drew ahead and turned his prey and drove
him back over the palace once more. NailBiter closed
within a length, and Shadow was almost ready to blinker
him and pull off, but then the gap widened slightly—
NailBiter had seen the joke. He was still just young
enough to enjoy the sort of game that young wilds
played. His comb faded to a more reasonable color and
began rippling gently—and the astonished Shadow could
relax. Suddenly it was easy. All he needed to do then
was keep the contest as close to the palace as possible.
He drove his hapless quarry a half dozen times over and
through the palm garden until finally the devastated Ja
Liofan ran out of air, landed his bird in a bush, and the
game was over.

NailBiter had shown he could be controlled. Back at
the aerie, Shadow rubbed his comb until the eagle quiv-
ered like an earthquake, and then broke more rules by
rewarding him with a mutebat.

When he returned to the royal quarters, the king rose

and shook his hand—an extraordinary honor. "Magnificent, Shadow," he said. "We have not seen a display like that in many kilos." He was about to pull off a ring, the standard royal gratuity, and then paused. "No, we shall issue a renunciation, freeing Hiando Keep from taxes for a kiloday."

Shadow stammered his thanks; his father would bless him with raptures. It was astonishing that the king would remember the name of his father's house. Vindax was frowning.

"Such an anticlimactic ending," Jarkadon mourned. "After all, it was only a trooper."

Vindax made no comment on the affair, not even when he and Shadow withdrew. Even now the prince did not retire for private relaxation or recreation; he sent instead for Lord Ninomar, vice-marshal in the Guard and hence the third-ranking military officer in the kingdom. He was also commander of the crown prince's flight. A ruddy, wiry little man of about fifteen kilodays, with the self-confidence of impeccable ancestry, he sported a bristly red mustache which clashed oddly with his thinning brown hair. He had apparently been called from table, for there were crumbs in the mustache, but his uniform was a tailor's masterpiece, glittering with decorations. Shadow wondered how good his flying might be, but then, breeding was more important than skill.

This was a formal audience. The three men remained standing in a corner of another terrace flanked by mosaic walls and a marble fountain, with guards, aides, and other observers safely out of earshot behind windows.

"You have had time to prepare your plans for the journey to Ninar Foan?" Vindax asked.

"Certainly, Your Highness." Ninomar smugly produced a sheaf of papers and proceeded to read them. He read them as though he had never read them before.

Vindax listened with an impassive face, Shadow with steadily increasing horror. His estimate of his own life expectancy slid from a hectoday to almost zero. This would be self-inflicted carnage.

At the end the prince nodded. "Impressive," he said. "You seem to have thought of everything." He turned his head slightly. "Shadow, have you any comments?"

For a moment Shadow was not sure if this was a mere formality, and then decided he had better not treat it as such.

"A few, Prince. The twelve spare birds...even the Guard never attempts to move more than three spares at a time."

"That is not in the regulations!" the vice-marshal snapped, reddening.

"Nevertheless it is the practice," Shadow replied. "And even three are too many. Spares are the commonest cause of accidents. I should take none. The size of the party...true, the Guard will sometimes fly in troops of fifty, but control is hard to maintain in an emergency."

Vindax was still silent, so Shadow plunged ahead. "We shall not be a flight of skilled troopers, for—with all respect to your entourage, Prince—many will be civilian. To fly in drill spacing..."

"Perhaps hunt spacing," Ninomar conceded.

"Wider still—range or greater. Space is our best defense for the prince. And that is my business, Vice-Marshal."

Ninomar's face grew as red as his mustache, but Vindax remained impassive. Shadow tore and savaged the marshal's plans to a shower of feathers. The problems of provisioning and perching so many in a poor countryside...no more than six troopers, and not the moguls and scions named by Ninomar, but able young archers, competent also to tend the birds...paired birds so far as possible, with only a few singles for communications if needed...one lady's maid was plenty...the itinerary to be flexible and not advertised except in general terms...

No point remained unblunted, no facet unscratched. The marshal was crimson and beyond speech by the end —he knew what rank this insolent stripling had held until the previous day.

"Thank you, Shadow," the prince said. "I had envisioned a larger retinue, though. The numbers were mine."

"Then divide it into three, Prince, flying a watch apart."

"No," Vindax said thoughtfully. "A small group may even impress more by demonstrating confidence, and your point on provisioning is good. What of baggage, if we have no spares?"

Shadow was beginning to feel more hopeful. "I was thinking only of your personal safety," he said tactfully. "Certainly we could use a small advance party, perhaps several, two or three men in each." That was so obvious that he hadn't thought of it himself until then. Damn, he had had no time to plan! "They of course could take spares, inspect accommodation and security..."

Vindax nodded gravely. "My Lord Marshal, I accept your proposal..."

Lord Ninomar took a deep breath.

"...with the few amendments which Shadow has suggested. Possibly he may offer further advice in future."

The crumbled remains of Ninomar departed—even his decorations seemed to have lost their shine. Then Vindax broke the rules by spinning right around to look at Shadow, still frowning.

"Feel any better now?" he snapped.

It was trust absolute: Shadow was to have supreme command.

Yes, it felt better. All in all, Shadow decided, that interview had tasted as good to him as the mutebat had to NailBiter.

4

"Don't put all your eggs in one nest."
—Skyman humor

AND SO, sixty-four days later, Shadow had brought Vindax safely to Vinok and almost to Ninar Foan—

"What rank is Shadow?" the girl demanded. She was red as a half sun, raging at having mistaken him for the prince, and he wondered how so tiny a form could contain so much anger.

"No rank, lady," he said. "I fly cover for the prince. But NailBiter needs to eat sometimes, so today I was advance scout." He tried a smile, but it died unanswered. "We saw two unexplained visitors arrive ahead of us—"

"How can you have no rank?" she snapped. He thought that in calmer moments she would be quite attractive, almost a beauty, and she had none of the buckteeth or other deformities which had worried Vindax. She qualified politically; physically she might very well satisfy his need for a royal breeding partner.

"I am just Shadow. I fly cover for the prince, bird fodder." She opened her mouth to argue, so he added, "By birth I am a commoner, lady."

That helped not at all—she had knelt to him. Why the rage? She was not the first to have made the error, for the subtleties of court insignia were little understood in

these remote parts, but no one else had taken it so hard.
And the starry eyes had not been for him, obviously.

The horizontal sunlight was cut out momentarily as an
eagle came in to perch. This was the second stranger,
then, the failed hunter, and he had found easier prey, for
a vicuña hung from the great beak.

"Who's this, lady?" Shadow demanded.

"My groom. And you address me as Lady Elosa, or
my lady: not just lady!"

"Not me," Shadow said. "They have special rules for
me. Come along, I must check him for weapons before
the prince gets here."

She stalked along beside him angrily. The groom had
come through the bars and was looking for a hooding
pole so he could pull back his bird's blinkers to let her
eat. He flashed Elosa a huge grin.

"Got one!" he crowed. He was very young and no
obvious threat.

Then he saw Shadow. He shied, whipped off his helmet, dropped his goggles, and made a deep bow.

"Who the hell are you?" Shadow demanded. The
nose, the eyebrows, the whole face and the build—it
was uncanny.

The lad went pale under his dust streaks and
windburn. "Tuy Rorin, Your Highness, groom to His
Grace—"

"I am not the prince," Shadow said, and almost
added, "*But you are!*"

Of course there were innumerable royal bastards
floating around Rantorra. Perhaps one of those by-blows
had been banished to the far end of the realm and this
was some impoverished descendant, a royal cousin.

"Oh! Beg pardon, my lord," the boy said, but his eyes
flickered momentarily toward Elosa and then downward
to hide a smile.

"Attend to your mount, groom," Shadow said. Then
he roared: "*NailBiter!* Oh, crap!"

Elosa uttered something very like a scream.

NailBiter had decided it was cawking time.

Lady Elosa's magnificent silver had agreed.

The two were side by side, with a futile length of chain dangling from NailBiter's ankle. His comb was fiery and thrashing with excitement, his plumage blown up until he looked twice as large as normal. Holding his kill with one foot, he had ripped off a leg and was offering it, and at the exact moment Shadow noticed what was happening, the silver accepted. NailBiter seemed to swell even more; he tore off the head and offered that. And that was accepted also.

"Stop them!" Elosa wailed.

"Ha!" Shadow said ruefully. "You stop them, lady! It's too late. Much too late."

"IceFire! She's priceless! And a bronze! Father will kill me!"

Eagles mated for life, and those two had just signed the contract.

"Do something!" Elosa demanded, stamping her foot in frustration.

"There's nothing we can do," Shadow said. "Except decide what to call their firstborn—IcyFingers, perhaps? Or Hotfoot?"

The groom guffawed, and Lady Elosa switched from woe back to fury.

Shadow walked over to the courting couple; they were much too intent on each other to be a threat to him. He checked to make sure that his bird had not injured his leg, and he removed the useless leash—the ancient staple had come out of the wall. NailBiter offered a tasty beakful of offal; IceFire gulped it and nibbled playfully at his comb.

Shadow refastened NailBiter. The bird needed no special liberty for his wooing, for it would be a long time in human terms before the two got around to consummating their union. Then he slipped back through the bars as more birds came soaring in.

Lady Elosa was still raging. "Careless oaf! Why did you not check that staple when you tethered your bird?"

"Did you check yours?" Shadow asked, tiring of this tantrum thrower.

She gasped. "Insolence! My father will have you flogged!"

Shadow was not afraid of the duke, but the king was another matter. "Will he so? But it is your father's responsibility to maintain this aerie. NailBiter belongs to His Majesty, who has breeding plans f~r all his birds. He will certainly judge the case himself. Perhaps he will have your father flogged."

She was too outraged to reply.

More birds arrived, carrying a couple of troopers and the countess, Lord Ninomar, and the lithesome lass who professed to be his wife. Those two had both caught goats. Where was Vindax? The aerie was filled with laughter and the clattering of shackle chains.

The groom was openly grinning now—with Vindax's grin. "My lord?" he asked diffidently. "That was a magnificent kill you made, if I may say so." He had Vindax's charm, also.

"I'm not a lord," Shadow said. "And you certainly may say so." He smiled. "I didn't see it myself—I had my eyes shut."

The kid looked at him carefully, wondering if he was serious. "Would you mind explaining how you did it, sir? How can you control a bird at that speed?"

"I don't try to," Shadow said. "His reflexes are so much faster than mine that it would be stupid, like fighting with the flat of an ax instead of the edge. That's my opinion, anyway. We saw you try and fail, and the prince asked if I could do it. Well, I could barely see the cliff from that height, but NailBiter obviously thought he could make the strike. So I gave him the signal and let him try."

NailBiter had dropped like a house.

Elosa frowned. "Father says that an eagle carrying a man is very different from an unloaded one. If you don't keep control in the heat of the chase, then its instincts will fly you both into the ground."

Ninomar and the others had started to approach and then stopped to stare in astonishment at Rorin.

Shadow shrugged. "I'm sure your father is very

knowledgeable, lady, and I admit that most trainers follow him. But some don't! After all, NailBiter has never flown without a burden. Even on his first glide, I suppose he bore a pack. So I have always just made sure that I chose the prey and the locale, and then let him teach himself to hunt. He hasn't gone after moles yet." But he had almost turned his rider's hair white a few times. "Perhaps you or your groom can answer a question for me, though."

"What?" Elosa demanded.

He nodded to the cawking pair. "How do eagles tell unpaired females? Could NailBiter have known? Did he do what he did just to impress your IceFire?" They had been very high, and it seemed incredible that even eagles could have eyesight that good. And how much risk had NailBiter taken?

Before he was answered, Ninomar and the countess came over. The prince's WindStriker landed at last, and three others. The troopers were removing saddles and helmets.

"Lovely kill, Shadow!" Ninomar said.

"Thank you, Vice-Marshal," Shadow said. "Countess, may I have the honor of presenting..." He was unpracticed at formal introductions but eager to unload this minx. The countess took charge. Rorin stepped back, noticing now how he was being studied, uneasy at the untoward attention. More birds came in to perch.

Then, at last, Vindax. "Beautiful kill, Shadow."

"Thank you, Prince." Shadow moved into place behind him as the countess began her introduction.

"Your Highness, may I—"

"Bastard!" Lady Elosa screamed, and fainted.

"It isn't possible!" Vindax said for the fourth time.

The floor below the aerie was divided along three sides into stalls for humans, primitive stone boxes, most containing only a leaf-filled mattress. Someone had attempted to furnish one in a style more fitting for royalty, with a bed, a small rug, and drapes on door and window. And even that was remarkable, thought Shadow, when all of it had probably been flown in on birds' backs over the wild and barren landscape. Now the prince was slouched on the bed, glaring furiously, and Shadow leaned patiently by the doorway.

They had put the hysterical Elosa in the care of the women. They had interviewed the terror-stricken groom and sent him off under guard. Now they were trying to make sense of it all.

Tuy Rorin had admitted to being the keeper's bastard and to looking very like him. He had gone so far as to give an opinion that the prince was even more like him. Elosa's shock was now explained—but how to explain the explanation?

Laughter drifted in from the stairwell. The courtly gentlefolk of the royal party had scorned the little castles and towns they had met at the beginning of the trip; they had complained and grumbled. As the habitations had grown more humble and conditions worse, the complaints had increased. The first of the lonely and primitive post aeries had shocked the courtiers speechless, but thereafter their attitude had changed. They saw themselves then as heroes, pioneers. The journey would not last forever, and they could dine out at court on the strength of their stories; they would be experts in hardship, seasoned campaigners. Now they seemed almost to relish the worst, greeting each new privation with black humor and joyful predictions of even bleaker things in store.

"It is just not possible!" That was the fifth time.

Then Vindax looked up at Shadow. "My parents were married on the kiloday of Father's accession, of that I am certain. I was born on 1374. The siege of All' 'an was somewhere around 750 or 760..."

"745 was the day Foan reached the palace," Shadow said. "I heard Ninomar saying so when we were talking about it in Gorr."

"So they got back to Ninar Foan around 765 or there-abouts? It doesn't matter..." Vindax was very pale, a gleam of sweat on his forehead. This was no ordinary paternity problem they were discussing—this was the succession. "I'm sure Mother has told me that she stayed about a hectoday there, so say 865 was when she and the others set out for Ramo. Foan went with them for a very short way...

"That's still five hectodays before I was born!" he shouted.

Shadow put a finger to his lips. "He has never been to court?"

Vindax dropped his voice. "Never! I asked why, of course. All I was told was that his post was here, defending the frontier." He frowned. "It is odd, isn't it? The frontier's been quiet ever since—Karaman has never tried to attack Ninar Foan. You'd think the premier noble of the realm would have visited the court at least once in... in my lifetime."

His distress was painful, and Shadow wished he could think of some comfort to offer. "Isn't Foan a relative, a distant one?"

Vindax shrugged. "Just about every peer in the kingdom has some royal blood in him." He pondered for a moment. "He's the great-great-grandson of Jarkadon IX, my great-great-great-grandfather. That makes us third cousins, once removed."

He went back to glowering at the floor. Shadow wondered why he had been chosen as confidant in this crisis; he felt both flattered and worried by the honor. "How about the royal portrait gallery?" he asked.

There he scratched gold—Vindax brightened. "By God, Shadow! This beak of mine—it shows up in some, but a long way back. Before Jarkadon IX, anyway. So, if it's the sort of thing that jumps generations..." Then his black mood returned, and he brooded for a while. "You ever heard of fair-haired parents having dark-haired children?" he asked.

"Yes," Shadow said, "but it always causes gossip."

"Gossip!" The prince lowered his voice to a whisper. "It isn't gossip that bothers me, Shadow. It isn't illegitimacy. It isn't Jarkadon IX. It's Jarkadon X."

Shadow knew of no Jarkadon X, so he raised an eyebrow, and Vindax nodded. "He's an ambitious bast—

he's not notably scrupulous. If he thought he could make a case, he's quite capable of starting a civil war."

But who was the legitimate heir?

Shadow decided to take some risks. "Prince, I think you're overreacting...and being very unfair to your mother. And your father. They wouldn't have concealed ...I mean your mother wouldn't have..."

He dried up and got a mocking smile. "Hard to put into words, isn't it?" Vindax said. "Why did they never summon Foan to court? Why was my mother so frantically against my making this journey? She raised every objection she could think of, even bad dreams. She's been failing ever since I suggested it—I thought she had some serious disease. I wanted to get the trip over with and get back as soon as possible. Now I think it was the thought of the trip doing it to her. You realize that until now almost no one else in the kingdom has met both him and me?"

"What did your father think of the idea?"

"He never met him," Vindax said grimly. Then he laughed harshly. "I was told to invite him to court! He'll be a sensation!"

Boots stamped outside, and Shadow reached over to lift the drape, unveiling Vice-Marshal Ninomar, soldierly, precise, and utterly brainless.

"Yes?" the prince said wearily.

"The men have been unable to locate any fuel, Your Highness," his lordship said. "We have virtually no provisions except raw goat meat. I wondered if you still wish to remain here over third watch or press on to Ninar Foan?"

He did not say that the countryside was barren for hours in all directions, that he had been against stopping at Vinok at all, that he had recommended bringing spares which could have carried supplies—food, perhaps, but hardly firewood, thought Shadow—or that the aerie might have been properly prepared for the royal visit had Shadow not tampered with the schedule.

Vindax sighed at this petty interruption and looked to Shadow—he seemed to be doing that more and more.

"There are spare mattresses," Shadow said. "Dry mute pellets burn very well, and I believe that the roof is made of timber."

He dropped the curtain without another word and was pleased to see a smile on Vindax's face.

"How do you do that?" the prince demanded. "The trooper found no fuel. So he reported to the trooper who was going to do the cooking, I suppose, and he told the ensign and he told the colonel . . . it works its way up through six or seven men until it reaches the heir to the throne. Then you solve it with a snap of your fingers! How?"

It was not a subject Shadow would have chosen, but anything was better than letting Vindax brood on his own paternity.

"From my father, I think," he said. "The Guard doesn't teach men to do things; it teaches them *how* to do things. You build a fire with kindling and logs. No logs, no fire."

"So?" the prince asked, puzzled.

Shadow smiled. "The locusts eat my father's crops, one corner of the Keep is subsiding, the wilds and the Guard steal the livestock, the neighbors deepen their well and his dries up, the serfs don't work if they're not watched, and the royal tax collectors demand more than he's got. But if he doesn't solve those problems, his serfs will starve, and he feels responsible. So he finds another way. No one tells him *how*."

Vindax nodded. "Practical! That's the sort of thinking I want in my staff, Shadow. I want to meet your father. When we get back—"

The drape rustled aside to admit the countess.

The countess of Dumarr was not a person, she was an office. Appointments to that office were neither gazetted nor bestowed at dubbings, although they might as well have been from the speed at which they were known around the court. The countess of Dumarr was the crown prince's current mistress, a position of some importance in palace politics. The present incumbent was a sweet little cuddly blonde with a heart of steel and a very

practical attitude to her work—Shadow approved of her.
Normally there was no count of Dumarr, but the chief of
protocol had been told to use that name for the duration
of the trip. Some of the country gentry may even have
believed that he was her husband.

She slipped by Shadow, sat down next to the prince,
and looked him over appraisingly. Then she cuddled,
getting little response.

"It's more complicated than we thought," she said.

"I thought it would be," Vindax said sadly.

"She's a woolly-headed spoiled brat, full of romantic
notions and her own importance, but I don't think this
jaunt was truly her idea. She was put up to it by her
mother and someone called Ukarres, an uncle." The
countess glanced up to include Shadow in the conversation, then back to Vindax. "She was led to believe that
her father was coming here—to warn about a plot on
your life."

Shadow stiffened.

"Her father knows this?" the prince asked.

"I would guess not," the countess said. "He can certainly deny it. She didn't want to be cheated out of meeting her dream prince, so she came herself."

Vindax frowned and looked to Shadow.

"Then her father will be coming also?" Shadow
asked.

The countess shrugged. "She told them she was going
off in the opposite direction, so he will probably be starting a search for her about now."

"Considerate little bitch!" the prince muttered.

The countess nuzzled the side of his neck.

"Was she told to bring that Rorin kid with her?"
Shadow asked.

The countess was smart enough to have seen that
point. "No. That seems to have been chance."

"Why does that matter?" Vindax asked sharply.

"Because that chance sort of scrambled the egg,"
Shadow said. "Without him along, this would have come
out in private, even if she did faint at the sight of you."

But the egg had been scrambled—the whole royal

party knew now. Vindax could turn tail and run back to Ramo, but the court would still hear how he looked so much like the duke of Foan's groom.

"Should I see her?" Vindax asked.

The countess shook her head. "Not yet. She's still in deep shock. She equates you with Rorin."

"Thanks."

She kissed his ear. "Silly! I mean that ever since childhood she has been dreaming of marrying the crown prince—and now she's discovered that he looks like her half-brother."

Vindax drew back his teeth in a snarl and looked up at Shadow.

"You will have to marry her now, you know," the countess said cheerfully. "It will be the only way to squash the rumors."

"Think of the wedding," Vindax snapped, "and the jokes about the father of the happy couple. I suppose you will now forbid me to visit Ninar Foan?" he demanded of Shadow.

"Who's behind the plot?" Shadow asked, needing time to think. "The rebels? Karaman?"

The countess said that neither Elosa nor her mother knew.

"Oh—*hell*!" Vindax said. He went paler than ever. "The duchess of Foan did visit the court once. I remember her being presented. I must have been about four." He stared in horror at the countess and then at Shadow. "So there may be no assassination plot at all— just a plot to keep me away from the keeper. Perhaps the duchess of Foan has been playing the same game as my mother?"

And that nasty question raised even more nasty questions.

"You could send for the duke," the countess suggested.

"Shadow? Advise me, dammit! What do we do?"

Shadow shrugged. He was not sure who was playing what games, for he knew he could never understand these prickly aristocrats with their convoluted principles of honor. Security, however, he thought he could handle, and unless someone launched an open assault, the lonely aerie was safer than anywhere. "We send Rorin back to explain that the girl is safe. We'll send one of our people along." Not a trooper, he decided. They had better keep the armed strength up. "The chief of protocol, perhaps? Have him ask the duke for reassurance—he'll probably come himself. Meanwhile you stay here. You can't avoid the scandal now. The damage is done."

Vindax nodded. His arm had gone around the countess, apparently of its own volition. He smiled at her, and she wiggled her tongue at him. He looked up and dismissed Shadow with a nod. "See to it!"

Shadow slipped out and closed the drape carefully, knowing that he was leaving the prince in good hands.

5

"...even nestlings are dangerous."
—Manual of Training, Royal Guard

IT was his birthday. He was sixteen kilodays old today, and no one in the world knew it. Probably no one knew his name, either; he often wondered if even the king remembered. For almost five of those kilodays he had been Shadow, and his real name had not been spoken in all that time. He had probably established a record, for it was very unlikely that any previous King Shadow had lasted five kilodays, certainly not in recent reigns.

He was standing in the royal cabinet, staring out a window and brooding on being old: sixteen.

At the far end of the cabinet the king was sitting at his desk with the royal breeder and the deputy royal breeder, talking bloodstock. Birds! Shadow hated birds and had never flown in his life.

The cabinet was an egg-shaped room, high and huge, decorated in white and gold and blue. Normally the king worked outdoors, but he was very careful not to establish a pattern. He changed his work place at random and never announced in advance where he was going unless there was some big formal function planned. Today he had chosen the cabinet—and he seemed to use that only when he had some particularly dark purpose in mind. Shadow thought of it as the spider's parlor, for the tiny king in his white clothes always reminded him of one of

64

the nasty little bleached spiders that turned up under
rocks. From the very nature of his position, Shadow
must know all the royal secrets, but the cabinet provided
an exception. What the king said or heard there was not
overheard by Shadow.

Or so the king thought.

That day the king had talked taxes with the chancellor
and honors with Feather King of Arms, and now he was
wasting hours with the royal breeder, which was what he
seemed to enjoy most of all. Nothing nefarious had
hatched so far.

The doors were at the wide end of the egg. Anyone
coming in was first faced with a big wooden chair, almost
a throne, elaborately carved, high-backed and winged
and imposing. That was Shadow's seat. The arrangement
was deliberate. A would-be assassin who had eluded the
guards outside would certainly be in a hurry and probably nervous, and he would see that chair and an occupant dressed like the king—chances were, he would
strike there in error. That would give the real quarry a
little extra time.

To see the king it was necessary to step around that
chair, for the royal desk and a group of flanking chairs
stood at the far end of the hall, the narrow end, a long
way from the doors.

There were other exits from that room, two of them,
behind the desk: hidden doors. One led up to a makeshift
aerie on the roof. Aurolron never used it and had had it
netted over, but some of his predecessors had kept birds
there. Another exit led down to the labyrinth of secret
passages which wormed through the palace like giant
termite tracks.

Five kilodays as Shadow—it was time now to give
him an honorable retirement, a better peerage, an estate,
and the royal thanks. Any decent monarch would have
done so long since, but not Aurolron. And Shadow did
not dare suggest it. A hundred times he had almost
broached the subject, and always he had backed away.
He feared that his retirement would be arranged to a
wooden box.

He knew too much.

And he knew a lot more than the king thought he knew.

He was not a brave man. He often wondered what he would do if he saw the flash of the sudden stiletto, whether he could ever find the courage in that split second to move in front of it. If he had time to think, then he probably could, for when a king of Rantorra died by violence, then Shadow was guilty of high treason and the penalty for that was much worse than a stab wound.

The king made a joke, and his companions laughed heartily.

There were eight windows along both sides of that big room, carefully slanted so that the sun did not shine in directly but caught instead the sides of the deep embrasures and illuminated the room by reflection. The king could see out the windows from his desk; a visitor coming in saw no windows, only the royal dais glowing brightly ahead of him, subtly magnified by the taper of the egg shape. Whoever had designed this place had been full of little tricks like that.

Shadow was standing on the darkward side, staring up at the mountains behind Ramo. He had a good view of the palace aerie and the birds that came and went constantly. Horrible, savage monsters!

Ironically, it was his very dislike of the brutes which had landed him in his terrible job. Almost five kilodays earlier his immediate predecessor had died in an attack by one of those terrors—not a wild, even, but one of the royal stock which had escaped from the aerie and then launched a deliberate attack on the royal party returning from a hunt. With a peculiar irony, it had chosen the king himself for its target, almost as though it knew. Shadow —the previous Shadow—had acted in the heroic tradition of his line, blinkering his mount and steering it into the attacker's path. His bird had fallen with a broken wing, and the fall had broken his neck.

The court had been loyally horrified at the attack and loudly joyful that His Majesty had escaped. Baron Haundor—there! he had thought that name—Baron Haundor had rejoiced with the rest of them and had been discussing the matter with a group of friends when he had been summoned to the Presence.

The king had been badly shaken. Never before or since had Shadow seen him show fear, but that day he had been trembling.

Baron Haundor had begun his congratulations on the royal good fortune; the king had cut him off with the terrible words: "You are to be Shadow now."

He thought briefly of that eager, fresh-faced kid who had been made Prince Shadow less than seventy days ago. He had looked ready to die of shock. He wondered if his face had looked like that. Probably.

"But why me?" the horrified baron had demanded.

"Because you know how to keep your mouth shut," the king had said.

In his terror, he had argued. "I have never flown a bird, Majesty!"

"And we never shall again," the king had said. "It is an unsafe practice for a reigning monarch. If Shadow cannot fly, then we cannot, so we shall not be tempted to change our mind." He had meant it, too. Before that day he had been a keen skyman, but thereafter he had confined his interest in the eagles to their care and breeding. He had flown no more.

Baron Haundor had been heard of no more. Only Shadow.

The royal breeder was gathering up the papers—the schedules and the genealogies and the lists. The audience was almost over then, and Shadow wondered who came next. Perhaps now he would discover what unsavory matter had provoked the king's choice of the cabinet for this day's session. He walked across and sat himself quietly in his high-winged chair.

"...progress in pairing SaltSkimmer and Rock-Eater?" the king asked.

Shadow knew one secret which the king did not. Any word spoken at that royal desk was clearly audible in Shadow's chair at the far end of the hall. It was another of the clever tricks built into that room, a brilliant use of

freak acoustics stemming from the curves of the walls.
Perhaps it had been an accident and some long-dead
Shadow had discovered it and suggested putting a seat
for himself in that exact spot. More likely it had been
deliberate and the kings had once known of it. Aurolron
certainly did not, and if he ever discovered that he had
been overheard there for five kilodays, then there would
be a new Shadow within the hour.

The conversation about pairing droned on.

What sort of a man had he been, King Shadow wondered, when he had been a man and not merely a
shadow? Not like that dashing young trooper the prince
had chosen, that was certain. Not handsome, even then,
when he had had hair. A politician, an impoverished
noble with a minor title and a real need for a favorable
marriage, a schemer. He had lacked looks and charm to
win such a marriage by romance—women had never
liked him. To be honest, he had been planning a little
blackmail as soon as he found the right key. A great col-
lector of gossip, a fair manipulator, he would have
worked his way up in the murky world of court politics
quite well, given a little more time. One day he would
have found a suitable heiress with a suitable secret, and
then he would have proposed and been accepted.

Five kilodays! Any decent king would now retire him
with a better title and an estate and marry off one of the
royal wards on him, some supple maiden aged about six,
with firm little conical breasts.

Once he had recovered from the initial shock of being
appointed Shadow, he had rather fancied himself as chief
of the secret police. If the king never flew, then
Shadow's duty must be to become familiar with the palace jungle and know what stirred in the undergrowth.

Wrong! He had quickly discovered that there was already a chief of the secret police: the king himself. His
knowledge and the extent of his spy network had astounded Shadow. Two assassination attempts had been
made on Aurolron early in his reign, but none since.
Would-be conspirators were invariably outconspired by
their intended victim and died to the dirge of their own

screams and the savory smell of themselves cooking. Shadow was merely the last possible line of defense, the human shield, and his longevity had been due to Aurolron's skill, not his—the dangers had never reached so near.

Little white spider.

The royal breeder and his deputy retired at last, bowing. They did not even glance at Shadow as they opened the door and went out.

He got a clear view of the anteroom through the doors, and he knew at once who was next. The equerry came in, stepped around the chair, and bowed.

"Your Majesty, His Royal Highness Prince Jarkadon awaits your pleasure."

Shadow turned his head. In the prisms hidden in the wings of the chair he could see the king at the far end of the room, and he saw the royal nod. The king did know of those spy holes; indeed, it had been he who pointed them out to Shadow. Any visitor would believe himself unobserved when he was beside the king's desk—if Shadow was in his chair, as he usually was, out of sight and mind. But the visitor would not be unobserved, so no silent overpowering could succeed.

Jarkadon stepped in, jauntily dressed in green and blue, a flaxen-haired, blue-eyed younger version of the king. He paused for a moment as the doors were closed behind him, and he eyed Shadow thoughtfully as one might eye a watchdog or a drawbridge. Shadow decided he was tense and trying not to show it. Then he walked around the chair and bowed toward the king.

He was nasty. Jarkadon had been a nasty child, and now he was a nastier adult. His father could still handle him, but he would be serious trouble for Vindax when he succeeded. Shadow trusted him even less than the king, if that were possible.

Queen Mayala, now, was a human being. Too nice a person for her position and hopelessly ground down by her husband, but basically decent. She never failed to give Shadow a smile when they met, and no one else did that. Yes, he could have liked Mayala were she not queen; her recent deterioration pained him.

Vindax was headstrong, too inclined to clash with his father in ferocious arguments that he must inevitably lose. He was smart, and charming when he chose to be. He was not truly trustworthy—none of them were—but certainly a better prospect for future king than Jarkadon would ever be.

Shadow made himself comfortable and prepared to enjoy a juicy royal outburst. The court was agog with a new scandal—and here was the prime suspect.

No! Jarkadon was going through a full ritual approach, with bowing and gestures, which was a mockery when father and son were alone, an impudence almost. But it was a petitioner's ritual, meaning that he had asked for this meeting. Curious! Aurolron took ceremony seriously and did not interrupt, although he frowned. Then the prince had reached the desk.

"What was all that for?" the king snapped, pointedly not inviting his son to sit.

"I come to crave a boon, sire," Jarkadon said. "Did I make any mistakes?"

"You have three minutes."

The prince nodded inquiringly toward the back of Shadow's chair.

"He can't hear," the king snapped. "What do you want?"

"My birthright," Jarkadon said.

Shadow wondered if he had heard correctly. Perhaps the king did also, for there was a long pause.

"Sit down."

"Thank you, Father." The little bastard was always cocky, but his impudent manner was even more marked than usual. He was being given the famous royal stare and not wilting at all.

"Talk," the king said.

"Well," Jarkadon said, leaning back. "It began with Mother, of course, and her curious reluctance to let her favorite son visit Ninar Foan. She thought she was being subtle, but it was obvious. I even mentioned one day that you had changed your mind, and she dropped two kilodays in front of my eyes—and put on three when I confessed I was lying."

"You little bastard," the king said quietly, and the prince chuckled.

"Hardly me, Father! But it made me curious. When you sent a courier off with news of the impending visit, I decided to have a chat with him as soon as he got back. He seemed to take a long time returning, so I investigated the aerie and found a bird wearing Foan's anklet. Of course the courier would have exchanged mounts."

"Of course," the king said.

"But the rider was nowhere to be found. Sir Jion Paslo? If Vindax can associate with commoners, I assumed I could. But he had vanished. I was told he had gone to Hollinfar, a very dull place, from all accounts, given over to sheep raising and similar obscene practices."

"You found him, though."

"Yes," the prince said. "The fourth cell on the right as you pass the thumbscrews."

Never, in five kilodays, had anyone spoken to the king like that, and his response was ominous. "The jailors you bribed are now in the third and fifth cells, respectively."

Jarkadon merely shrugged. "An occupational hazard of the corrupt. Yes, I did talk with poor Jion—implying that I might secure his release, of course. I gather that the resemblance is incredible."

The king's angry glare was perceptible even to Shadow at the far end of the room

"If you studied bloodlines, in birds or in people, as I do," Aurolron said, "then you would know that such resemblances can turn up in quite distant relatives, and they are related, distantly."

"Closely, I suspect."

The royal fist thumped on the desk, and then both men turned to look at the back of Shadow's chair. The king half rose and then settled back uneasily. To order

Shadow out of the room would be unprecedented, and therefore cause for speculation.

"You realize," the king said, "that any other man who said that would be guilty of high treason. However, I suppose that it does concern you, so I shall be lenient—just this once. We will discuss it, and then the subject will never be raised again! Is that clear?"

"Certainly," Jarkadon said. "If I may make a couple of comments afterward? Please explain, Father."

Now the king's face was white with anger. Anyone else in the kingdom would be groveling at this point. Shadow was shaking and perspiring as though he had a fever.

"I also talked with the courier. Of course your mother knew, and that is why she is so upset. Obviously there is going to be gossip when it becomes known. I have never doubted your mother's honor—and I am appalled that you would. I have accepted Vindax as my son, and I shall continue to do so. Resemblance or not, I can assure you that it was physically impossible for the duke of Foan to have fathered him. Your mother is notoriously unpunctual, but even she could not carry a child for five hectodays. She was a virgin when we married, anyway. Foan has never been to court. Yes, there will be gossip when Vindax and his party return. But not in my hearing."

The king leaned back and glared.

"Why did you let him go?" Jarkadon asked, still unruffled.

"Because it must come out eventually. It is a miracle that it has not already done so." The king paused and then spoke reluctantly. "He was born blond; his hair grew in dark. The facial resemblance became obvious only when he reached adolescence, although the duchess came to court when he was a child, and she noticed even then, I think. She could not take her eyes off him. That was when I . . . when I suspected."

Jarkadon nodded. "You have met the duke, though?"

"Never," the king said.

The prince chuckled. "And you didn't warn Vindax, did you?"

"No." Again the king paused. "Perhaps it was unfair, but it is his problem, and I thought it would be a good test for him. He, I am sure, will not think evil of his mother. But then, he is a man of honor."

Jarkadon's fair-skinned face reddened.

"I am the fount of justice," the king said. "I try many cases myself, and invariably I try cases dealing with inheritance among the nobility. The law is quite clear and quite universal: A child born in wedlock is legitimate unless the husband can prove beyond doubt that he could not have fathered it. In this case, I can prove beyond doubt—should anyone have the temerity to ask me—that Foan could not. There is nothing left to discuss."

Shadow was paralyzed with terror and yet more fascinated than he had ever been.

"Oh, we are not talking certainty," Jarkadon said. "I do not claim so. But we are talking of a direct male line unbroken for forty generations—on so polished a scutcheon, even a fingermark will show up. Especially one made by the wrong finger."

"Be careful!" his father warned between clenched teeth.

Yet Jarkadon seemed to relax even more, and clutched his knee with both hands. "Around day 1108 of your reign would be the fateful moment, wouldn't it? 266 from 1374: I have been doing research, you see. Or later, possibly—he was a small baby."

The king did not speak.

"Schagarn," the prince said. "And Kollinor?"

There was a long silence while the monarch stared at his son and Shadow wondered who or what or where Schagarn and Kollinor were. Obviously the king knew and they were words of power—the silence was very long, and when Aurolron broke it, his tone had changed.

"How did you find out about those?"

Jarkadon slipped a hand into his doublet and produced a piece of paper. "All those interminable records you keep of your feathered pets, from egg to pillow. I never could see the point of them—until now. This is a copy, of course, but you can call for the original. It is an extract from the journey record on a bird called Death-Beak, one of your mounts in those days, apparently. I see that you rode it to Schagarn and then it went to Ninar Foan. It returned later—with a message, I suppose, or else it had started pining. The name of the rider who took it from Schagarn has been scratched out, but it must have been a very short name. 'Foan,' perhaps?"

He laid the paper on the desk, and the king stared at it. Then he almost snarled. "Your mother was never at Schagarn," he said. "And the duke never went to Kollinor. I know that for granite fact!"

"Quite possible," Jarkadon agreed. He pulled out a second paper and laid it beside the first. "Another copy, of course. WindStriker. Remember her? Day 1165?"

Aurolron was always most dangerous when he was quiet, but now the silence dragged on, and it seemed to be the king who was at a loss for words.

"I think you did meet the duke, Father?"

There was an even longer silence, and then Aurolron sighed. "Yes. But you will not report that to anyone—anyone at all, is that clear? Many men have died to keep that secret."

The unseen eavesdropper shivered, but the prince was undeterred.

"Is it fair to me, Father? Look at me. Look in a mirror. When—in a long time, we all hope—you die, you are expecting me to kneel in homage to a bastard, sitting on your throne? I am your son! Would you do that?"

"What are you suggesting that I do?" the king demanded in a low voice.

"Obviously if you disown him, then you would have to put Mother to death," Jarkadon said, "which would certainly provoke gossip. Also Foan, which would mean a military campaign to catch him. I think you already found an easier solution."

Shadow shivered again.

"What are you hinting?" the king asked.

"Ingenious and simple, Father. All you had to do was

say yes! But you are a perfectionist for security," Jarkadon continued. "Yet you let Vindax go off along the Rand, and you put *Ninomar* in charge. He sent out proclamations announcing the plans! His family tree is very solid, but his head was carved from the trunk. You were not in character there, Father! And Mother—she detests scandal, I know, but even scandal could hardly upset her like this. She suspects!"

The king was still looking down at the papers. "She fears for his welfare, naturally."

"Naturally? But it would solve the problem, wouldn't it?" The prince was looking very pleased with himself. "However, they have been gone a long time, and they have singles. We should have heard. I began to wonder if you had overlooked something, Father, so I thought I would point it out."

"What?" the king asked, without raising his eyes.

"Harl."

"Harl!" The reaction seemed to astonish even Jarkadon.

"He's good!" the prince said. "I went along on a few of their practice flights, and I admit that I was impressed. And Vindax has put Harl-the-churl in charge. He lets him overrule Ninomar."

"Shadow?" the king muttered thoughtfully.

"Shadow," his son agreed. "Obviously he has kept Vindax alive this long. Perhaps he is too good for you."

A trace of the earlier anger flamed at that, but it was the prince who was in command now. King Shadow had never seen anything like this before.

Then Aurolron seemed to make an effort to assert himself. He picked up the two papers and started to tear them into small shreds. "You are a meddlesome, snooping busybody—but I suppose you inherit some of that from me. Your paternity, at least, is not in doubt. You will find curiosity useful. Who else knows of this? Have you discussed it with that rat pack you favor?"

The prince flushed. "With no one, Father."

"Good," the king said. "Very well, I congratulate you. I agree that I may have overlooked something. Forget this conversation. I shall take steps to uphold my honor, and I suggest that you now be more concerned with your own. You may withdraw."

Jarkadon rose and bowed low, but as he turned for the door, his face broke into a wide smile. Hastily Shadow closed his eyes and leaned his head against the wing of his chair, feigning sleep, afraid to meet the prince's gaze. His clothes were soaked with sweat.

He did not hear the equerry enter across the thick rug, and he jumped quite genuinely when the man spoke. He saw a few grins out in the anteroom. Shadow asleep on duty! Why had he never thought of that before? He must start dropping such hints, and perhaps he would win his retirement yet.

No more audiences were scheduled, only a few petitioners.

The king would not see them.

The equerry withdrew, and the door was closed. For an endless time the monarch sat at his desk and stared at Shadow's chair, making its occupant melt with terror. *Did the king know?* Had he been pretending ignorance all this time? If he as much as suspected that Shadow had overheard, then Shadow's death was very near.

And which story was correct? The king's mind was infinitely tortuous, and he had switched positions like a moth. Obviously he was betraying one son or lying to the other, but which? Or both?

Aurolron ended his brooding. He reached for the bell rope and summoned his most trusted secretary and another man, whose name was enough to send shivers down Shadow's back—ostensibly an armorer, he also applied his skill with hot iron as one of the royal torturers. The door was closed and then opened almost at once as the secretary scuttled in.

The king waited until the man was ready and then began. "To the crown prince: usual greetings . . .

"*By our royal command: Terminate your journey at Gorr and do not continue to Ninar Foan. Return with all your companions as fast as practical. You may give your mother's health as a reason, but she is well.*

*"While you are in Gorr, a man named Ovla will seek
audience with you. Admit him privily and receive him in
private, with only Shadow present. You may allow a day
or two for him to appear.* Usual ending. Also, prepare a
warrant for the arrest of the holder of Hiando Keep—a
baronet, last name Harl. Look it up. And his wife. To be
held incommunicado during our pleasure. We will receive the aerie archivist after lunch."

The secretary rose.

"Wait!" the king said. "There is more." He paused
until the man was ready once more. "Add this to the
prince's letter: *I know that this revocation will distress
you greatly, but I have good reasons for it, and the man
Ovla knows them and will disclose them to you. Then
you will understand that I am acting in your best inter-
ests only. We have much to discuss when you return, my
son, and I regret that I have not taken you into my confidence sooner.* That's all. Bring the private seal; I shall
have another."

Shadow watched the secretary's stooped shoulders
hurry through the door and puzzled on what all that had
meant. Even after five kilodays, he could never unravel
the spider's webs, the depths of his duplicities. Aurolron
prided himself on never having to cancel an order. The
feint of a recall, the double feint of that apparently sin-
cere and personal addition to the impersonal command,
the irresistible hint of secrets to be disclosed by Ovla...
then what? What else would the mysterious Ovla bring?

Now the king had taken pen and parchment himself
and was writing—and that was rare indeed. Only the
most contrived machinations ever provoked him to use
his own hand. For what seemed a long time he sat and
wrote, while Shadow cowered in his chair and listened to
the pen scratch like a fingernail on a coffin lid.

The king finished, read it over, folded it carefully. He
rang once more, and then received the armorer, who
smiled at Shadow as he went past. The man enjoyed his
work.

"There is a Jion Paslo in the cells," the king said
quietly.

"Yes, Majesty?"

The king sighed. "He is very sick."

Not expected to live.

"Any questions, Majesty?"

"None," said the king. "Quick and painless. I expect the warden's report within the hour." He passed over a ring as payment.

The man bowed. "About one hundred breaths, sire."

He paused at the door and gave Shadow another friendly smile. He always did that, and Shadow always wondered if he were being measured for a griddle.

The secretary returned, and the two letters were sealed.

"Both to be sent by the bird from Ninar Foan," the king said. "Take them to the aerie yourself and see that the lord eagler attends to the matter in person."

He rose and wandered along the room behind the secretary, looking amiable.

"Well, Shadow," he remarked cheerfully. "I think we have earned some lunch—are you well?"

"A touch of the grippe, Majesty, perhaps."

Aurolron frowned. "Then we shall send you to bed. We should not want you to become very sick."

Shadow shivered convulsively, as though he had an ague.

Someone was going to be very sick, he was sure, when that letter reached its destination.

6

"Give a man the whole sky and he'll break his neck."
—*Skyman proverb*

WHY did the world always feel colder when a man awoke from sleep? Shadow climbed quietly up to the top floor of the aerie, shivering and wondering. The sun was the same and the wind was the same, but he had not shivered when he had arrived at Vinok. The two troopers on sentry duty straightened when they saw him; nineteen eagles paid no attention.

The primitive toilets were on ground level, a long way down. No one else was awake, so Shadow moved to leeward and relieved himself over the perching wall.

A desolate place! The Rand here curved away from the sun, almost across the terminator. The lower hills were sheathed in perpetual shade, and the higher peaks glowed against a somber sky. The air was thin and bitter, the sun a bloodstain on the horizon.

He had slept badly, his mattress stretched across the door of the prince's room. That was an excess of zeal, perhaps, but that was no fault in a leader, and everyone in the party knew who made the decisions. Zeal, unfortunately, was little protection from either drafts or frequent giggling and rustling sounds—the countess had been working overtime at cheering up her prince. Raising the spirits by raising the flesh, she called it.

It was now forty-five days since they had left Ramo,

and Vindax was still alive. The wild birds—and they had seen several flocks—had avoided so large a group. If wild men were planning violence, Shadow's precautions had confounded them so far.

His business ended, Shadow wandered over to the nearer guard.

"Good sky, trooper."

"Good sky to you, Shadow." It amused the troopers that he need not be saluted and yet could overrule a vice-marshal.

NailBiter and IceFire had stopped nuzzling each other. Shadow stared hard along the ridges rightward, seeing nothing but barren rock and rare wind scrub. "We are about to have visitors," he said.

The trooper blinked and turned to look. "I see nothing, Shadow."

"Nor do I. But I'll go and warn the others. Make spaces, in case they have spares."

Smiling to himself, Shadow headed for the steps. The eagles were all gazing rightward, and their combs were flickering as they did when they got excited. They could see something, and the timing was right—it must be the reply from Ninar Foan.

The trooper was still staring blankly at the hills.

It was a uniformly shivering and rumpled party that assembled on the aerie floor shortly afterward: gritty eyes, hunched shoulders, and—with four exceptions—bristled faces. A scent of wood smoke and scorched goat meat was drifting up the stairwell. Shadow's stomach knotted at the thought of more goat, and he was pleased to see that the newcomers did include two spares. The duke had thought to send supplies.

A spare would follow its mate without trouble—usually—but landing was tricky. Many a rider had been savaged on the perching wall before he could dismount. Shadow felt a quiet satisfaction at having ordered the troopers to clear spaces—the only safe place to land when there were spares loose was between two other birds, both safely hooded. The spares circled a few times, angry at not being able to perch next to their mates, and then settled down as close as possible.

Five eagles; three men. The first man rode a spectacular male silver; he must be the duke, Shadow decided, and his guess was confirmed when Elosa ran forward to hug him as soon as he cleared the bars.

But the duke did not merely return her hug momentarily and then gently set her aside so that he could approach the prince—which would have been proper. Nor did he boot the young lady all the way to Allaban—which might have been a natural parental reaction. He held her for a few minutes as though he were comforting a small child. Or were they getting their stories matched? The back of Vindax's neck began to grow hot as he waited.

Then the duke stepped away from Elosa, pulled off goggles and helmet, and advanced.

And the welcoming party froze like the ancient rocks of the Rand.

Tired and dusty in his flying suit, this man was Alvo, duke of Foan, keeper of the Rand, hero of the battle of Allaban, premier noble of the realm—and possible traitor, seducer of his sovereign's wife.

It was bitterly unfair, Shadow thought. Rarely do two men truly look alike, be they brother and brother, father and son, or cousin and cousin. Family resemblances are usually subtle, a feature here and a mannerism there. A skilled and keen skyman, the duke had retained his trim, athletic figure; even appproaching middle age he still looked youthful, and his body and his face were the body and face of the prince. There were differences: lines on the forehead and slight sags below the eyes. His neck and shoulders had thickened, he held himself with the greater authority of age, and he lacked the quick restlessness of the younger man, but the similarities far outweighed the differences. The beak nose, the bushy brows, the dark, deep eyes—seeing that astonishing identity, it was suddenly very hard to believe in a freak throwback in third cousins once removed.

Even if they were father and son, then nature was being infinitely ironic: Shadow had never seen father and son look quite so much alike. Remembering Jarkadon's resemblance to the king, he wondered if Queen Mayala had some curious property of not imparting anything of her own looks to her sons—and realized that he was now a believer.

"Your Highness," Elosa mumbled to the dusty floor, "may I have the honor of presenting my father, His Grace, the duke of Foan."

The two men bowed. Normally they should then have embraced, being relatives, but neither seemed capable of moving his feet. The duke's windburn showed like red blotches on white paper; his face was rigid. Shadow could see little of Vindax's face, but he suspected it was no more relaxed.

"Well met, Cousin," the prince said at last.

The duke took a deep breath and then made an appropriate speech. Vindax replied in a monotone. Neither took his eyes off the other.

Then Vindax seemed to shake himself. He proceeded to present his companions.

Prince and duke and Shadow stood in the tiny bedroom cubicle. Vindax had passed from shock into quivering rage. The older man had recovered his composure and seemed to be totally at ease.

"I deeply regret the misunderstanding, Highness," he said. "My wife and Sir Ukarres agree that they spoke with her, but only by chance meeting. The rebels were mentioned in passing, but there was certainly no talk of plotting or treachery. Young girls sometimes come up with strange fancies. They have romantic ideas."

The back of Vindax's neck turned pink—he did not like that obvious fiction. He did not reply.

The duke smiled cheerfully. "And your royal parents, they are in good health? The queen? It has been a long time since she illuminated my halls with her beauty, since I said farewell to her—at Gorr."

Deny, deny!

"She has been failing lately," Vindax said. "I think she was distressed at the thought of my journey. She may have thought that I would fall in with questionable characters."

The duke ignored the barb. His voice had a rough, country sound to it; the prince's carried the softer lilt of Ramo, but the two were one voice.

"And His Majesty?"

"Well, thank you, when we left. You have never met my father?"

"No," the duke said. "I never had the honor."

There was the obvious moment to extend the king's invitation to court, but it did not come. Instead Vindax suddenly snapped, "We are strangely alike, you and I!" Tension raised his voice above its normal pitch.

The duke laughed. "So I was informed by the royal courier, *Cousin*. He was quite astonished."

"He did not inform your daughter; she was very astonished."

That shaft struck; certainly the duke would have dragged all the details out of Tuy Rorin. He colored.

"I repeat, Highness, that she has romantic notions. You are most welcome to my home. You will be quite safe—as prince and as relative. Our hospitality is genuine and heartfelt, although conditions will be more humble than you are used to."

There was a pause, and then Vindax obviously came to a decision—anger was useless, and the situation must be resolved with at least a public display of fellowship.

"So humble that you and I must share a dressing room, Your Grace?"

Foan blinked. "Certainly not, Highness. Why?"

"We could save on a shaving mirror," Vindax said.

And so Crown Prince Vindax flew on to Ninar Foan, a bleak and forbidding castle looming over a drab town, its rough stone walls swept by the chill winds of the Rand and lit by a reluctant red sun.

The proprieties were observed—there were formal presentations and a dinner in the great hall. The participants went through their paces like puppets, royal party and castle dwellers alike. It was unfair! Even an unusually close resemblance could have been tactfully ignored in public and passed off with a wink in private, but not this twinlike identity. There were eighteen in the royal party. They would not all remain silent; they could not all be put to death. There had been others; thinking back, Shadow could remember looks of shock and disbelief from some of the gentry they had visited, the near or far neighbors who knew the Keeper. Already the word must be working its way back along the Rand like an infection, heading for the court.

The scandal made his job harder, now and in the future. If Jarkadon did not already have a faction of his own, then he certainly would soon, whether he wanted it or not. He would. The death of Vindax might seem like a very logical and desirable solution to many people: the duke, the queen, the king, Jarkadon, the duchess, Elosa . . . the list ballooned in his mind. Surely none of those was capable of murder, but the thought must be there, and there were always fanatics and overeager supporters.

Three days of festivities were three days of vigilance. In one sense, Shadow had an easier time than the rest, for his attention had to remain fixedly on the problem of safety and he had no time for brooding about politics, no need to edge around verbal precipices.

There was a reception for the local gentry, who stared aghast at this younger reflection of their duke.

There were discussions of crops and taxes, of justice and order, and those were safe subjects.

There was a tour of the aerie to examine the celebrated Ninar Foan silvers. The duke was gracious over the problem of NailBiter's illicit seduction; he had more serious problems than that to worry about.

"She made an understandable choice," he said. "Your bronze is a big, handsome fellow. The silvers need an outcross, anyway, to restore the vigor of the line. Elosa must console herself, and I most happily give IceFire to you, Highness, as a memento of your visit."

"You are very generous, Cousin," Vindax said. "I shall accept on behalf of my father, who is the enthusiast in our family. He will be overjoyed; and I am sure that he will send you the firstborn, as is usual in such cases."

"Your father is a great expert," the keeper said. "The priests uncovered much relevant material in the sacred texts for him. As you know, he can talk on the subject for hours. The progeny will all be bronzes, but breed one of those bronzes back to the silvers and . . ."

They were at the precipice again.

"And the recesssive characteristics reappear," Vindax snapped. "I have heard my father lecture. I always have a problem knowing which features are recessive."

The duke's face flushed equally red, and they exchanged identical furious glares.

But how, Shadow wondered, did the duke know that the king would lecture for hours?

Late on the third day, close to two bells, the duke and his royal guest sat and drank mulled wine by a roaring fire in the duke's study, a shaggy, incoherent room full of trophy heads and faded frescoes and mismatched furniture. It was a friendly, informal place, reflecting the varied tastes of generations of dukes, all of whom seemed to have added and none subtracted.

Perhaps Vindax thought he could drink his host into indiscretion, but the two of them seemed to share the same remarkable capacity for alcohol as they shared so much else. Ukarres fidgeted on a chair between them, while Shadow sat beside and a little to the back of Vindax, sipping sparingly and bone-weary from the continuous tension. WindStriker was overdue for a kill, and Vindax suggested a hunt.

The duke agreed with enthusiasm and promised good sport—he kept a couple of peaks as his own reserve, he said.

"Not Eagle Dome, though?" Vindax asked.

Earlier that day they had peered out at the distant shape of the great massif which broke the normal slope of the Rand and marked the boundary between Rantorra and the lost realm of Allaban. Sun-bright and faint, more like a cloud than a rock, it had obviously tantalized Vindax.

The duke laughed. "Hardly! Shadow would not approve."

"No-man's-land," Ukarres said, "but not no-bird-land!" It had earned its name in remote ages, he said, from the number of wilds inhabiting it, and now the wilds had taken it again. Its slopes were too steep for cultivation but were well watered and therefore rich in game. The eagles of Eagle Dome had become peacekeepers between human factions, for to attempt a flight around that great jutting mountain was certain suicide.

"Whose side are they defending?" Vindax asked, amused.

"Both, I suppose," the keeper said. "I scouted that way about a kiloday ago, I think it was. They flocked by the dozen—I fled faster than I ever have in my life. Allaban was never an integral part of Rantorra, as you know. In theory it was a vassal kingdom, but in practice it was always more or less autonomous, with its own royal family. Had it not been for the rebels, then your dear ... your honored mother would be reigning there now."

They could never stay away from the precipice for long.

"Eagle Dome has always been something of a barrier," he concluded weakly.

"The rebel, Karaman," the prince said. "Have you ever met him?"

"No," the duke said, "but Ukarres has."

The old man looked up from his forward-hunch position and smiled, revealing his scattered teeth. "He's an interesting character, Your Highness—if he's still alive, of course. A religious fanatic, but with a certain charm. He was what you might call a low-key fanatic, I suppose ...underpowering? On normal subjects he came across as a quiet, rather earthy man. But not to be underestimated. And a fantastic trainer of birds."

"So the eagles of Eagle Dome stand guard," Vindax

said thoughtfully. "To retake Allaban, wc should have to
fight our way past them first and then take on the
rebels."

The keeper frowned. "Are you considering such an
attempt, Your Highness?"

"Not seriously at present," Vindax said. "Maybe
someday. After all, I am heir to Allaban . . . also."

The precipice again.

At last Vindax declared himself ready for bed; the
duke had drunk him to a draw. Neither man seemed
more than tipsy, although they had each downed enough
to have laid Shadow on the carpet. The prince hardly
wavered as he headed to his room.

There he flopped on a chair, folded his arms, and
glared blearily at Shadow. "What would he say, do you
suppose, if I asked for his daughter's hand in marriage?"

"He might say yes," Shadow said, wishing Vindax
would go off to bed and end the day. "Would you like
that?"

Vindax pulled a face. "Never! I know what she'd do.
She'd marry me fast as a stooping eagle—and then
refuse to consummate the affair on grounds of consan-
guinity."

Shadow thought that seemed likely. "Let Jarkadon
have her, then?" *Damn!*

Vindax did not seem to notice the lack of tact. "Why
not? She had the gall today to ask me what color his hair
is."

Shadow decided to change the subject. "Let me warn
you of something, Prince? When you tell a lie, your right
ear twitches."

"Oh, great!" Vindax said, scowling. "Try not to stare
at it, will you?" Then he smiled. "Thanks. I appreciate
knowing that. But I haven't been twitching too much
today, have I?"

"You told Elosa she looked charming in that outra-
geous dress," Shadow said. "No, there's something else.
When you asked the duke if he had ever met Karaman,
he said no. But his ear twitched."

"Yes," Vindax said quite soberly. "I think His Grace has been twitching the truth quite a lot lately."

The hunt was to be restricted to a small party: the prince and the countess, the duke and Shadow, and four troopers as escort. When they assembled after breakfast, however, Lady Elosa was already supervising the dressing of Icefire. The duke frowned but did not intervene. Shadow almost exerted his unlimited authority to order her away, but relations were strained enough without making a scene over a badly spoiled brat.

Shadow dressed WindStriker himself, checking every scrap of harness twice. True, the story of a plot seemed to have been unfounded, but few things were easier to arrange than a hunting accident. NailBiter was sulking, not wanting to interrupt his dalliance with IceFire—they preened each other and nibbled combs by the hour, a parody of honeymooners.

Standing in the high aerie, overlooking the drab and pinkish countryside, the duke pointed out the local thermals and upturns, warned of downdrafts, and suggested a route to the higher, sun-bright locales with a good chance for goats, the most sporting of quarry.

Or perhaps, he suggested, the prince would like to try some archery against game birds, leaving the goats for later.

"No!" Shadow said firmly. The troopers must be armed, but he would not have unnecessary arrows flying around his ward.

The duke frowned in astonishment at such insolence; the prince merely smiled and agreed.

They mounted. The troopers launched and took up station. They were followed by the hunters: the duke, the countess, Shadow, the prince, and finally Elosa.

Shadow soared over the town, sparing a passing thought for the frozen poor in this bleak place, then turned into the updraft and began circling, watching as the prince settled in below him, as always. Upward they floated, and then he thought he heard a shout—and saw to his astonishment that Vindax was breaking out of the thermal, as though heading back.

Then WindStriker seemed to balk, beating her wings furiously, and in a moment had taken Shadow's air. What the hell was His Royal Crazy Highness up to?

Reluctantly he urged NailBiter upward, knowing that powered flight would soon exhaust the mounts. Still he could not reach the prince—indeed the gap was widening. An old relic like WindStriker outclimbing NailBiter?

Then he knew.

WindStriker swayed and veered above him, and momentarily he had a clear view. Her blinkers were shut, and the prince's face was white below his goggles. He shouted, and Shadow heard the word he expected: "Bat."

A single mutebat would send an eagle into an hour or more of ecstatic intoxication, hunched down on its perch with its eyes closed, drooling and quivering, its comb blue and rigid. But batmeat took time to act—get a bird into the air before the effects appeared and it was a flying maniac. The drug produced visual hallucinations, so that blinkers had no effect, and the bird would fly where and how it liked, soaring in downdrafts, beating its wings, turning upside down. It was capable of flying straight into the ground. It was also capable of heading to heights or depths where human lungs could no longer cope—and Ninar Foan was already very high for men.

The castle aerie had been cleaned of mutebats; Shadow had noted that with approval. This was human doing—treachery—and there was no recourse. He could only try to follow and hope. WindStriker was old, and NailBiter young and unusually powerful, but NailBiter could not match the frenzy of a batted bird.

Even if he could approach, there would be nothing he could do. No bird could carry two men; there was no way to move the prince to Shadow's mount and no way to exchange mounts. The only help he could offer was to keep in view—and watch Vindax die.

WindStriker locked herself into a soaring mode and rode the thermal, higher and higher and higher. Shadow followed with his lungs heaving, his ears popping constantly, his nose starting to bleed. He was gradually closing, for NailBiter had the greater wingspread, but dark spots began to flow in front of his eyes.

He remembered what a guard was taught to do in the prince's predicament: "Tie your reins, close your eyes, and pray loudly."

The thermal was dying out. Its curve had carried them over darkness, the lower slopes of the Rand, the mountains and chasms below showing only as wrinkled, indistinct patterns of shade. It would be deathly cold down there, where sunlight never shone.

Then the prince vanished into the cloudcap. Shadow felt his senses slipping and knew that he could do no more. Choking for air, he put NailBiter into a dive.

Vindax was gone.

7

"Where there's shadow, there's light."
—*Proverb*

T HE castle commons was a vast, dim hall with a barrel ceiling darkened by the smoke of centuries. The tables were of stone, for lumber had never been plentiful near Ninar Foan, but the great ovens and hearths kept the place warm, and the smell of food made it cheerful. Shadow shuffled in across the worn stone flags. He collected a giant tankard of steaming coffee, a large black roll, and a bowl of stew, without looking to see who gave them to him. Then he limped to a convenient stool.

He gulped the coffee, burning his mouth and throat and feeling the lip of the tankard rasp on his unshaven face. His face, raw from the constant wind, burned also, and his eyes were so loaded with fatigue that he could hardly focus. His head throbbed like a drum. All around the room there were others in the same plight, humped by the tables, many being anxiously tended by wives or daughters and some already asleep, head and arms spread out among the dishes.

He laid down the tankard and blearily regarded the stew bowl. He ought to eat, he told himself firmly, but his gut rebelled at the thought.

He had never been so tired in his life.

A cool hand ran its fingers through his tangled hair, slid down the side of his face, and came to rest in the neck of his flying suit. He looked up with a sad smile and leaned his head back against softness.

"Anything I can do?" asked Feysa, one of the royal party.

He shook his head. "It will be a long time before I can call on you," he said. "But thanks for a kind thought."

"You are going to get some sleep, though, aren't you?"

"One more patrol," he said.

Frowns did not suit her lovely face. "Sleep first, Shadow. You'll go to sleep in the sky."

"No," he said firmly. He picked up the spoon and forced some of the meat into his mouth. Then more. He started gulping it down, suddenly aware of being famished.

Feysa vanished as silently as she had come.

"Who is that, Shadow?" It was a boy sitting across from him who spoke, but when he focused the face out of the background haze, it was Elosa, chalky and hollow-eyed in her flying suit. He had not realized that she was there.

"That's Feysa," he said. "You haven't been to bed, either, have you?"

She shook her head. "If you can do it, then I can."

He slowed his eating, partly from table manners and partly because he knew he was being stupid to hog so fast.

"You fly like a man, lady."

"Is that a compliment?" she asked.

He could still smile, apparently; he hadn't known that. "It was intended as one. I'll rephrase it. You're a wonderful skywoman, lady. You look in better shape than any of us."

She smiled back coyly. "Then I'll accept the amendment and thank you. Now, who is Feysa?"

He bit into the tough roll. The coffee was beginning to work. "She's a lady's maid."

"She doesn't act like a lady's maid," Elosa said, frowning.

Shadow took another bite and chewed to gain time, studying her. She was obviously exhausted, as they all were, but he was honestly impressed by her courage and stamina—those could compensate for a lot of woolly-headed romanticism. Elosa was hill-bred—there was granite inside that elfin form. Perhaps he owed her a little wisdom.

"At court, and under her own name, she outranks both the countess and Lady Ninomar," he said.

Elosa studied his face gravely. "Explain."

He shrugged. "The countess is the prince's mistress, right?"

Obviously she had not known that, and a trace of color crept into her pale cheeks. He outlined a little palace politics.

"And Lady Ninomar?"

"Well, the countess obviously could not travel alone, so Lady Ninomar came also. Not his real wife, I shouldn't think."

Elosa bit her lip and said nothing.

"And two ladies cannot travel without a lady's maid. So Feysa. There happen to be three main factions in the palace at the moment, and each one got to place a lady in the party. It was all carefully planned."

"Spies?"

"Certainly," Shadow said. "Reporting what the prince says, who he favors, spying on each other. Some of the men are spies also, of course."

"I see." She looked very prim and suddenly very young again. "And whose mistress is Feysa?"

"Mine."

Now she truly turned pink. "Nice for you."

"Yes and no," Shadow said. He was deathly tired, and suddenly his bitterness overflowed in a torrent. "I had no say in the matter. I was told that the lady in question was coming and I would service her as required. Very practical—if she were assigned to anyone else, there would be arguments over precedence. Furthermore, I have no time to myself, as the others have—I attend the prince three watches out of three. So the others can find their own entertainment. Vindax was quite blunt—he did not want his bodyguard getting too horny to think straight."

"That's disgusting!" Elosa snapped.

"I agree," Shadow said. "At the palace it works the same way. The countess—whoever she happens to be at the time—comes at third watch to the royal bedroom. She is always attended by a maid, who sleeps in the anteroom—where I sleep. I tried to complain and was told to shut up or I would cause a scandal. Sometimes they're very pretty. I understand that I'm regarded as a great improvement on my predecessor, so now they roll dice for me. Flattering, isn't it?"

Elosa turned very red and said nothing.

"As Shadow I have no life of my own, lady. My body functions are part of palace politics. I'm a naive little country boy, and I don't approve. I rapture the ladies provided, but I don't approve."

"Why are you telling me this?" she demanded angrily.

He took a long draft of coffee, watching her. "Because I think you could benefit from some truths about the court. If you get the choice—stay away from it."

She tossed her head, but before she could speak a voice behind her said, "Leave us, Elosa."

Vindax! Shadow's heart jumped and then sank again. It was only the duke, bristly and sore-eyed like all of them, hair tangled and clothes filthy. He sank down on the stool his daughter had left and nursed a mug of coffee. Vice-Marshal Ninomar materialized at his side. Then a tapping noise sounded behind Shadow, and Ukarres hobbled up. Some days he seemed more crippled than others, and this day he was using two canes. Despite his haggard senility, he alone looked as though he had slept within living memory.

That left only one missing, and in a moment Vak Vonimor, the rubicund eagler, hurried in to join the meeting.

"Rorin's back, Your Grace," he said. "That's the lot."

Shadow's stew bowl was empty, polished, and he thought he could eat more, but it would put him to sleep.

"I suppose the big question," he said, "is whether we extend farther or quarter the same ground yet again."

The others glanced at the duke.

"No," he said. "First we're going to take a break. The men are past their limits; we all are. Why we haven't had accidents, I don't know. Even the birds are exhausted, and I've very rarely seen that in my life. Sleep for men, rest for birds. In another watch we'll start again."

"I have to agree," Ninomar said in his fastidious, military fashion. His close-trimmed mustache was drowning in encroaching stubble.

"And I say we fly one more patrol," Shadow said firmly. "He's been two days out there. If he's lying injured, then every hour counts. While we sleep, he dies. No, we keep going."

"Shadow?" said a voice like leaves blowing over stone.

"Seneschal?"

"Have you ever known a man to survive a batted bird?"

"No," Shadow admitted. "But it can happen, and this is no ordinary man."

"You're looking at one," Ukarres whispered. "It happened to me. I survived. No—half of me survived . . . sky sickness. They said I was lucky; I have often wondered about that. I have very few parts that work properly. I hurt all the time."

"But," Shadow said, and then stopped.

"It was my fault—I should have noticed. SkyBreaker was his name, appropriately. He went down. Then up. Then down. Then he sauntered back to his roost as though nothing had happened, and they lifted me off and I screamed for three days. Believe me, lad, you may be doing your prince a kindness by not looking anymore."

Shadow was carefully not thinking those thoughts.

"Look at the odds, Shadow," the duke said quietly. "You almost blacked out in the first few minutes. Most likely he died in that cloud, and we don't know which direction WindStriker took out of it. If the prince was alive after the cloud, he almost certainly died in the next hour—up and down as Ukarres says. The bird probably dropped from exhaustion when the batmeat wore off—

she's old, remember, and had been thrashing hard. In that case he was killed on impact, or else he's been lying unattended for two days. There are very few places around here where a man could survive that, even if he was uninjured to start with."

Shadow banged his fist on the table, but the stone made no sound. "We have to find him! Dead or alive!"

Foan nodded patiently. "But admit it—we're looking for his body. We can't risk living men to find a body. We must break it off for at least a full watch."

"If someone saw him come down . . ." Shadow began. But that was a futile thought. The country was almost a desert. Near Ramo no one could fall out of the sky without being seen, but there were few peasants on the Rand, at least not here.

"We've asked at every cottage," the keeper said patiently.

More than half the men in the room were now asleep, slumped on the tables, and some were even stretched out on benches, snoring.

"You will send a second message, then?" Ninomar asked while Shadow was struggling to find words.

The duke nodded. "I reported the accident and warned that there was very little hope. I think now we should say that although we shall continue to search, chances are almost nonexistent and he must be assumed dead. Perhaps you will wish to add your own report?"

"Did you tell them it was murder?" Shadow asked angrily.

He got four very steady, very cold stares.

"No I did not," the duke said. "Have you evidence of that?"

"There were no mutebats in the aerie. I had looked." He turned to Vonimor. "You cleaned them out. What did you do with the bodies?"

The eagler hesitated and then said, "Threw them over. There's a megaday of junk at the dark side of the tower. Go and see."

"Somebody did," Shadow said. "It is possible to get to that junk pile?"

"Yes."

"Then somebody found one and took it up to the aerie. When no one was watching, he threw it past WindStriker. Any bird will snap up a mutebat—we all know that."

The silence was deadly. Then the duke spoke. "It must have been done within minutes of our departure. There were very few of us there. Whom do you accuse?"

Shadow dropped his eyes. "I don't know. But it was one of us."

"I think we might have missed a couple of the bats," Vonimor muttered. "They're hard to see . . . hard to get every last one . . ."

"It was murder," Shadow said.

This time Ninomar broke the silence. "If the prince dies by violence, Shadow, or is even injured, then you are automatically guilty of high treason, I believe. Is that not so? Whereas if he had an accident, then I expect a court would be lenient."

And yet another silence. Again Shadow said stubbornly, "It was murder."

Ninomar and the duke exchanged glances.

"You are the civil authority, Your Grace," the vice-marshal said. "You now believe that the crown prince is dead?"

"Yes, I am afraid so."

Ninomar nodded. "Then, Shadow, you are no longer Shadow. You are Ensign . . . Harl, wasn't it? You are therefore under my orders. When we have all had some rest, the search will be resumed—and His Grace and myself will be in charge. You may continue to fly Nail-Biter, as no one else seems to be able to. There will be an inquiry—"

"I am Shadow!" Shadow shouted, scrambling to his feet. "The king appointed me!"

"The king will kill you," Ukarres muttered.

"I am Shadow!"

Ninomar waved an arm, and two sleepy-looking troopers hurried over.

"Take this man to his quarters," he said.

"I am Shadow! I give the orders!"

As they dragged him from the hall he was still half weeping, half shouting: "I am Shadow."

8

"Plain eggs can hatch strange chicks."
—*Skyman proverb*

"I will see that bet," Aurolron XX said, "and raise you three."

The baby-faced trooper licked his lips. "I believe I shall have to fold," he muttered hoarsely.

The king's eyebrows rose. "With a pair of queens showing?" he murmured. "Where is the courage we expect in our Guard?"

Ensign Rolsok turned even paler—if that were possible—and pushed five gold royals toward the center of the table. It was a kiloday's pay for an ensign. He lived on his family's money, not on his stipend, but the tiny beads of sweat on his upper lip shone like fine jewels in the sunlight.

It was a long, long time since Shadow had enjoyed himself so much. Even sitting behind the king, he could not view the royal hand, for Aurolron played all cards close to the chest, but that did not matter—the king was playing with a marked deck, and Shadow could read all the other hands as well as Aurolron could. They had been at it since dinner, and the king was systematically, progressively, and mercilessly ruining his opponents. It was a vintage performance by the royal spider.

The balcony was crowded round by heavy trees, sheltered and private. Two bells had already rung, yet the game showed no signs of ending. It was an unusual group, the king and five youths: Prince Jarkadon and four others. The only persons close were Shadow and an elderly secretary whose job was to keep track of debts, while waiters and guards hovered at a distance. There was heaped gold, shining and clinking; there was fine wine; there was gracious conversation—a little strained at times—and there was gambling. There was no mercy.

Perhaps there was even a smell of justice.

The court might gossip and censure, but it was rarely shocked. Certain things were a known peril for scullery maids and other minor menials—no one was interested in those private lives. Yet even the court's tolerance had its limits. When the daughter of a baronet was grievously abused, then full-scale scandal erupted.

A half-wit gardener was arrested, tried, convicted, and impaled.

The court was not deceived. The girl's family was displaying sudden new wealth, so silence had been purchased—and that was not done for dead gardeners. Stories were whispered of a group of young sadists who called themselves the Lions. The Lions, it was said, included representatives of some of the best families. The Lions had been indulging their peculiar taste in recreation for some time and had only just started to seek their victims among the better classes . . . and so on.

The royal spies brought all of the rumors and most of the facts to the king, and so to Shadow. Shadow knew very well who were the Lions and who was the leader of the pride. He knew who had bought the silence.

For a while the atrocities must have stopped or returned to the kitchens. Then a second case occurred among the gentry: this time two girls, one so damaged that she might never recover. The king defended his own—a couple of minor lackeys were hauled into court and duly found guilty. Again money and sinecures were dispensed to the families.

But this time the king had decided to act. Four young men were unexpectedly invited to a game of cards with His Majesty. Such an invitation was never refused, al-

though each of them must have been surprised by it—
they were friends of Prince Jarkadon, not of the king.

Surprise turned to terror when they saw who else had
been invited. They waited grimly for mention of their
sadistic diversions—and it did not come. They were
there to play cards. The cards and coins were produced.
The play began.

Understandably, the guests were not at their best. The
king was. He could probably have beaten them handily
without the marked deck. He was charming and courteous and lethal.

"Five?" muttered the next boy, the one they called
Crusher. He moved his lips as he counted out the coins
with massive peasant hands, although his cards were
quite worthless. His family was rich also, but four young
men were going to have to crawl to their respective fathers bearing news of sudden incredible debts.

Bills from merchants could be ignored. Not a debt to
the king.

By Shadow's rough calculation, the king had already
won enough to run his palace for thirty days. The families would be crippled, forced to sell estates to pay for
this evening.

Aurolron had shown that he knew exactly who were
the Lions, and brutality had never been mentioned.

"Son?"

Jarkadon was eyeing the cards thoughtfully. He had
been as shocked as his playmates when he arrived, but
he had recovered his poise as soon as he saw the nature
of the plot. The king might keep his son on a slack rein,
but he could hardly bankrupt himself, and he was obviously not about to go public with his knowledge, so
Jarkadon at least was immune. The chief Lion was safe.
Yet Jarkadon was also in a trap. Two cheaters working
together could manage a crooked game much more easily than one. Whose side would the prince take? He had
made the wiser choice.

"I'll see your raise, Father," he said, smiling, "and
raise you another five."

Four pairs of eyes turned to him in agony. Treachery!

The stakes were becoming even more colossal as the game proceeded, with no sign of an ending.

The next young man had some trouble speaking, but he asked the secretary for another hundred.

It was a vintage performance.

Then a herald came running out the door and was intercepted at once by a hovering equerry. Shadow saw the document passed, saw the glance toward the king. The equerry approached. As a welcome relief from long sitting, Shadow rose and stepped over to intercept in turn. He recognized the seal as he carried the letter back.

The king muttered a polite apology to his guests, but he had noticed also, and he read the letter as close to his chest as he had played his cards. His expression did not change by an eyelash, but one does not stand by a man for five kilodays without coming to know him well. This was the high one, Shadow decided. He glanced over at Jarkadon—and the young devil was watching him, not the king. Damn!

The king read the letter through a second time, then folded it up. He put his hands on the arms of his chair to rise, and the whole group was on its feet before him. Wild relief shone in four young faces.

"Our regrets, gentlemen. Perhaps we can continue this another day?" Still no trace of expression, but the mere lack of it was ominous. They were courtiers; they could vanish gracefully and yet quickly. Jarkadon stood expectant, eyes gleaming. The king beckoned the equerry. "Find Her Majesty. We believe she is attending a chamber concert somewhere. We would meet with her —in the cabinet, we think would be best. At her convenience."

He eyed Jarkadon and nodded. Jarkadon was trying very hard to conceal excitement, and not succeeding. The king walked toward the door; by the time he had reached the corridor beyond, he had collected guards before and behind and was moving within a convoy. Shadow could feel the emotional temperature rising steadily and the palace web beginning to quiver: The king has received a

message from Ninar Foan and has summoned the queen
—and to the cabinet, not the private quarters.

They moved through corridors and cloisters and passages . . .

The great egg-shaped room seemed hot and airless
after the balcony. The doors closed silently on the curious faces outside. Shadow stopped beside his chair; Jarkadon followed the king to the far end.

"Bad news, Father?"

Aurolron did not reply until he was seated. "I think it
must be, because of the odious smirk on your face. Remove it."

Jarkadon flushed in silence and did not presume to sit
until invited to do so. He was left standing.

The king read his letter again and then laid it face-
down on the desk. Then he stared at it in oaken silence,
and nothing seemed to happen for a long time.

At last the doors opened and Queen Mayala stood in
the entrance. Shadow rose. She looked at his face, and
for once she did not smile.

She wore a high-necked gown of dark green which
merely emphasized the pallor of her face. The dull-dyed
hair was coiled on top of her head and surmounted by a
tiara of emeralds, her hands concealed in a white muff.
Muffs had suddenly become fashionable because the
queen had taken to using them—probably, Shadow
thought, to conceal the constant tremor of her hands.

He saw at once that it was one of her bad days.

Then she swept past his chair and the door closed
again, but the antechamber was filling up with ladies who
had come with the queen and men who had sensed the
tremors in the web and heard the tap of drums.

The king rose and held out a chair for her. He remained standing on one side, Jarkadon on the other.

"Vindax?" she said.

"It is bad news, my dear."

"He has not reached Ninar Foan yet, though?"

"Yes," the king said. "He arrived on the thirty-third
—sooner than we had expected. There has been an accident."

The queen made a dry sobbing noise and said nothing. Shadow was trying to watch Jarkadon also, but he was too distant to see the young man's expression clearly.

"He went hunting. Apparently his bird had taken a bat."

"Oh, my God!"

"They have not found him yet. The letter was written the same day, so the search had just started. There is still hope."

"Hope?" she said. "In that country? Up that high? Those hills?" She doubled over and buried her face in her muff.

Silence.

Aurolron put a hand on her shoulder. "We must have faith, my dear. It is bad, but there is still hope."

The queen straightened up and leaned away from him, dislodging his hand. She looked at Jarkadon. "Why are you smiling?" she asked quietly.

He was startled. "Mother . . . of course I am not smiling. It is terrible news."

The queen lurched to her feet, facing the king, and suddenly screamed. *"You did it!"*

Shadow rose also; he could have heard that without the trick acoustics, and screaming near the monarch was his business. He hurried over toward the desk.

"Mayala! Control yourself!" her husband snapped.

"You planned this. Taken a bat! How often does that happen? You expect me to believe that it was an accident?"

"Mother . . ." Jarkadon said.

She ignored him, glaring at the king. He reached for her shoulders, and she backed away.

Shadow slipped into position behind the king, and they did not even see him.

Now Mayala's face was suffused, her eyes wild and rolling. "You did it! You put one of your foul assassins in his party. You have murdered my son!"

"Our son!" the king said angrily. "Don't be absurd!"

"You have killed Vindax!" she insisted. "You want to

put that *pervert* on the throne?" Jarkadon turned almost as red as she.

Aurolron was startled also at her vehemence, but he paused to glance at the prince. "That is another decision entirely," he said. Jarkadon went just as suddenly ash-white.

"Monster!" Queen Mayala hissed. She pulled a knife from her muff and struck at the king. He yelped and jumped sideways, tangling with a chair and half-caught by Shadow. Jarkadon grabbed the queen, who was screaming wordlessly.

Then the king's knees buckled, and Shadow lowered him to the rug. Blood was spreading hideously over his white doublet; Shadow ripped it away from the wound.

High treason!

"Get a doctor!" the prince shouted.

"No!" Aurolron snapped from the floor. "It's only a scratch."

Shadow's ripping had exposed the skin—a gash on the king's ribs was pouring blood, but it did not look deep. He wadded a corner of the cloth and pressed it against the wound.

"I think it is superficial," he agreed, "but it needs stitching."

He was King Shadow, and the king had been stabbed. What was going to happen to him now?

The queen had collapsed on her chair again and was sobbing helplessly into her hands. Jarkadon knelt down also, ignoring her.

"We should get a doctor, Father," the prince said.

"Wait!" Aurolron said. He had gone very pale from the shock. "Perhaps we can keep this quiet."

But that would be impossible. His clothes were blood-soaked; so was the carpet.

"I wonder how long she has been carrying this," Jarkadon said suddenly, holding up the knife. It was small, slim, but quite adequate. Shadow was starting to tremble. His mind was jittering around so much that he did not know what he was thinking. He was not supposed to stay close to the king in this room; he could not have possibly moved fast enough; no one ever searched the queen for weapons; they did unspeakable things to traitors.

"We must keep the queen out of this," the king muttered.

Stabbed by his own queen? He would be a public laughingstock. It would be shame, not danger or pain, which would be troubling him most. Scandal!

"Perhaps we can," Jarkadon said.

He looked across at Shadow.

The king turned his head and looked up at Shadow.

Sheer terror froze him. Three quite unimpeachable witnesses: the king, the queen, and the new crown prince. He was lost.

"Then I think you had better call a doctor," the king said quietly.

"No immediate hurry," Jarkadon said. "Let's have a look. Yes, it's not deep. Fortunate that Mother doesn't know how to use a dagger, isn't it?"

By some terrible precognition, the paralyzed Shadow knew what was about to happen—and knew that he was not going to be able to move to prevent it.

"Fortunate that she doesn't even know anatomy," Jarkadon said. "She should have put it *here*."

The king's eyes rolled up, and with no sound at all he went limp, the silver hilt ornamenting his chest like some macabre heraldic symbol.

For a moment that seemed to outlast the ages, they all stared in silence: Shadow with disbelief, the queen perhaps not comprehending, Jarkadon with a thin smile of satisfaction. Then the prince leapt to his feet.

"Treason!" Jarkadon screamed. "Murder!" He went running down the room to the doors. "Guards! Murder!"

Those outside could not hear him through those doors, and in his haste he tried to push instead of pull. Then he got one open and renewed his yelling. The guards jumped forward; the other spectators back. There was confusion. The guards forced their way through, and then all jammed together in the doorway.

When the would-be rescuers finally rounded the big chair and came rushing along the room, they froze in horror at the sight of the king's lifeless body.

There was no one else there.

9

"If you see a shadow move, don't blame the sun."
Proverb

*C*LINK.

Clink . . . clink . . . clink . . .

He opened one eye.

Clink!

Both eyes open, he saw that a table by the bed held a tray. Someone was mercilessly rapping a spoon against a cup.

He peered past the table: Ukarres, hunched forward in a chair.

The old man grinned with the usual display of stumps. "Good sky to you, Prince Shadow."

Shadow sat up fast. "What time is it?"

The old man dropped the spoon and squirmed back painfully in his seat. "You have slept about one watch and a half."

Shadow glanced around a fine, luxurious room, with bright hangings to hide the stone walls and thick rugs on the floor and well-carved, shiny furniture; bright sunlight shone through good, clear glass. He recognized the ante-room—through that door was the prince's room, probably the ducal bedroom in normal times, empty now, of course.

He threw back the covers. "The patrols are ready?"

"Oh, they left hours ago," Ukarres said in his wheezy voice.

108

Shadow put his feet on the floor. His head was whirling, but most of the ache had gone.

"Stop!" Ukarres said. "You can serve your prince better by staying where you are and listening to me."

Shadow stared at him skeptically.

"I mean it. I know things you do not. So eat that meal before it gets cold—it may be the last decent one you will ever see."

He smelled coffee. Yes, he was hungry again, so he had been out for a long time. This had not come from the commons; the ducal kitchen itself had spawned the white bread and the plate with thick, glistening slices of ham and a huge fried goose egg. His mouth watered.

He reached for the coffee, noticed that he was grubby and smelly and naked, and decided he did not care. "Then speak."

"Do you trust me?"

Shadow shook his head.

"Wise of you," Ukarres said. "I am a trickster. I never tell the truth when a lie will do as well. Deceit is almost the only pleasure left to me, and it was always one of my favorites. This time, though, I find myself forced to be honest."

"You lied to Lady Elosa," Shadow said with his mouth full.

"Of course. I knew that the sight of the prince would dumbfound her—enough to be obvious, so that he would get the reason out of her. I never thought that Rorin would be sent along. That ruined it. I had a slight hope that he would have the sense . . . well, it didn't work." He sighed. "No need to hurry. You aren't going out to search with the others."

"NailBiter?" Shadow barked, sputtering coffee in his alarm.

"No, he's still there. But Lord Ninomar left written orders: You are to return to duty at somewhere called Jaur."

"The sun will move first."

Ukarres squirmed again and regarded him with some amusement.

"He is trying to save you, you know."

"Ha!"

"Yes, truly. He maintains that only you can fly Nail-Biter. Of course that is all feathers—the duke can handle anything ever hatched. He's on your side, too."

Shadow chewed for a while, wondering how much to risk. "I can understand the duke wanting me out of sight. But Ninomar hates me down to the hairs on my big toe."

Ukarres shook his head, his one live eye shining, his wrinkles emphasized by a smile. "He admires you."

"Mutes!"

"I asked him about you before the accident. He said you were an insolent, smart-aleck peasant but one of the finest skymen he had ever met and fanatically loyal to the prince. Loyalty is one of the few things he understands. He despises you, yes, but secretly he thinks you deserve to escape. The king will have you publicly ground and roasted like a coffee bean as a warning to all future Shadows. No, the vice-marshal is risking a serious reprimand, but he has left the door open for you, the door to the world."

Shadow started to eat more slowly. "To be an outlaw? No rank, no name, no honor?"

"The king of Piatorra would accept a good skyman with his own mount."

He shook his head. "I shall stay and help search."

Ukarres sighed.

"Loyalty!" he said. "It is rare. Yet, in spite of my devious ways, young Shadow, I was always loyal to my duke. He trusts me. Nobody else dares to. I have served him all his life, kept his secrets, done a few things he wanted done but could not ask for..."

He was silent for a while, as though pondering the next most likely strategy. "Vak Vonimor and I are blood enemies. He runs the aerie and I run the household, and Eagle Dome itself lies between. When I was there to greet your prince, it was the first time I had been in the aerie in...well, in almost your lifetime, I should guess. He is fiercely loyal to the keeper also, but we detest each other."

"So?" Shadow said. Ukarres was a slimy old ruin, but he had a curious attraction about him.

"Today we are friends," Ukarres said solemnly.

"I don't understand," Shadow said, still working his way through the ham.

"You were right—it was murder. You can work it out."

Now Shadow paused, fork in hand, staring at the old man, trying to guess what message lay in that single watery eye.

He thought back to the departure from the aerie. Ice-Fire had been perched in a corner, with NailBiter next to her—it was standard practice to isolate a cawking pair. Then there was old WindStriker, then the duke's Ice-Flame and a group of birds that were not being used . . . Before the dressing, Shadow had laid all the equipment nearby on the floor. The prince had stood just inside the bars, facing into the aerie so that Shadow was properly at his back. He would have seen a bat being thrown from in there, and by the time he turned around to mount, WindStriker had been blinkered and unable to react.

"Only one man had the opportunity!" he said. Why had he not seen that before? "You are accusing the duke himself?"

Ukarres's eye slid away from his. "His Grace must take some blame. And so must I. And so must you, Shadow."

"Me?" By God, that was unfair! "What more could I have done?"

"Oh, you did too much, not too little," Ukarres sighed. "Now I must betray a trust. Listen! About four hours before the deed was done, in the middle of third watch, the duke came to my room and woke me. He had received a message from the king."

"What?" Shadow shouted. "How?"

"By bird, of course. The royal courier who came to announce the prince's plans, Sir Jion Something . . . he left his mount and took one of ours. It returned with this." He reached inside his old brown doublet and pulled out a letter, a seal still dangling from it. "It is an extraordinary document!"

Shadow held out his hand, but the old man hesitated. "My duke is a passionate man, lad, in all ways: lust or rage or joy, but I have not seen him cry since he was a child. Yet this made him weep. The king would have my head . . . he would have the duke's for showing it to me, I think. Well . . . read it."

Astounded, Shadow unfolded the parchment. The seal was certainly genuine, but the writing was scrawly, not that of a professional scribe, and the usual flowery preliminaries were missing. But he had seen the king scribble notes, and recognized his hand. It began even more starkly than the summons he had received at Hiando Keep.

> The King to his cousin of Foan: Greetings.
> Send the enclosed letter to intercept the crown prince at Gorr. It bids him terminate his journey there and forbids him to come to Ninar Foan.
> I was aware, as you must be, that for you to meet him in public would provoke scandal. I had decided to pay that price, in the belief that the gossip would be harmless and would eventually die. Now I have learned that I was wrong—not only has it already stirred dangerous thoughts in certain quarters, but I see that it could lead to the uncovering of other matters which must remain hidden. You will know to what I refer. Therefore, the isolation of your house from mine must be continued.
> Doubtless he has already met persons on the Rand who know you, but the court is where the danger lies, and so long as none of his companions see the two of you together, the harm will be small.
> Yet you should meet him. I have told him that a man named Ovla will seek him out in Gorr. Be careful that you are unobserved. Only Prince Shadow will be present. Inquire into his background—it is relevant.

Shadow looked up in astonishment. "What has my background got to do with all this?"

Ukarres shrugged. "If I knew, I would probably lie about it."

He did know—Shadow was certain. Angrily he returned to the royal letter.

It is a sadness when the scion of an ancient family lacks a son. I propose to give you one of mine. As soon as Vindax returns, I shall send Jarkadon to you. I hope that you will consider favorably a marriage between him and your daughter, that he may ultimately succeed you as keeper of the Rand. In return I shall issue patents that your titles may descend through the female line.

He has merit, yet is scathed by the temptations of court life. I believe my older son does credit to my rearing. Perhaps you, in your more wholesome lands, can improve on the younger.

I think you owe me this.

Written in our own hand, this 9234th day of our reign in our capital of Ramo.

Aurolron R.

"Great fires of the Ark!" Shadow exclaimed, and read it all again. Then he stared at Ukarres. "He as much as admits that the duke is the prince's father!"

"He does not!" the seneschal snapped. "But then, the duke would know that better than the king, would he not?"

"Is he? Was there opportunity?"

Again Ukarres knew, but the wily old man was not going to say. "I told you it was a strange missive. The comments on Prince Jarkadon? Even the royal admission of error! Yes, we had better both keep quiet about this, my lad."

Banish Jarkadon? They would have to tie that young man on a bird's back before they would get him to the Rand.

And if Vindax were truly the duke's son, then the

king's letter was utterly incredible. No wonder the writing was shaky—it must have been written under great stress.

"But the message to the prince?" Shadow demanded.

Ukarres shook his head. "The duke erred. He said, 'Well, he wants a hunt, so I shall give him this afterward. The damage is done now.'"

Of course! Shadow moaned aloud. The damage was done because he had juggled the royal itinerary in the name of security. That was what Ukarres had meant when he said it was his fault. He had innocently thwarted the king's plan.

For a few moments his mind seemed to dance all over the Rand like a batted bird. The he remembered something else.

"You said you also bore blame?"

Ukarres nodded sadly. "The duke departed at last, and he left that terrible document in my charge, for I am archivist, among many other things. I should have taken it at once to the castle vaults. But I am old, Shadow, and a cripple, and it was only a couple of hours until three bells. I thought a short delay . . ."

Who else saw it?

A curious reluctance came over Ukarres. "We are all downside up here just now, with so many guests. But while I slept, the person in the next room must have passed through mine. I am certain that the letter had been moved . . . it was on the chair by my bed . . ."

Then Shadow knew and was horrified. "But why?" he said. "To protect her father against a charge of treason?"

Ukarres rolled his single eye. "It would not occur to her."

"Why, then?" Shadow persisted, even more appalled. "Why would she do such a thing?"

"Motives make poor bandages, as they say," the old man muttered sadly. "She would not be the first to seek a throne through violence, would she? No . . ." He fell silent for a moment, as though he had not previously thought about motive. "She has five brothers that she knows of," he said at last, "in the town and castle—all

illegitimate. She cannot inherit the title, nor most of the
lands, for she is a woman. How does she feel about bastards, do you suppose? Contempt? Fear? How would
she feel about one becoming king?"

"And her destiny is to be queen?" Shadow groaned
again. "It must have been done just as the blinkers were
opened. I thought at first he was trying to return to the
aerie. He must have heard or seen, too late. But if he is
alive, then he knows who did it."

The old man squirmed to relieve his back, or perhaps
just his feelings. His dry whisper became even quieter.
"That is why Vak and I are suddenly allies. We are loyal
to our duke, but even great men have weaknesses. He
has fathered seven bastards that I know of, all sons.
From wedlock he obtained a single daughter. He must
know she did it. But he will protect her. He has never
denied her anything."

Breakfast was forgotten. Shadow stood up. "I must
join the search and warn the others at the next break. If
the duke finds the prince first . . ."

Ukarres shook his head angrily and thumped his cane
on the rug. "Never! The prince was his guest! He would
not stoop to that, and none of his men would support
him in so dastardly a crime. Elosa is being watched—I
know that. I meant only that he will not bring her to
justice if the prince has died. And, strangely, I find that
my lifelong loyalty has choked at last. Sit down! There is
more."

There could not possibly be more. Shadow sat down.

"Now," the old man wheezed. "We all know that the
chances are very, very slim. Perhaps one man in twenty
survives a batted bird. But the bird usually does, right?
If the rider tied his reins. They do not often fly into a hill,
for there is just too much sky. So where did she go, afterward?"

Gods! For a moment Shadow had a foul vision of
WindStriker arriving back at the palace with the lifeless,
rotting body of the Prince . . . but no, she was a widow.
He had inquired carefully. A bird removed from its mate
for long became fractious, which was why he had

brought only pairs and widows, with very few singles. So she had no mate to go back to.

"I expect she is wandering the hills."

"Who chose her?"

Shadow shrugged. "The prince. I suggested a mature female. She came from the family private collection. She is the queen's official mount, although the queen has not flown in kilodays."

Ukarres nodded. "I remember her, and Vonimor knew her the instant she arrived. We were on the Allaban expedition, both of us, and Princess Mayala flew on Wind-Striker. She has been here before."

The story was quite plausible. She might have belonged to the queen's grandmother also. "She had a mate back in Allaban?"

"We're not sure, but Vak thinks she might have done." He smiled ruefully. "Our departure was hardly orderly, you know. It was almost every man for himself. But I think that if the prince lives, then he lives now in Allaban."

"She would have flown into certain death on Eagle Dome."

The seneschal shook his head gently. "Not necessarily. There is another way to Allaban. A more direct way."

Shadow smelled treachery. "How?"

"It is known as Dead Man's Pass. Quite simply, you fly around the back of Eagle Dome. It is very high. The wilds can use it, of course, but they do not live there, in the dark. It is not guarded, as the sun side is. It is extremely dangerous for men, but a few have made it throughout history, for one reason or another. More have failed. It takes an exceptional mount and an exceptional skyman, but it can be done."

"Would WindStriker have known of that way?"

Ukarres shrugged. "The eagles have strange ways of finding the best route, Shadow, as you know."

It could be a trap. He was the one shouting murder, so the duke and Ninomar and now Ukarres were all trying to find ways to make him leave and shut him up.

Treachery?

"Vonimor will confirm what I have said," Ukarres suggested. "Of course, we are both the duke's servants and you can doubtless find reasons why the duke may have put us up to this. Basically you have three choices, though. You can stay here, helping in the search, but you will only be one more pair of eyes among seventy.

"Ramo has no more of our birds, and no courier can be here within twelve days at a minimum. He will certainly bring orders for your arrest. You know what will be done to you then. Or you can go through the window the vice-marshal left open for you—dress NailBiter and flee.

"Or you can gamble your life and health and sanity and go to Allaban."

"The rebels?"

Ukarres shrugged. "They will certainly not hand you over to Aurolron. They may take NailBiter from you, of course. If you release him first, he will return here, to IceFire. If the prince is indeed alive, then perhaps they will treat you well—they may be holding him as hostage. The possibilities became innumerable, and we cannot guess..."

Shadow weighed the odds. One more added to seventy was very little, true. Flight to exile was somehow unthinkable, although he did not know why. He rubbed his prickly face. Off the prince's chamber was a bathroom with a bathtub, the only one he had seen on the Rand. A tub of hot water was one of the greatest luxuries in the world.

"Let us talk more while I shave," he said.

"Don't," Ukarres said. "Stubble keeps the cold off."

NailBiter sat alone on the perching in a strangely empty aerie, with only Vak Vonimor in attendance. Ukarres had provided Shadow with a magnificent flying suit in brown calfskin lined with lamb's wool. It would have cost a trooper a kiloday's pay; Shadow had not inquired who owned it. Vonimor eyed it and said sadly, "You fly to rightward, then?"

Shadow nodded.

The older man shook his head. "It is a slim chance for him and not much more for you. But you will need this." He had laid out a daunting heap of equipment.

"I'll fly straight underground with that lot," Shadow complained.

"You'll need it all," the eagler said grimly. "Ever seen one of these?" He produced a metal cylinder with a black triangular thing on the end of it, and Shadow shook his head.

The object was very ancient, Vonimor told him, dating from the Old Times, and perhaps even from the Holy Ark itself. It contained air, which he had forced into it with an equally ancient pump, and he showed how the black thing fitted over a man's face and how a twist would release a puff of the air. Such a rarity was beyond price, and Shadow now began to believe that the two men were indeed betraying their duke and not him. There was also food and a great coil of thin rope—and that also must be a sacred relic, for it was made of neither silk nor hemp nor any material he had ever seen. There was a grapnel attached to one end.

"Kiting?" he groaned.

"Take it," Vak insisted. "And pray you don't need it. Lad, I would not try that road for anything. I know it's been done, but more have failed."

So NailBiter was dressed and the baggage attached; the bird crouched low in complaint, knowing his master was still to come.

The eagler hesitated. "Did Ukarres say anything about the wilds in Allaban?" he asked. "About the birds there?"

Shadow thought back. "No."

Vonimor seemed surprised—and reluctant to continue. "Well...he has some funny notions that he got from Karaman. I don't hold with them, but I saw less of Allaban than he did."

"What sort of notions?" Shadow asked.

The older man shrugged vaguely. "Just keep your eyes open, lad. There are funny stories—you may see birds doing funny things. Even that NailBiter of yours. Birds act queer when they get to Allaban." He changed the subject. "Good luck, my lord," he said gruffly, holding out a hand.

"I am no lord," Shadow said. "Are you going to be in trouble when the duke returns?"

The ruddy, honest face turned dark. Vonimor turned away and then stopped. "I saw it," he whispered.

"What? Then why did you not speak?" Shadow demanded.

"There was no time," Vonimor said. "It was just as he launched, and I did not believe my eyes." He stalked away across the aerie floor.

Shadow mounted his bird and launched automatically, his mind pondering the monstrous crime and the agony of followers whose lifetime of loyalty to a noble family had been betrayed. They were blaming the duke. Perhaps they were right.

NailBiter soon forgot his sulks, and Shadow followed the fast route that he had been given, the landmarks familiar to him after the long days of search. Twice he saw lonely birds soaring in the far distance, the patrols still hunting for traces of the missing prince, but they were too far off for him to recognize birds or riders, and therefore he would not be identified either. He discovered that he had become convinced—if WindStriker had survived her frenzy, then she had gone to Allaban, and the only question remaining was whether she had been carrying an unconscious cripple or a corpse. Certainly the latter was more probable, and he resisted an inner voice which told him he was crazy and should be going the other way, to sanctuary and refuge in Piatorra. But he knew that then his burden would not be rope and food and bottled air, but a lifetime of wondering and guilt.

Eventually he was over country new to him. It was the first time he had flown alone since his mad rush over the desert from Rakarr to Ramo on the day he became Shadow, and now he had the same problem he had had then: to find the thermals. In theory any especially warm surface created a thermal, but in practice many of those were dissipated by the cold wind and unusable. Path-finding was the best test of a good skyman. Now he did what he had done in the desert—he let NailBiter choose, for the birds could apparently see the warmer air. Here, high on the Rand, there was little risk in trusting his mount. In the desert things had been different, for had he sunk too low in the red air and been unable to find a good thermal, he would have died, and long before his eagle did. NailBiter could have killed him easily on that journey to Ramo.

Eagle Dome was farther away than he would have believed, the sheer size of it almost beyond comprehension. From Ninar Foan it had seemed smooth and symmetrically rounded; when he at last grew close, he could see the frost cap and the vertical ribbing of the lower slopes that told of springs. The thermal on the sunlit side must be enormous, and a permanent cloud hung above it, streaming away sunward on one edge, continually re-forming on the other. He came at last to the great flanking valley which cut back into the Rand and which would provide both his gateway and his trial.

Choosing a projecting rock above a sun-bright cliff, he brought NailBiter in to roost. Having no shackle, he had to leave the bird blinkered, and the scarlet comb throbbed angrily. Shadow dismounted and stretched aching joints; he estimated he had already flown almost a full watch from the castle. Shivering and panting in the cold, thin wind, he sat down in the lee of the rock and ate some of his rations.

He studied the great valley before him. He did not need Ukarres's description to warn him that a monstrous torrent of cold wind flowed down that gully—if he were caught in that, he would be swept out into the darkness over the plain and would die.

But if the cold wind dropped low, then the hot wind must drop also, and also the shear zone between them. Rarely, it was possible for human eyes to detect the shear zone, and he convinced himself at last that he could see it now, faint whirls of mist, vanishing almost before the eye made them out. His objective, then, was to climb as high as he dared and then glide NailBiter into that valley and hope to ride the hot wind around to the dark side of Eagle Dome.

It sounded simple.

The climb in the thermals was easy; NailBiter did not care, for his lungs could handle the altitude with ease, and perhaps he was even impatient with the rider who held him back, easing gradually to humanly impossible altitudes. The top of Eagle Rock seemed no lower when Shadow reached his nose-bleeding limit and tried a twist of air from the ancient bottle. It smelled foul, and seemed to do very little to clear his head. He risked a few more minutes' climbing and a few more puffs, then signaled for a dive. He probably blacked out briefly after that, but a sudden surge and a torrid breath told him that he had entered the invisible trough of the shear zone.

It was like riding a batted bird—NailBiter was hurled and buffeted and tossed. At times the two of them were turned right around and thrown toward the plains. Then a saving upwelling would loop them over and swirl them back again. Shadow's head throbbed, and his stomach heaved—he had never experienced anything like this before. He suspected NailBiter was enjoying it, but the strain on his wings must be immense. How much of their progress was due to his eagle instinct and how much to Shadow's skill and how much to sheer luck was impossible to know; all they could do was try to climb in the ups and avoid the downs, with neither visible in advance and their mutual boundaries unpredictable—a great game for lunatics.

Just once, and only briefly, they caught a sky wave, a smooth ripple between hot wind above and cold wind below, moving in the right direction, and for a few minutes they rushed in silent flight up the valley. Then it ended abruptly, or they lost it, and it was back to the turbulence again.

Inch by inch, it seemed, they fought their way up the narrowing gorge. The sun sank lower, the plains behind began to shrink, framed between the mountains of the

Rand and the flank of Eagle Dome, and the land below was a darkness faintly glimmering with traces of ice.

Yet the topographic valley climbed relentlessly, and the invisible valley in the sky climbed also. Eventually the shear zone was too high for Shadow, and that came just where Ukarres had warned it would: where the valley swung around the mountain and the black bulk of Eagle Dome cut out the sun. The air bottle was exhausted. Shadow put NailBiter into a dive, and they plunged down through the icy wind toward the side of the mountain.

A jagged spur loomed out of the darkness, and he signaled for NailBiter to perch.

He had never experienced such cold; it soaked through his flying suit like ice water—and met the cold of fear working outward. NailBiter clutched fiercely at the rock and hunched down, his feathers fluffed out and rippling in the hurricane. The valley was lit by a dim reflection from immense sun-bright peaks on the High Rand, ragged and taller even than the Dome. On one side the black valley, on the other an equally black cliff stretching up . . .

Stars! Shadow had never seen stars, but his eyes had adjusted to the dark, and the sky above him glittered with billions of tiny points of light. He had heard of them—and there they were. Even in his terror and exhaustion he was overwhelmed by their beauty. The poets and the ancient texts had never done them justice.

But if he sat and looked at stars for very long, he would freeze to death. Somehow he had to fight his way up the next stretch of this valley. Eventually, Ukarres had said, he would come to a junction, where the torrent of cold wind from Darkside flowed down off the High Rand and split against the back of Eagle Dome. After that, it would be downhill all the way to Allaban. Until then, it was upwind and there were only two ways to travel upwind: on the power of NailBiter's wings or by kiting.

"Let's go, fellow," Shadow said through chattering teeth, and pulled on the reins.

NailBiter did not want to go—he could see no reason whatsoever to fight against the wind into darkness. Food and warmth and his mate were in the other direction, and he balked and argued and struggled and was kicked as he had never before been kicked. The wind would be least strong near the ground, so the first leg was easy—a nearly vertical, ear-bursting dive toward the surface of the glacier to traverse the cold blast as quickly as possible and gain maximum speed for a glide—but after that it was powered flight all the way, NailBiter fighting the wind and Shadow fighting NailBiter.

The glacier itself was a rock pile, with only small traces of ice showing and deadly teeth looming unexpectedly out of the night. Some of the boulders were as large as Hiando Keep, small mountains. Those giants provided lee air and slightly easier flying for a moment—and then made up for the respite with the icy fury of their turbulent edge winds.

Shadow had lost all count of time, and he had no idea how long the battle went on, until he suddenly realized that the ground was right there in front of him, and NailBiter grabbed a rock and stopped. He was finished—a bird could not carry a man far on muscle power. Shadow was lying prone, with his head against the feathered back, and he could hear the pounding heart.

They rested, man and bird, as the wind moaned its triumph and dug ice talons deeper into Shadow's bones. When NailBiter's pulse rate had dropped to a more normal level, Shadow moved to the next stage. He took a sheep's leg from his baggage and tossed it forward.

Snap!

Two minutes later they were airborne once more—the mutton had been doped with a trace of batmeat. In very small doses it acted as a stimulant. That was how his predecessor had died, he remembered, when some young aristocrat had tried the trick while in the prince's company. The difference between stimulation and madness was razor-narrow, and now he risked the same fate as Vindax, if he and Vonimor had misjudged the amount.

But even batmeat had its limits. Four times he doped

his eagle and NailBiter surged forth with new strength. But Vak and Shadow had agreed that four was the most they could risk—a dead bird would be of little use. The final dose produced only a short progress, from which NailBiter took a long time to recover, crouching low to his rock and trembling violently. He could fly no farther.

The frozen desert of dark and rock and cold still held them, sloping more steeply now, but still they had not reached the crest of the pass. There was only one desperate measure still to try.

"Good old buddy," Shadow said. "You've done your best. Now for a new trick."

NailBiter had never been taught kiting; Shadow had never seen it done. He untied his coil of rope and grapnel, slid from the saddle, and started to walk, scrambling in the dark over the boulders. Every step was a torment for tortured lungs, and he needed to stop frequently just to get breath.

When he guessed that he had come far enough, he wedged the grapnel between two rocks and started to return, paying out rope, stumbling, falling, panting... Idiot! He should have tied the other end first. What if he could not find the bird? The thin air was shriveling his brain.

But he did find NailBiter, and with fingers already numb inside his mitts, he fastened the other end of the rope to the saddle girths. He threw the rest of it loose on the ground, climbed aboard again, and took a hard grip on the end closest to the grapnel.

"Okay, Naily," he muttered. "Let's kill ourselves."

He made the signal that meant "spread wings," and bird and rider whirled upward while Shadow let the rope run through his mitts, waiting nervously for the jerk when it was all gone. NailBiter sensed the drag of the rope and almost panicked. Shadow needed about four extra hands, but somehow he kept control. Then came the jerk, spinning the eagle around, and for a moment Shadow thought they would be smashed down against the rocks.

They were not; the rope did not get tangled around

the bird's neck; the grapnel held. Now NailBiter was a
kite—the wind lifted him, and the rope held him. Man
and bird rose higher and higher until the tether was very
close to vertical. Then Shadow called for a dive. That
was the trickiest part of all, for the rope must now stay
slack or it would slingshot them into the rocks below.
They landed roughly, and NailBiter showed every sign of
wanting to become hysterical; Shadow stroked his comb
and muttered words of comfort that he knew could not
be heard.

He tugged on the rope, but he could never be so lucky
as to retrieve it that way. He clambered down and
started to walk. It was not walking, it was rock climbing,
but at last he reached the end of the rope, collected the
grapnel, and started back. Now it was rock climbing and
rope coiling combined. He reeled and choked in the thin
air, but at least the exercise helped warm him a little, and
eventually he was back beside the huddled shape of his
mount.

Again he stumbled forward and planted the grapnel
between two monoliths.

Two steps forward and one back—time and again he
kited, walking his bird up the glacier. NailBiter caught
the idea of it, as he always did, but showed no signs of
enjoying the process. Shadow's mind was blank with fatigue, his feet and hands numb, and NailBiter was trembling and rebellious. Several times the grapnel slipped
and then caught again, jarring bird and rider and threat-
ening to snap the girth. The hardest part of all was paying out the rope away from NailBiter, for feathers and
bird skin were not designed to resist friction, and if a
wing became entangled, then their adventure would end
at once. At last a sudden agony in Shadow's hand told
him that his mitt had worn through. He let go by reflex,
and the end of the rope came with a jarring crash—the
rocks were close below and very nearly caught them.

That was enough. When that last kite soar and dive
were done, Shadow knew that he must stop. Perhaps
some food and sleep would revive him enough to try
again. Perhaps a break would even revive his bird

enough for some more flying. They could go no farther now. The top of the pass must be very close, but it would have to wait.

They were lucky. They had landed in the lee of a huge rock, and the ground beneath was relatively smooth, although anywhere else he would have called it a rock pile. NailBiter needed little urging to crouch down like a brooding hen; no doubt he was just as tired and hungry and frightened as his rider, although he would be suffering much less from the cold and the lack of air.

Without dismounting, Shadow reached into his baggage and pulled out NailBiter's reward: one last, undoped sheep leg, a mere snack. He opened the blinkers and tossed the meat forward. *Snap!* NailBiter waited hopefully, but there was no more.

Now Shadow climbed down, which was easy when NailBiter was crouched. He was shaking so much with cold that he could hardly unfasten the saddle, but it would be unfair to leave it on any longer. He pulled it around and spread it below the great curve of the yellow beak, which was still higher than his head. He sat down on it and cuddled close to the feathery chest to eat. The food was frozen solid, and so was his canteen. He should have guessed.

Sleep first, then, and thaw out the food at the same time. In an emergency, an eagle made a very good tent. It would not be the first time he had played egg to NailBiter, for that was part of standard Guard training.

He found the bird hood and he had to stand on tiptoe to work it over NailBiter's head. He unfastened the helmet and let it fall.

"There, Naily," he muttered. "You have a nice nap, also, and we'll try again." He reached up and rubbed the comb.

His arm spread the bag. The wind caught it and whipped it off and took it away.

In his numbed, air-starved confusion, he had forgotten to tighten the drawstring.

Shadow found himself looking into the huge golden eye of an eagle at a range of about a foot. He had never done that. He had never heard of anyone else doing that and living to tell of it. He froze—and for a long moment nothing seemed to happen in the world.

Hopefully he continued to rub the bird's comb, but he felt no answering rumble of pleasure. NailBiter was probably as surprised as he was.

At least, Shadow thought, he had undressed the bird. Once he had digested his meal, NailBiter would be free to fly back to IceFire. His chances of reaching Allaban had been slim anyway, Shadow told himself. He was destined to die in this hellish cold, rock-infested darkness, and this way he would provide his bird with nourishment and one of them would escape.

Still no attack?

Shadow lowered his hand. Very slowly he crouched, fumbling around his feet to find the helmet. Was it possible that he could get it back in position before the beak bit him in half?

NailBiter bent his head and nudged, and Shadow fell flat on his face.

Then there was another long pause.

"Well, get on with it, you idiot!" he yelled. "Don't play with your supper!"

NailBiter started to rock, shuffling forward awkwardly, first one foot and then the other. Then a great wing scooped—and Shadow found himself in a warm, musty darkness, pressed between wing and breast, downy feathers tickling his face. The saddle was still below him, and NailBiter was above and all around. The wailing of the wind had stopped. There was only a steady thumping of the eagle's heart.

And there was warmth.

Perhaps the bird wanted to thaw his food also?

No. Shadow was being mothered. NailBiter had apparently done something that no other eagle in history had done—he had decided to make friends. His rider was cold and needed rest, and he was treating him like a fledgling. It was unprecedented and unbelievable, but it was warmth and safety. Indeed it was very comfortable, a living tent and sleeping bag combined. But Shadow had never heard of it being done with an unhooded bird.

Now he remembered the strange remarks that Vonimor had made: Birds did funny things in Allaban. Nothing could be stranger than this, so it was true, and the effect extended beyond Allaban itself.

He shivered as the heat seeped through him; the pain in his feet and hands made him want to scream, but in time it must have gone away because he slid easily into sleep.

10

"Look before you launch."
—Skyman proverb

THE walls were paneled in marble, carved in bas-relief. One slab showed a goat being seized by an eagle; King Shadow hit the edge of it with his shoulder and thrust with every atom of his being. It was magnificently balanced, and the bearings were still smooth, even after so great an age, but its sheer mass made it slow to yield. Reluctant as a glacier, it pivoted about its center, and a welcome slit of darkness appeared beside him. He squeezed himself through as soon as it was wide enough. He had forgotten, though, that the opening did not reach to the floor, so he cracked a shin hard against the high lintel and fell forward, striking the opposite wall of the very narrow passage and collapsing sideways on a soft layer of filth.

Heedless of his pains, he struggled to his feet. Now the panel stood wide. He grabbed it and, with the advantage of leverage against the wall, swung it back on its pivot once more. He caught a last glimpse of Aurolron's body starkly bathed in sunlight; he heard the yells as the rescuers piled up in the doorway, then the slab closed with a gentle thump. He fumbled in the dark to find the massive bolts and slid them into place . . . one . . . two.

He leaned against the slab, gasping and breathless, hearing the thunder of his own heart and an angry twittering of birds overhead. Just for a moment, perhaps, he had won safety.

"It's very dark!" the queen said, and he choked back a scream.

It was not quite perfect blackness—he could just see the glimmer of her face and hair. While he had come by one side of the slab, she must have stepped through the gap on the other.

"Majesty!" he wailed. "What are you doing here?" The stone was quite soundproof; there would be bedlam out in the cabinet, yet he could hear nothing.

"Hiding from that madman," the queen said in a very normal, conversational tone. "He'd kill us all, you know. He's quite mad. He pulls wings off spiders."

Great flames of the Ark! He had panicked, yes, but if he had any chance of life left at all, then he must flee at once. He had never intended that the queen should come with him.

The guards were out there—she would have been completely safe. Right behind him was a blank wall; the passage was barely wide enough for one person, and she was between him and the way out, the way down to the secret tunnels. A lifetime of training held him back from brashly attempting to thrust by her—if he could—and what would she do, anyway? She might well scream. She might reopen the panel and give him away. She might not be strong enough . . .

He would have to kill her.

"What are you doing here?" he demanded again in a low voice.

"Waiting for Vindax," the queen said calmly, in the sort of voice she might have used to discuss wallpaper or the temperature of soup.

"He is dead! He had an accident! There was a letter—"

"Lies!" the queen snapped, but not loudly. "Alvo would never do such a thing. It is a trick."

Shadow was stopped short. Was that possible? With a schemer like Aurolron, anything was possible. "But the letter?"

"The letter?" she repeated. As his eyes adjusted to the deep gloom, he could make her out better. "Yes, the letter. Read it to me." She thrust a crackling parchment into his hands.

She had brought it with her. The implications of that struck him like a lightning bolt. The guards would have found the dead king in an empty room. Jarkadon would now be claiming that he was king, for his father and brother were both dead, but he did not have the letter, and no one but Aurolron had seen it. So they would only have his word for it, and there must be limits to how much credibility would be afforded even a prince in such incriminating circumstances.

So there would be even more chaos than Shadow had expected, and his tiny, tiny chance of escape might just be a little bit greater because of it.

The passage was merely a rough-textured gap between double walls, starting where he stood and curving away around the arc of the egg-shaped cabinet itself. In spite of its narrowness, it was very high; small gaps at the top admitted a trickle of light and air. They had also admitted swallows, whose nests encrusted the upper walls and whose litter had piled thick on the floor. The swallows were jabbering angrily at the intruders, darting in and out of the holes.

"I can't see to read, either, Majesty," Shadow said. "Perhaps in a little while . . ."

"Well, we have lots of time," the queen said. She steadied herself with both hands and somehow managed to sit down in her fine, rich dress on the heaped bird droppings on the floor. She leaned her arms on her knees.

She had gone mad, obviously.

Aurolron and he had shared one thing: They had both hated the dark and never closed drapes. Yet he knew that the human eye could adapt to darkness for some inexplicable and useless reason. Twenty minutes it took, they said, but already he could see much better. Yes, the document he held was the letter from Ninar Foan, but still not decipherable.

"It was very stupid of me," the queen sighed. "I should have explained to Vindax and warned him." She sounded as though she were talking to herself.

"Warned him of what?" Shadow demanded. He ought to be running like hell, yet he had to plan his moves carefully. Was there any possibility that the queen could be of assistance—or of use? A hostage? The uproar and search going on outside must be mind-wrecking.

"Alvo must have got such a surprise," she said. "How proud he will be of Vindax!"

Gods! Was the queen about to admit it?

"They are twins, you know. When I look at Vindax, I see Alvo exactly, as he was. I expect he has aged, but I remember him as he was then, as Vindax is now."

The passage led to a stairway, and that led down to a cellar. Through such passages and cellars and store-rooms, it was theoretically possible to move almost any-where around the palace complex, if he could remember them all. He had shown many of them to the new Prince Shadow. Aurolron, who had liked to be sure of his backups, had inspected secret doors once in a while. Vindax knew of them. But only those three and himself, he was sure. Two were dead. The fourth might also be dead and was at the far end of the kingdom anyway. He did have time, but not much.

"A man would not kill himself," the queen said. "That was what Aurolron thought, but he would never."

A man ought to kill himself—suicide would be much better than a traitor's death. It would have done no good to have stayed and done his duty, denouncing Jarkadon as the assassin, for when the king died, Shadow died. Even if the queen had supported him and he had been believed, he would not have been saved.

"What?" he said, confused.

Now he could see the queen's expression as she explained with great patience, "The king thought that Alvo would kill Vindax, of course. He thought that Alvo would think that Vindax was his son and had been sent to him to be put to death because it would be a breach of honor for a man to let his own bastard sit on another's throne."

Now, that had to be the craziest thing the crazy woman had come out with yet. Honor was not something that Shadow had ever claimed to understand, but he knew that some men had it. Whatever it was, though, no one carried it to those extremes.

"His own son? Madam, is the duke of Foan Prince Vindax's father?"

"You never asked me that before, dearest," she said reproachfully. The clothes had confused her—now she thought he was Aurolon.

"But why do they look so alike?" Suddenly he thought he would go happier to his death if he could get this confounded mystery solved.

"Ah!" The queen sighed blissfully. "Well, you see, I was very much in love with Alvo before I learned to love you. But royalty had obligations, as you told me—you were very patient, my dear. And I gave you what you wanted, didn't I? Two sons? 'An heir and a spare,' you said." She giggled and then sighed. "I should have liked a daughter, but a king likes to have two sons."

He would need different clothes. Servants' clothes, preferably. There was no way he could escape by air even if he knew how to fly those damned birds. An escape on foot into the town was his only chance. Then —Piatorra? Aurolron had sent the king of Piatorra some sculptures once. That meant carts, so it must be possible to reach Piatorra on foot somehow.

Shadow peered at the letter and saw that the words were becoming distinguishable. Astonishing! It had been quite dark when he first came into this smelly stone slot. The twittering of the birds was dying down. He would need money...

"I only thought of it a few days ago," the queen said. "All these kilodays it has puzzled me, and I only thought of it now, too late!" She began to weep softly.

"Thought of what?" He had no money of his own. When he had been Baron Haunder, he had owned an estate somewhere a long way rightward on the Range.

He had never been there—the rents had come in regularly, and he had relied on the manager.

"Why Vindax looks so like Alvo."

Great Ark of God! "Majesty," he said, "why *does* your son look so like the duke of Foan?"

"Because I was so in love," the queen sobbed. "All the time I was carrying the king's son I was thinking of Alvo, Alvo my love. I made a baby that looked just like him."

Balls! Shadow thought. It wasn't love that made babies, it was balls.

"Er . . . did the king know this?"

"Yes!" she sobbed. "I just told you I just told him because I just thought of it—too late. After he had sent Vindax away to die. And he said of course that was why it was and not to worry about it."

Even King Shadow did not get to hear all the private conversations within the family itself.

"That was why he sent a letter to call Vindax back," the queen explained, wiping her eyes with a lace handkerchief that had appeared from nowhere.

No, it wasn't. It was because of Jarkadon.

The former Baron Haunder dragged himself back from his planning. Was it possible that Aurolron had been sending Vindax to his death? He had claimed as much to Jarkadon. Or had he been leading Jarkadon on to see how much infamy the young man was capable of suggesting? Did it matter at all now, especially to a fleeing traitor? He held up the parchment, and some of the words could be made out, some guessed at.

"No, I still can't see well enough," he said. He lowered the letter and looked down at the queen.

"Lies!" she snapped, and reached up to rip it from his hands. She tore it in half. "It was WindStriker! She wanted revenge. She has never forgiven me for escaping from Allaban. The eagles have never forgiven me." She ripped the document in four.

Shadow leaned back wearily against the end wall. He could think of no way he could use this madwoman— she would merely be a ball and chain on him.

Money? The queen wore jewels; he could take those, and if he could get into town, he could cash them in. But what in hell did he do with her? He shivered. He would have to kill her. She was the only one who had always smiled to him.

Now she had stopped ripping the whole letter and was working on it one fragment at a time.

He needed clothes first, obviously. But from where? Perhaps down in the kitchen cellars he might find some discarded rags. He might club down some servant from behind. The trouble was, most of them would be hulking lunks who could turn right around and break him in half. Then he'd have to head out into the city.

Then?

Then nothing. Even if he knew where his former estate was, he could never get to it, and it would not be a safe place anyway. When Baron Haunder had become King Shadow, his estate had been put under royal wardship—which meant that the crown had plundered it, of course. The men there would never have heard of Haunder and would have no interest in him anyway.

"Clever eagles!" the queen muttered, reducing sixteenths to thirty-seconds.

And who was king now? If the queen recovered her wits and both of them testified against Jarkadon, then who was next in line? He had no idea—one of the decrepit royal dukes probably. If he did do the honorable thing—return the queen and testify against Jarkadon—would the successor be grateful enough to pardon him? Somehow the chances did not seem very encouraging.

He would have to hide out. Now he recalled the bolt hole under the royal quarters. It had been built for just such a purpose. It was never used, and he had not even shown it to Prince Shadow; he had not even seen it since his first day on the job, five kilos ago. Perhaps even Aurolron had forgotten it. But it was furnished with two cots and a chair, water, and even books. It had three entrances, one of which led into the larders of the royal kitchens, so a fugitive could hope to sneak in there during third watch and steal food. It had spy holes. Perfect!

It would be a prison, but a comfortable one, and he could vanish for ages, until long after he had been forgotten. Then he could make his escape to Piatorra.

"Come, madam," he said. "We must go." The guards might start taking sledges to the walls of the cabinet soon, seeking the secret passage.

"Where to, dearest?" she said, holding up a hand. Now he was the king again.

"Let us go and find Vindax." He helped her up.

"Good idea!" she said, and walked obediently along in front of him. He guided her down the stairs, fearful she would stumble in her long dress. At the bottom the passage ended, but there was an opening in the wall, with a massive metal door. He slid this into place and shot the bolts. Pursuers would have to break through that from a space almost too narrow to move in—the long-ago genius had planned well. He found flint and steel and ancient dried-out candles.

This way was long and complicated, and he would have to take care not to get lost or sidetracked, but his first problem, obviously, was the queen. He was not man enough just to strangle her.

The solution proved surprisingly easy. They were stumbling along a dusty underground passage, and he found a massive door standing open. Flickering candlelight showed a small empty cellar, apparently carved out of the rock itself. A dungeon, perhaps? He did not know.

"In here, Madam," he said.

She smiled thanks, thinking he was following, and then stopped in surprise. He pushed. He heaved the door closed and shot the bolts as the echoes rolled away. Then he shivered uncontrollably. Hunger would kill her? No, thirst. He would come back for the jewels—after a long time, hectodays. Poor woman! But it was her fault that he was in this mess. He stumbled away down the corridor, expected to hear screaming or banging behind him, but there was only silence.

Passages and trapdoors and concealed panels...he detoured through cellars and once through shrubbery, scuttling along like a hunted rat. But no one saw him or heard him, and all he saw of the search was once when he looked out through another spy hole and saw a band of men running. The whole palace must be in turmoil, and even the cellar areas and kitchens were stripped of people, which made his journey easier. It was the middle of third watch, too—those who had not heard the news would be in bed.

At last he reached the royal quarters and began to advance more carefully than ever. One entrance to the bolt hole was from the king's bedroom—he could forget that one. Another was from the larders, and a third from a cloakroom off a public corridor. The larders were the best bet.

He had to leave the secret ways and enter a wine cellar through the back of a cluttered and apparently useless closet. He tiptoed in the dark around great fragrant barrels, wondering if he was leaving marks in the dust. He crept up steps and peered around the corner. He scurried through a deserted kitchen and down more stairs.

The larders were pitch-dark. Wearily he went back up and found another candle and lit it. Then he descended again and picked his way cautiously between the racks and bins to the far corner. Damn! A great stack of boxes stood in the way. Sweating with fear and exhaustion and effort, he moved the whole pile forward one row, leaving a narrow space behind. With luck, no one would notice and the pile would conceal the door, for he would be coming back this way many times in the future.

At last the job was done and he could slide behind the pile and find the panel. It creaked like a clap of thunder, at least to his ears. Then he was through it, had closed it. There were no bolts or fastenings; on this side it looked like a boarded-up passage, and perhaps once that was all it had been.

The candle's glimmer showed more stairs, but this was a wide and passable corridor compared to most he had used. The steps were thick with dust. He plodded up them, wishing he had thought to grab some food while he was in the larders. At the top he reached the door to the room, but the corridor continued, running on to the cloakroom entrance. He had better make sure that that was sealed, and then he would attend to the royal bedroom exit, which was off the far side of the hideaway. Then he could go to sleep for a few days.

The cloakroom entrance was already bolted on the inside. That surprised him. Indeed, that was astonishing and quite beyond understanding. Perhaps if he were not so exhausted and emotionally battered, he could figure it out, but he was very glad he had not tried to come in that way.

He followed his flickering candle flame back to the bolt-hole door and threw it open.

The first thing to strike him was the light—the place blazed with lamps. The next thing was the heat, from the lamps and from the people. The walls were lined with mirrors or draped with scarlet cloths. The simple furniture he remembered had gone, replaced only by thick rugs and piles of cushions.

There were five people there: a whimpering, naked girl, two young men still in the process of undressing, and two already busy. He had last seen those four men a couple of hours earlier around a card table. Jarkadon was not present, but his friends were celebrating in his absence. Shadow had walked into the Lions' den.

"Let's take it from the beginning," the archbishop said wearily.

It was all too confusing. A man of his age should not be dragged from his bed before three bells and then expected to deal with some sort of major crisis on the spur of the moment. The messenger from the court—he had some fancy title which the archbishop had already forgotten—was a blithering moron who made no sense at all.

"The king has been stabbed, Holiness," the dean said.

"Yes!" the archbishop said. "I got that. Doesn't surprise me . . . I've been expecting it for kilodays." His first reaction to that news had been one of great annoyance. It meant a state funeral and then a full-blown coronation,

and he dreaded the thought of all that effort and work.
At his age, he deserved to be left in peace.

"The crown prince is out of town," the dean said,
"and he may be dead also."

The archbishop held up a blue-veined hand to stop
him while he thought about that. Normally the dean
made sense. He was his nephew, of course, and he handled all the routine and gave advice and so on. "What do
you mean, 'may'? Is he or isn't he?"

"There was a letter, Holiness, saying he had had an
accident. But his body has not been found."

"Let me see this letter!" the archbishop said triumphantly.

"It has vanished," said the idiot from the court, and
the dean hushed him.

"It is apparently not available, Holiness," the dean
said. "The only persons to have read it were the king and
Prince Jarkadon. The prince is too upset to remember
exactly what it said."

"Humph!" the archbishop said. He still could not see
why they needed to involve him. He huddled in his gown
and wished he could go back to bed or have breakfast or
something.

"It may be a few days before we know about the
crown prince," the dean explained slowly. "So there will
have to be a regent appointed."

"The next in line, isn't it?" the old man asked. They
had told him that twice.

"Yes, Holiness, but the next in line is Prince Jarkadon, and there is some doubt . . ."

The two younger men glanced at each other and
shrugged. The dean winced and put it into words: "It is
possible that it was the prince who stabbed the king!"

"What!" The archbishop blinked. Why couldn't they
have said so sooner instead of all this flapping around?
"Then he must not be regent! He could not succeed. It
would not be proper! Or legal."

"Exactly, Holiness."

This really was a matter for the lord chamberlain or

the lord chancellor, thought the archbishop; none of his business. "Why not the queen?" he asked.

"The queen is distraught, Holiness. Quite incapable."

This was where he kept asking them to start again. He pondered. "Well, if not one of the princes, who comes next in succession?"

"You do, Holiness."

"Rubbish!" That was a ridiculous idea and rather frightening. "What about my brother, for heaven's sake?"

The dean and the messenger exchanged glances again. "He had a stroke two days ago, Holiness. He is still in a coma—and the doctors do not expect him to recover."

"What?" the archbishop said again. "Why was I not told?"

"I did mention it to Your Holiness, I am sure."

"Well . . ." Yes, he remembered, now that he thought about it. "Well, you mentioned that he was sick. You didn't say he was that bad. I should have been told. I ought to send him some grapes or something."

"So you are next in line, Holiness."

"Oh . . . pish!" the archbishop mumbled. "I refuse to get involved. Separation of church and state. That's why the cathedral is at the far end of town from the palace, you know. Ancient law. It will have to be the prince. Damn, don't you know who killed the king?"

"There were only three people present, Holiness. The prince says that Shadow did it, and Shadow says that the prince did."

"Shadow?" the archbishop muttered. "What possible motive could Shadow have?"

The other two glanced at each other again hopefully. The old relic had seen the problem at last.

After some more thought the archbishop said, "Three, you said?"

"The queen was present also, Holiness. But she is under sedation, and not making much sense. She has had a terrible ordeal . . ."

"Bah!" the archbishop said. "Surely someone asked her who stabbed the king? Eh?"

"Well, yes," the messenger admitted. "She said she did. And her ladies identified the dagger as being hers."

There was a pause.

"Let's take it from the beginning," the archbishop said.

11

"Coming down is easy."
—*Skyman Proverb*

How long Shadow slept he never knew. Sleep was supposed to be very difficult at great altitudes, but exhaustion belied that theory. He awoke choking, but suddenly and completely, knowing where he was and astonished that he was still alive. He was hot. At some time he had unfastened his flying suit, but he had no memory of that. He closed it up once more, fumbling in the dark, and wondered if he dared search for his food and water. NailBiter felt him move, tightened his wing slightly, then relaxed it again. The bird would not have slept, of course, but he must be growing perilously hungry.

Shadow crawled out from under the wing and stood up and looked at that deadly stare.

"Breakfast?" he asked. "No? Well, let's get going."

Would he be allowed to dress the monster? He picked up the helmet, and NailBiter lowered his great head slightly to make it easier. Incredible! Birds were smart, Shadow knew, and if they were to be cooperative also, then things were going to be a lot different. The saddle went on, and he clipped back the blinkers as soon as possible, knowing it was a risk but anxious to show appreciation. Perhaps he had just gone mad and this was not happening at all. He scrambled back down the length

142

of the rope to collect the grapnel and then scrambled up it again, coiling. NailBiter turned and stared at him.

Then he opened his wings a fraction.

He wanted to fly! He was trying to say that he did not want to kite!

Shadow was definitely insane.

"Okay, Naily," he said, tying the coil to the saddle, "you're the boss now." His teeth were chattering again. Every bone in his body was chattering. The stars were still there, but the shining mountaintops had changed since he last studied them; there was certainly a gap in them. That might be a shadow from Eagle Dome, or it might be the central windgap he was seeking—in either case, he must be close to the crest. If it got any higher, he was dead anyway.

NailBiter rose erect and turned his head back and forth. Then he took a few unsteady steps and stopped.

Shadow dismounted. The bird paced over the rocks, picking his footing with care—eagles were never good on their feet. He found a better launch pad, where the wind was stronger. Shadow climbed back into the saddle, tempted to pinch himself awake.

"If only you could talk, old buddy!" he said.

NailBiter crouched, spread, and leaped. For a tense moment rocky fangs snatched out on all sides, and then man and bird were airborne, fighting once more against the icy wind.

The bird was allowed to make the decisions now. Once he stopped for a rest, buffeted so roughly by the wind that his talons made scraping noises and he was continually seeking a better grip. Shadow could not have dismounted there if he had tried, so the message was clear. He was not supposed to. No more kiting!

Then there was turbulence and cold beyond belief, and he knew that he had reached the divide. And suddenly the wind was behind them. They soared and whirled up a steep cliff which must be the back of Eagle Dome, swept forward and upward relentlessly by the great wash coming down from the High Rand, starting to curve over to the right. Shadow heard himself cheering,

and he reached out to rub NailBiter's comb in triumph.
Then he blacked out.

He was awakened by a headache worse than anything
he had ever known. NailBiter was gliding, floating down
a vast gorge with the sun climbing over the horizon
ahead. Shadow was stiff and frozen. His fingers and toes
were numb, and when he was conscious enough to think
about it, he decided that he probably had frostbite. But
straight ahead must be Allaban—he had made it through
Dead Man's Pass. One more for the history books.

Then a turn took them out of the gorge, and they
drifted over a green countryside. He had been told that
Allaban was a richer spot than the rest of the Rand, but
he had seen nothing like this since he had left the Range:
terraced fields and cottages and even small woods, and a
prosperously cultivated hillside facing toward a white
and brilliant sun. Not here the great tilted steps of the
typical Rand, but gentle ridges and valleys running sunward, with many tiny dams to catch the springs, and
canals bearing their lifeblood to the crops.

Suddenly the flying suit was outrageously hot and his
feet and hands began to thaw in agony.

NailBiter's head flicked from side to side. Wilds! Several of them, above and to either side.

Shadow's heart sank again. His bow and quiver had
vanished somewhere in the pass—but he probably was
not capable of shooting an arrow into the side of a castle,
let alone hitting a bird. Frantically he searched the
ground below for shelter and selected a group of farm
buildings.

He decided to steer for that. NailBiter ignored his signals.

On the point of imposing his will by closing the
blinkers, Shadow changed his mind and decided to wait
and see. He stretched out prone once more, almost too
weary to care. Two of the wilds took up station to his
right and three more to his left, but they stayed distant
and seemed to be posing no threat—he had been given
an escort. Was he being taken in under guard?

He wondered if this was what Vonimor had been warning him about. And Ukarres had said something about Karaman being a fantastic trainer of birds. Was it possible that the men of Allaban could teach eagles to perform without a rider, like dogs?

The fields raced by below him, and he saw a few men working; they glanced up to stare—as though a skyman were a rarity. There were few fences, and he could see no livestock, but there seemed to be more bicycle traffic than he would have expected.

Then NailBiter banked without warning, circled around a large huddle of farm buildings, and swooped deftly down to a landing post nearby. A place not large enough to boast an aerie would usually have such a structure, a flight of steps up to a stout wall from which the eagles could take off again.

Two weary beats of the great wings and NailBiter landed. Then there was stillness and peace and warm sunshine.

Shadow reached up and stroked the bird's comb—and this time he felt the rumble. NailBiter was pleased, too.

Shadow pulled off his mitts and counted: eight fingers, two thumbs. They hurt enough for sixty. He started to dismount but slid, fell, and crumpled limply on the platform. He sat there for a moment, trying to gather his wits. His head was spinning, and his throat and lungs felt burned raw.

First problem: There were no shackles. So NailBiter would have to stay blinkered.

Second problem: He looked around and could see no hoods or hooding poles.

With an effort he clambered to his feet, thinking that at least he could remove the saddle.

"Let us help you," a quiet voice said behind him. In turning around he staggered and sat down again, hard. He was looking at a pair of worn, patched brown trousers and two skinny bare legs. Then a hand took his and he was helped to rise; his arm was draped over thin, bony shoulders.

"Six steps," said the voice, an elderly voice. "Take your time."

Shadow wobbled down the steps, leaning on this frail little man. Then he stopped and turned around. The bare legs belonged to a young boy who had scrambled nimbly into NailBiter's saddle and was reaching up, fumbling with the buckles of the helmet.

"No hood!" Shadow mumbled urgently, feeling as though his mouth were full of sand. "Stop him!"

"That's all right," the old voice said calmly. "He won't hurt us."

Then bigger, stronger arms gripped Shadow and made a human chair and lifted him from the ground—husky, bare-chested farm workers, smelling of hay and sweat, grinned on either side of him. NailBiter's helmet fell away beyond the perching wall. NailBiter turned his head and looked ferociously toward Shadow.

Shadow tried to shout a warning and produced a hoarse croak. The boy jumped down to the platform and started on the saddle girths, and the two bearers turned Shadow around and began to carry him away, ignoring his pitiful struggles.

He had a vague impression of trees and buildings. The first speaker, the elderly man in brown, who was small and stooped and had a great shock of white hair above his weather-burned face, was walking alongside, regarding Shadow with some amusement, and the two young men were setting their pace to his.

"Congratulations," the old man said.

With an effort Shadow managed, "Why?"

"Dead Man's Pass," the old man said.

Then a dark shape flashed above them, and Shadow jerked his head back in alarm. A brown wild eagle whirled around once more. He twisted his head to see, so the men stopped and turned him so he could watch as the wild settled down beside NailBiter, a sheep dangling from its beak.

"What the hell?" Shadow said. At least, he tried to say that, but it didn't sound very distinct, even to him.

"Your friend is being helped too," the old man said.

The wild passed the whole sheep to NailBiter, who began tearing it up and swallowing it. That was not cawking ritual—it wasn't anything. Eagles did not do things like that. Vonimor had warned him. The wild spread its wings, jumped, and went flapping away over the meadow.

"He's a fine fellow," the stranger said. He wore a brown smock and brown trousers and a curiously placid, friendly expression.

"Who are you?" That came out clearly enough.

"I am Ryl Karaman."

If Shadow had been standing, he would have fallen.

"The rebel?"

Karaman chuckled, motioned for the helpers to bring their burden, and walked alongside once more.

"I suppose. And you are Shadow . . . and Master Nail-Biter?"

"How do you know that?" It was very hard to talk, and the world was fading and solidifying all the time.

He received no reply, but he was carried up steps onto a porch and laid down on a couch, boots and all. Someone gave him a mug of something wet.

"Try not to gulp it," Karaman said. "Sip it. Oh, well. Sip the next one, or you'll throw up. You're dried out like a prune."

Shadow finished the second cupful and wanted more, but they took the mug away and firm hands were stripping his clothes off. He was suddenly racked by coughing.

"Fingers all right. Looks like you may lose a couple of toes, though. And half an ear, possibly." Karaman laid a blanket over him, and someone else was tucking a pillow under his head. The roof swayed pleasantly overhead.

"The doctor will be here shortly," the old man remarked. "Try to stay awake until he gets here." He settled into a rocking chair, and the others faded back, out of Shadow's field of thought.

Shadow turned his head and forced his eyes to focus; he saw that NailBiter had finished his meal and was feaking, the equivalent of picking his teeth if he had had teeth. Karaman's chair squeaked as he rocked quietly.

"How did you know my name?"

The cheerful expression faded from Karaman's leathery old face. "Your friend kept calling it out."

Now Shadow remembered why he had come. "He's here? Alive?"

"He made it," Karaman said cautiously, "but only just. He's in a very bad way."

"How bad?"

"Very bad. The doctors will not say if he will live— and he will never be the man he was."

Another Ukarres? Shadow choked back sobs. "Wind-Striker came through the pass with him?"

"Oh, no! Not at her age. She came around the face of Eagle Dome."

"Then the wilds let him through?" Shadow asked. Someone gave him another earthenware mug, and he tasted hot milk and honey.

Karaman rocked back. "They let *her* through—she was a returning native. They thought she was carrying a corpse, and they brought her to me to get it off her. I thought he was a corpse, too, at first."

"I want to see him. Now!"

"He isn't here. Yes, he's in Allaban, but we rushed him down to a little place called Femie, very low. He's being well treated, but I don't think he would know you yet."

NailBiter spread one enormous wing and set to work preening it.

Shadow's eyelids started to droop.

"You're the first man ever to make it through Dead Man's Pass," Karaman said.

The eyes opened by themselves. "Not what I was told!"

Karaman shrugged. "Eight or ten have done it from this side. None has ever succeeded coming from the left. Many have tried."

The words lay like a lump in Shadow's mind until meaning seeped out of them. Vonimor? No, not he. He was basically a decent man. He had known that the pass could be crossed, but not that it was a one-way proposition—he had been duped by Ukarres, and Ukarres had been trying to kill Shadow.

"NailBiter did it, not me."

Karaman nodded. "You unhooded him. That was very trusting of you."

Sleep was creeping up every limb, and Shadow was fighting it and losing . . . but now his eyes popped open again. "How do you know that? What did you do to him? How do you make the birds safe, like this? How did he know to come to this house?"

"That's too long a tale for now," the gentle old voice said. "But I did nothing to NailBiter in the pass—that was your doing. You must be a remarkable trainer. You must trust your bird greatly, and he knew that. He was greatly surprised when you unhooded him, but then he was sympathetic. He knows what you were trying to do, or thinks he does."

"What?" Shadow asked, getting sleepy again already. Karaman was trying to keep him awake until the doctor came. It wasn't going to work.

Karaman smiled, and his ridiculous comb of white hair waved back and forth as he rocked. "He had just cawked a few days before, right? A silver. Very beautiful, I am told, and very fierce. He was missing her greatly, and you were searching for your mate, too."

"I was doing *what*?" Shadow said, his eyes snapping open once more.

Karaman laughed shrilly. "People don't copulate in front of the birds—they have trouble telling the males from the females among us. You fly right behind the prince all the time, so NailBiter assumes that he is your mate. You were going looking for him—or her. He knew that WindStriker would have gone to Allaban, and you were going to Allaban. He was sorry for you, so he helped. It was nothing to do with me, and there have been very few trainers who ever won loyalty like that from their eagles."

"My God!" Shadow said, wondering if he was having his leg pulled. But Karaman seemed serious. In his weakness Shadow started to giggle at the absurdity—but to a bird his close attendance on the prince might seem like pair behavior. What would Vindax say to that? "Did WindStriker find her mate, then, too?"

"Oh, no," Karaman said. "He died years ago, in the fighting. She knew that, but she still had to go back to the last place she saw him. The eagles are much smarter than you think, my young friend, but that is a compulsion."

"Yet she knew he was dead?" The sleep was rising again, drowning him. "Somebody told her, I suppose?"

"There can be few more barbaric ideas ever invented by the kings of Rantorra," Karaman said, "than the post of Shadow. Yet you came after the prince. Why?"

"He gave me his trust, I suppose. I had to do what . . . I had to."

"You see? We have compulsions, too."

"Then you know who your prisoner is?" Shadow said. Karaman's voice was coming from farther away. "A guest, not a prisoner. He wears the trappings and the signet of the crown prince of Rantorra. I don't know his name; we get little news from the kingdom."

"Vindax."

"And Aurolron is still king?" Karaman asked. "And is Alvo still duke of Foan?"

"Yes," Shadow said cautiously. Why should Karaman ask about him when they were talking of Vindax?

NailBiter reared up and flapped both wings to ease them, then went back to preening.

Shadow suddenly found that his eyes were full of tears. "You won't let me shackle him, will you?" he asked.

"No!" Karaman snapped in a totally new tone.

"I'm going to miss that big mutt," Shadow growled, mostly to himself.

"NailBiter?" Karaman asked. "You're fond of him, aren't you?"

Fond of an eagle? Strange idea!

"Yes, I suppose so," Shadow said. "But he'll try to go back to IceFire. Will the wilds let him by?"

Karaman rose and stepped over to adjust Shadow's pillow. His face was a blur against the veranda roof. "Yes, and back again. But he isn't going back to IceFire just yet."

"Huh?" Shadow murmured sleepily. Doctor or not, he couldn't keep those eyelids open . . .

"I said NailBiter isn't planning to leave just yet," Karaman said from a great distance. "He is going to wait until you're recovered. He wants you to go back to Ninar Foan with him and release her, so they can both be free. He told me so himself. I told him I thought you probably would."

PART TWO:

PUNISHMENT

12

"A bird in a hood is worth two in the hills."
—Skyman proverb

VICE-Marshal Ninomar was drunk.

He felt good.

His face was streaming, possibly steaming, and probably as red as the logs in the fireplace. He sprawled on a cushion on an oak settle with his legs stretched out in front of him and an enormous tankard of hot mulled wine in his hand, and he was very, very content.

A jeweled star hung on a ribbon around his neck, and every few minutes he found himself fingering it and took his hand away quickly. Order of the Eagle, Second Class! That felt best of all.

There had been long days of waiting for orders from Ramo after the search had been called off, and he had not been relishing the prospect of returning to the capital to face a king whose son had been lost. Now the royal courier had arrived and there was a new king. The castle bell had summoned the townsfolk and the castle workers to the gate, and there the proclamation had been read:

> BY THE GRACE OF GOD
> and the Love of the People,
> JARKADON THE TENTH,
> King of Rantorra and Allaban,

155

Sovereign of Range and Rand, Lord of Land and
of Sky,
Fount of Justice and of Honor,
Giver and Upholder of the Laws,
Supporter of the Poor, etc.
Given under Our Hand this First Day of Our Reign,
being the nine
thousand two hundred and forty-third day of the
reign of our dearly
mourned and honored father, AUROLRON XX,
now deceased.
GOD SAVE THE KING!

And all had responded with loyal cheers for the new
monarch, led of course by the duke.

The vice-marshal was relieved. The new king could
hardly look so coldly upon Ninomar, for it was partly the
loss of Prince Vindax which had put him on the throne.
But the great surprise had been the award, the jeweled
star. The courier had produced it, and the duke had hung
it around the vice-marshal's neck in the king's name, and
there had been more cheers, although not so loud, naturally. It was astonishing, indeed almost embarrassing.
And there was no accompanying citation to explain.
Most odd. It was almost as though he were being rewarded for the accident. He took a swallow of wine and
dabbed his mustache with care, wondering uneasily
whether he would even dare wear the medal at court and
what sort of looks he would get if he did.

In law he had been responsible for the safety of the
prince—he was the officer. In practice Shadow had
made all the decisions but those sorts of things could not
be said. A commander must be a noble, naturally. He
could not be expected to know everything, and he might
well seek advice from the lowly born, but the prince had
not even made the pretense of letting Ninomar do that.
He had allowed the kid to give orders in public, and that
had been very annoying. Still, it seemed that all was
going to be well.

The duke lifted the copper jug from the hob and of-

fered it around. Ninomar accepted a refill, Ukarres declined, and the courier was given one without asking. Sir
Griorgi Rolsok was a tiny scrap of a thing, barely old
enough to shave from the look of him, but he had set a
new record from Ramo to Ninar Foan, even with nine
stops on the way, and was obviously proud of it. He was
also exhausted, and the duke was relentlessly plying him
with drink beside the roaring fire. Very shortly the other
three were going to get all the court gossip out of the kid.
That was not difficult to figure out.

Ukarres was only pretending to drink, but the duke
seemed to be doing so and holding it very well. Foan was
a fine gentleman; Ninomar had come to like him very
much. They were about the same age and both keen skymen, and it was a heady business to be a drinking buddy
of the premier nobleman of the realm.

Before sitting down again, the duke tossed some more
wood on the fire. "This is marvelous stuff, Ukarres," he
said. "Where did you get it?"

"From the aerie," Ukarres said with amusement. "For
years I have been scouring the Rand for firewood, and
Vak has been hoarding it, apparently. When he cleaned
up, he had it thrown over the side. I sent the lads out to
pick up. Have you any idea what happens to a table
when it drops that far? Some of it was halfway to Allaban. That junk pile had all sorts of..." He stopped and
suddenly took a drink—and it looked like a real one.

Ninomar drank also. Of course the junk pile had been
exonerated by the inquiry. The possibility of foul play
had been ruled out completely. He had not been present
in the aerie when the terrible incident occurred, so the
duke had appointed him and the local bishop as commis-
sioners; they had interviewed all the witnesses and
proved beyond doubt that the affair was an accident.
Their official report had already been sent off to Ramo
on the last of the single birds.

"Time!" the duke said suddenly. All eyes looked to
the table. There stood the great hourglass that was the
master timekeeper for Ninar Foan, both castle and town,

and beside it sat the three small hourglasses that every royal courier carried—and the sand was running out.

The duke reached for the big glass as it dropped its last grains and turned it over. The great bell of the castle rang: once . . . twice . . .

It was the start of third watch. "Bedtime, everyone!" the courier said with a giggle. He took another drink.

The other hourglasses emptied also, and the duke turned them. "Yes, we run a little fast," he said, frowning.

"Not enough to worry about, surely?" Ninomar asked.

"It mounts up," Ukarres observed. "When Sir Jion arrived, we were almost a whole day ahead of the court."

The duke rose and ceremoniously pulled the drapes, dimming the room. The firelight danced and flickered. It was curious to see so ancient a religious ceremony still being performed among these country folk; in Ramo people no longer bothered with such superstitions. Who knew how they originated, back in the mists of time? Whatever mists were. Whatever time was—now, there was a good subject for a drinking session. Ninomar took another swallow, and the duke lifted the big steaming copper jug from the hearth and politely topped up his tankard and Sir Griorgi's.

"How is Sir Jion?" the old man asked.

"I believe he has been sick," the courier said. "Haven't seen him around."

The duke had resumed his seat. He lifted a big roll of parchment. "You have proclaimed this all along the Rand, have you not, Sir Griorgi?" he said. "I may add it to the family archives, then? We have many similar."

"I am tired of hearing it," Griorgi said. "You can stuff it anywhere your ducal honor wishes, Your Grace."

Impudent young brat—they all laughed heartily.

The courier hiccuped, and that seemed to be a signal.

"I am a little confused," Ukarres said quietly. "When exactly did the terrible event occur?"

The courier blinked a few times and decided they

were speaking to him. "Just after His Grace's first letter arrived."

"And what day was that?" Ukarres asked.

"That was the thirty-eighth, I think," Griorgi said.

The other men exchanged glances. "It took a few days to straighten things around, then?" the duke murmured. "Normally a new king is proclaimed at once, I thought."

This was what they wanted to hear, of course. "Well, it was a little confusing," the boy mumbled. He proceeded then to make it seem very confusing. "...and then the traitor striking down the king and abducting the queen... There were no precedents."

Ukarres chuckled. "It must have been absolute chaos."

"Some of the high officials were a trifle perturbed."

Ninomar started to giggle and stopped when he caught the duke's eye. Then they both laughed aloud. Tragic... terrible... but the confusion in the court...

Ukarres nodded to himself. "Getting back to the timing of the new king's proclamation," he said, "the duke's third letter reported that the search had been called off and that there was certainly no hope. But that message can hardly have arrived before you departed, so when you left there must still have been some doubt about the fate of Prince Vindax."

The boy tried to think that through.

"There is no doubt now, though?" he muttered.

"None at all. Prince Vindax is dead," the duke said.

"Ah!" Young Sir Griorgi bent over and picked up his pouch, almost falling from his settle. "I have some more documents, Your Grace."

So that was what the duke was after! The courier produced a bulky package, wrapped in black ribbon. The duke rose and almost snatched it.

"One for you, my lord," he said to the vice-marshal.

Ninomar took the document and examined the royal seal carefully, then broke it open. It was the missing citation, explaining his star. He squinted in the firelight. For diligence in searching for the body of... well, that was better. A little weak, though. He wondered uneasily if he had merely been given a bribe to make sure that he was on the right side.

But there was more. He looked up in surprise at the duke.

The duke was scowling at another parchment. "I am summoned to court, Ukarres," he said. "At my earliest convenience, to do homage to the new king."

"Your post is here!" Ukarres said sharply.

"The frontier is quiet, surely?" Ninomar muttered.

"It may not be so much longer," Ukarres replied cryptically. He and the duke were frowning about something. The courier was slumping on the settle, sliding silently into one corner, his eyes closing.

"And here," the keeper said, "a death warrant for the man hitherto known as Prince Shadow, convicted in absentia of high treason, the sentence to be carried out in accordance with the law of..." He read on for a while and then growled. "That belongs with the cooks' recipes!" He tossed the parchment onto the table with an expression of disgust.

It was very fortunate, thought Ninomar, that the man in question had taken the hint and drilled a hole in the sky. Not a bad kid, really. He had even had the tact to leave the fake orders which Ninomar had made for him —and had so quickly destroyed when he recovered them. He hoped that young Shadow would find a better life in Piatorra, if he had the sense to go that far. He should be there by now.

"And," the duke said, "a royal letter addressed to my daughter."

He stared at it thoughtfully and again exchanged glances with Ukarres.

Ninomar coughed politely. "I am instructed to escort Lady Elosa to court, Your Grace."

The duke took the orders from his hand without asking and read them through. His face grew grimmer than ever.

"Her mother is not invited also?" Ukarres asked.

"No," the duke said. "And the letter to me suggests that she is to remain and hold the castle."

Sir Griorgi was asleep, snoring. The duke leaned down, peered in the courier pouch, and took out a second package, this one wrapped with red ribbon.

Ukarres chuckled.

"These, I suppose," the duke of Foan said, "were to be delivered in the event that Vindax had been recovered and was alive?"

"A reasonable supposition," the old man said, grinning.

Both of them glanced at Ninomar, who smiled politely.

The duke laid the package on the table and opened it.

"Another for you, my lord."

The vice-marshal felt his hands shake as he opened it. He peered at the writing, finding it very hard to focus. Then it was removed from his hand.

"You had it upside down," the duke said. "Let's see . . . an order for you to conduct the man calling himself Prince Vindax to court at once, regardless of his physical condition. Mmm? Also to conduct myself. At once. Interesting. I think you would have earned your bauble, my lord. Yes, here is the citation for it. Postdated, this one, I see. You would have had to deliver the goods."

Ninomar took a long drink, emptying the tankard.

"And a summons for me," the duke said. "To come at once, though—no mention of convenience. No mention of Elosa. And a proclamation of bastardy against the person calling himself Prince Vindax! Well, well!" He was almost as red as the unconscious courier now, flaming with anger. "It takes two to make a bastard, I understand. I wonder how the little punk's mother feels about this, if she knows. And here? A warrant, promoting Ensign Harl to flight commander!"

Ninomar was speechless.

"I wonder what he would have said? I think that young man's price might have been higher than flight commander." The duke glanced thoughtfully at the vice-marshal's chest.

Ninomar quietly tucked the Order of the Eagle, Second Class, inside the edge of his tunic, out of sight. Dukes should be humored when in this sort of mood.

Foan read on. "Ah! There's more. Sir Hindrin Harl and his wife have been released from jail." He looked thoughtfully at Ukarres.

"Aurolron said that his background was relevant," the old man wheezed. "It would be Schagarn he was covering, I should guess. Both, maybe. The new king would prefer willing witnesses?"

The duke frowned angrily. It was all well above Ninomar's head, but he was not going to ask.

"The little creep has been busy," Ukarres remarked, probably referring to his liege lord, King Jarkadon X of Rantorra.

"Very." The duke bundled up the second group of documents and stuffed them back in the courier's pouch. "We'll let this lad worry about these, I think. They are irrelevant, as the prince is dead."

He sat down and reached for the copper jug. "Now, Ukarres, do I run to court like a whistled dog? Or do I lock up my daughter and tell the king to—" He stopped. "Well?"

There was a thoughtful silence. Ninomar remembered that he had orders to escort Elosa and began to sweat even harder than before.

"Aurolron is gone," Ukarres said. "How long until they find out?"

Who?

"He will not know of that," the duke said. "Vindax did not. Do I write or dare I go in person and warn him?"

"He will not believe," Ukarres said. "It will be Schagarn all over again."

What? Where?

The door began to open even as someone knocked on it. Vak Vonimor came bursting in, panting, his straggly gray hair awry, his shirt half out of his belt. He was too out of breath to speak and just stood there, gasping, pointing behind him.

Ninomar felt suddenly less drunk.

"Well?" the duke demanded.

"Shadow..." Vonimor said.

Ninomar laid down his tankard. If Shadow had not gone to Piatorra...if Shadow had returned...

"He's back?" Foan asked, frowning.

Vonimor nodded. "Up in the aerie...wants to speak to you...and Vice-Marshal..."

"Then invite him here," the duke said, folding his arms and crossing his ankles. "I am not summoned to my own aerie."

The eagler shook his head. "I did, Your Grace. He won't come."

Foan scowled. "Bring him."

"I daren't...I can't..." A few more pants, and Vonimor said what Ninomar had been dreading. "He says he has a message from the prince."

Halfway to the aerie, Lord Ninomar concluded that he should properly have waited for the duke to move first, but it was a little late by then. Word had spread throughout the castle, and there seemed to be runners everywhere. He passed the duchess, tall and bundled in a burgundy robe with her gray hair flying loose; he was himself passed by Lady Elosa, still wearing the pink dress she had worn at dinner but with her black hair also unfastened and streaming behind her.

He went up all those hundreds of steps faster than he had run up an aerie since he was a cadet.

If the prince was alive, then there were two claimants to the throne...a proclamation of bastardy against one, which meant high treason against the queen dowager... and he had orders to find Vindax and take him to Ramo ...and also orders which effectively told him to arrest the duke of Foan also and take him...He ran.

He emerged gasping and panting in the brilliant sunlight, blinked, and pushed past a line of silent men. And stopped—like them, frozen.

There, certainly, was Shadow.

He was outside the bars—in fact, he was standing on the perching wall, with no safety belt visible, in a gap between the birds, but he was at one side of the gap, right next to Lady Elosa's silver, and he was keeping his balance by leaning a hand against her wing. *She was unhooded!*

Ninomar felt suddenly sick.

The bird had turned her head to watch the crowd gathering within the cage and was apparently ignoring the vulnerable human being beside her. He looked tiny in comparison; she towered over him.

A line of giant eagles and one tiny man. No hood?

It was impossible—Shadow's head should be inside her crop already.

"Good sky to you, Vice-Marshal," Shadow said. "I see you have a new pretty." The star had fallen out of the tunic.

Ninomar was beyond speech. He could only pant and gape at this miracle. He heard more feet on the stairs behind him.

Shadow was on the darkward side of the aerie, so the sun was shining through on him. He had unfastened the front of his flying suit, and his bony chest was shiny with sweat, but that must be from the heat of the sun only. He was showing no other sign of fear in spite of the terrible danger of his position. He held his helmet in his free hand, and he had a bandage over one ear. There were healing scars on his face, and that face held something that had not been there before: a hardness or wariness. It was not fear. It was perhaps anger or the stain of an ordeal.

Even if the bird did not bite his head off, she could topple him backward off that wall with the slightest movement. Ninomar thought of the drop and shuddered. Ukarres had talked of a table smashed halfway to Allaban.

There was something odd about that flying suit: some object fastened to the back of it and thick straps dangling down the front. Ninomar wondered vaguely what they were for, but mostly he was waiting for that eagle to strike.

The duke had pushed in beside him, and two gasping footmen were setting down Ukarres.

"Come off there!" Ninomar said quietly, not able or daring to shout. "You're out of your mind."

"I prefer to remain, Vice-Marshal," Shadow said. "Thank you." In his brown flying suit he seemed to glow against the dark sky behind him.

"Obviously you have been to Allaban," Ukarres said calmly. Having been carried, he was the only one not out of breath.

"Obviously," Shadow said. "I understand, Keeper, that King Aurolron is dead."

The duke nodded. The stairs were quiet now, but the entire population of the castle must be crowded in behind him, every one tongue-tied.

"He was murdered by King Shadow."

"That story I deem worthy of careful review," Shadow said. "God save King Vindax!"

There was silence.

"I was told you brought a message from ... Vindax," the duke said.

Shadow nodded toward one side of the group. "Tuy Rorin has it."

The groom edged sideways toward the duke, unable to take his eyes off Shadow. He held out a parchment. The duke snatched it.

"This should be discussed in private. Come down to my study. I promise you safe conduct."

The younger man shook his head angrily. "Your hospitality is flawed, Keeper. I stay here. Please read that out; it concerns the vice-marshal, also—and everybody, I suppose. I can quote it from memory, if you prefer."

The duke hesitated. "Very well." He raised his voice. "I shall read this document, but you will all understand that I am merely reading it and not making any judgment on it. Whatever it is, it may be total rubbish and a forgery. I quote:

"'Crown Prince Vindax of Rantorra to his cousin, the duke of Foan, etc., and to whomever else it may concern: Greetings. Know that I am alive and in good hands, although I have suffered serious injury from the . . .'" His voice trailed off.

"Read it, Keeper!" Shadow said. "Or I shall tell them what it says anyway."

The duke glared at him briefly and then continued. "'. . . serious injury from the attempt on my life, made by a person known to you. Please forward this letter to my royal parents at once, so that their worries may be relieved, and see to it that the would-be assassin is brought to justice. I shall remain here until I am well enough to travel, but this may be a hectoday or longer. I have been assured by the persons exercising authority here that no constraint will be put upon me. I am also assured by them that I shall not be required to recognize in any way their status, nor abrogate nor diminish in any fashion the claims of my mother or my father or ultimately of myself as their heir, in Allaban. Sealed by my hand in Allaban, this nine thousand two hundred and fifty-third day of the reign of Aurolron XX. Vindax P.'"

"God save King Vindax!" Shadow said again, quietly, and again there was silence.

"This proves nothing!" the duke snapped, crumpling the parchment.

"It is his signet," Shadow replied. "At least it proves that I found him. Or his body. Right?"

Ninomar took the crumpled ball from the duke and straightened it. "It is the correct signet," he said.

"I have permission to take a person designated by you to Allaban to meet the prince, the king now," Shadow said. "He will be returned safely within four days and will confirm that Vindax is alive, although still very ill."

"How do you propose to get by the wilds on Eagle Dome?" Ninomar demanded.

"I came that way," Shadow said. "They will be no problem. You agree, Keeper?"

Vonimor suddenly bellowed, "That Karaman! I told you in Schagarn—"

"Silence!" the duke roared.

"I know about Schagarn, Keeper," Shadow said. For

the first time his cold expression softened, almost into a smile. "It is suddenly very relevant, isn't it?"

He stood there, glowing against the sky, and it seemed that the whole audience was still holding its breath. Why did the bird not attack him?

Ninomar took a step forward. "King Jarkadon has been proclaimed. He has issued a declaration—"

"Silence!" the duke roared again.

"With respect, Your Grace," Ninomar said firmly, wondering how much of this sudden courage was from the lingering effects of the wine, "these are public matters. Very well! I have orders which do not recognize the status of Vindax as crown prince—"

"Or as a prince at all, I suppose?" Shadow interrupted. A quiet sigh went around the whole group.

"I have orders to take that person to Ramo."

"Go ahead and try," Shadow said.

"I also have, downstairs, a promotion for Ensign Sald Harl to the rank of flight commander."

The lone young man's face turned furious red in the sunlight. "Take that to Ramo and stuff it in his royal ear!"

"Shadow," the duke said quietly, "there is more. King Aurolron had apparently put your parents in the cells. King Jarkadon has released them."

Shadow's eyes narrowed, and he stiffened. "That would be because of you, Keeper, I suppose?" he said.

"I don't know," the duke said.

"How do you feel about tyrants who use family members as hostages?" Shadow demanded bitterly. "If you are suggesting that I should trust Jarkadon, then I can only say that I knew him when he was a small boy. He was a little turd then, and he is a bigger turd now. You know what his father said about him."

Ninomar gulped at such treason.

"Ukarres!" the duke roared, spinning around. "Did you show him that letter?"

"Yes, he did," Shadow said. "You knew Aurolron— he always offered the small end of the egg."

There appeared to be a standoff. IceFire turned her

head to look at something, and the spectators stiffened, but nothing more happened. The other birds were absolutely still, eerily so.

The duke stepped forward beside Ninomar. "Shadow," he said, "leave personalities out of this. We have matters of very grave import here. You say you know about Schagarn. I think that others do not. I also am summoned to court, and I would want to disclose those hidden things to His Majesty. Would you agree to allow me a hectoday to go to Ramo and return, without any change in the present status?"

Ninomar was getting very tired of hearing about this Schagarn and of not hearing about it.

Shadow shook his head. "I do not meddle in politics, Keeper, and I have no authority to do so. I will give you my personal opinion, though: Nothing is likely to happen within the next hectoday. But that is only my opinion, and it carries no weight."

"The king should know," the duke said.

"But who is the king?" Shadow asked. "You are the authority on the Rand. Do I return and tell King Vindax that he has your loyalty? Or do you support the usurper, Jarkadon?"

Nicely put, Ninomar thought. And he himself must make that decision also, on behalf of the few royal troopers he had with him. If his choice was not the same as the duke's, then he was going to be in the castle dungeon before three bells.

"I think I need time to consider," the duke said. "Again I offer you my hospitality, upon the honor of my house."

"And again I decline it. Decide."

The duke had gone very pale, and Ninomar suspected that he was not much better himself. Jarkadon's two sets of orders showed that news of his brother's survival would not provoke an abdication.

"You are accusing me of conniving in an attempt to murder Vindax," the keeper said at last. "Yet you want me to do homage to him? Would he accept it?"

Now it was Shadow who hesitated. "We did not know

of the king's death," he admitted. He shrugged. "It makes no difference. Vindax agrees that you were not privy to the plot, so he will accept your fealty. But the assassin must be punished—he is adamant on that."

Now—and much too late, he knew—Ninomar realized that they were discussing Elosa. After NailBiter launched, her bird had been next to the prince's. He and the bishop had never even considered Elosa. A child? But she could have done it, and the prince could have seen, albeit too late to stop his launch. The official inquiry had failed, then, and there was another problem.

The duke was silent, and his shaded face was visibly running sweat. If he supported Jarkadon, then the proclamation of bastardy effectively named him as a traitor for fathering Vindax and he must turn against his own son as a pretender. If he supported Vindax, then his daughter was a would-be assassin and therefore a traitor and he would also be in rebellion against the established court.

So the duke must choose between son and daughter. And if Vindax was not his son—and the duke at least could not be in doubt—then he was certainly the true king, but the duke's daughter must be sacrificed . . . while if Vindax was truly his son, then he was still a traitor and he and the queen dowager could suffer traitors' deaths, regardless of who was on the throne . . . Ninomar's head was spinning.

"Go back to your Vindax," the duke said, "and ask a pardon. Bring it here—"

"No!" Shadow said. "Kneel now, here, before me, and pledge your unconditional allegiance to King Vindax VII, or I return and tell him that you are in league with the usurper Jarkadon."

This was a commoner speaking to the premier noble?

"Then your Vindax will remain forever an exile in Allaban!"

"What was done at Schagarn is ended," Shadow replied quietly. "What if Vindax joins forces with the republic to recover his throne? You threaten war, Keeper? Kneel and swear!"

The duke moved as fast as an eagle. Two steps, and he had snatched a bow from one tub and an arrow from another and the bow was drawn and the feather at his eye before Ninomar knew what was happening.

But Shadow had moved also—he spun around and leaped out into space and was gone, as the arrow passed where he had been.

Women and men screamed in unison.

Deliberately, IceFire hunched and launched and vanished; Ninomar had not noticed that she had been unshackled. Elosa wailed loudly.

But Shadow? Ninomar thought of that terrible drop and the smashed table, and he suddenly slid to his knees and vomited up great quantities of mulled wine. When he had recovered, people were streaming down the stairs and a few others were having hysterics and yet others had hooded the birds and slipped between them to peer over the edge and look down into the darkness at the body.

"Well, that is the end of him," he said aloud. "He must have been completely crazy all along, and the prince is dead."

There was a dry wheeze behind him. "He was not crazy," Ukarres said. "He has been to Allaban. That was not the end of him."

After a moment he added, "But it may be the end of us."

13

"It served us damn well right!"
—*Ryl Karaman*

On the day after he arrived at Allaban, Shadow had flown with Karaman to Femie, there to meet his prince.

He had been warned, but no warning could have fully prepared him. Karaman had not thought to mention the nauseating stench of gangrene, or the madness that days of unbearable agony put into a man's eyes, or the flatness of the bandages on a face whose nose had been killed by frostbite and so amputated. There was irony in that. Vindax would not look like the duke of Foan now; he would not look like anyone.

There was more horrible irony. His hands were bandaged stumps, and the doctors thought the rest of the fingers would have to go also, but he had lost no toes. So he had feet but no real hands; yet his arms were uninjured and his legs paralyzed. Sky sickness was caused by bubbles in the blood, Karaman said, quoting the ancient texts. At some point in her frenzy WindStriker had plunged down almost to the desert floor, to air of great pressure. Then she must have soared high again. Eagles could do that; men could not. The return to the depths at hot, suffocating Femie had not been made in time to prevent the damage.

The doctors thought that the patient might live but were still not sure.

Shadow stared in silence at the bundled horror on the bed and said a prayer that Vindax might die. Ukarres had indeed been lucky.

But honor required that he speak the prince's name, and the eyes opened in the gap left for them within the bandages. They stared for a long time blankly, as though there were no mind behind them. Then the lips twisted into a smile.

"I knew you would come," Vindax whispered. After that, Shadow was looking through tears and did not need to see the details.

Karaman cut the visit short; he made the return journey slowly, stopping frequently at isolated farmhouses to chat with old friends. He introduced "Citizen Shadow" to innumerable people, all of whom offered food and hospitality and wanted to reminisce about old times. It was not mere socializing, he assured Shadow—a gradual ascent was more wisdom from the ancient texts. Shadow was too shocked and depressed to care.

These easy-living rural folk rang no watch bells, taking their time undivided. When Karaman reached home with Shadow, they sat on the porch, Karaman in his ancient rocker, Shadow slumped on the couch. His body was telling him that it was time for bed, yet between him and the view of fields and sunlit orchards glimmered that anonymous bandaged head and its mad eyes, and he doubted that he would ever sleep again.

Karaman disappeared briefly and came back with two mugs and a few large crocks. "We make an excellent cider here," he suggested.

"I'll get drunk," Shadow growled.

Karaman chuckled. "That was what I said."

So they sat and quaffed cider and talked, and Karaman told of many things which should have been unbelievable and were somehow not when wrapped in his gentle, casual good humor. Shadow drank three mugfuls to each of Karaman's and eventually spoke of politics and attempted murder and of Vindax. The generation-long silence which had hung over Eagle Dome was breached, and slowly the nightmare vision standing guard in his mind became blurred.

"When was the prince born?" Karaman asked.

"Why?" Shadow said cautiously.

The old eyes twinkled in their wrinkles as the old man saw that Shadow was not quite drunk enough to lose all discretion. "Just nosy. He looks so like the duke."

"He did!" Shadow said. "But the duke says he never met you."

"Then call one of us a liar," Karaman replied. "Me, by choice—it would be safer. Aurolron must have noticed. I wonder why he did not disown the prince? Not in character!"

"He never met the duke," Shadow said, wondering if that was a lie also, thinking of that strange letter Ukarres had shown him.

Karaman smiled. "Once I spent several days with both of them together. Certainly call me a liar before you try it on the king."

A meeting between the king and the rebel? Fuzzily Shadow pondered that. It must have been a very well-kept secret. Yet he could believe this threadbare, patched old man more easily than Aurolron or his premier noble.

"Where? At Ninar Foan? On the Rand?"

Karaman shook his head, holding out the cider crock once more. "On the Range, at a little place called Schagarn."

"I know it," Shadow said, surprised. "One of the royal manors. He used it as a hunting lodge before he gave up flying."

"Right," Karaman said. The two men stared out over the hills for a while, waiting on each other to speak.

"Was the queen there?" Shadow asked at last. He saw the twinkle return to Karaman's eyes.

"No. We're a pair of old gossips, friend Shadow."

Shadow giggled drunkenly, then became serious. "So far as Vindax knows, it was not possible for the duke to have fathered him. He was born on 1374."

There was a long silence, then Karaman said, "I

would not say this to anyone else, but you have earned his confidence and I shall give you mine. Yes, it was possible. Just. 1170 or thereabouts."

So the mystery was solved, here in far-off Allaban.

Karaman sighed. "It was my fault, I suppose, or at least I was the excuse."

"She betrayed her husband and her king at Schagarn?"

"Not there, but nearby. And I find it hard to think of it as a betrayal, Shadow. I suppose I am a romantic, or I was then. They were a tragic couple. He was noble, she was royal. He was handsome, she was beautiful beyond legend. They were as much in love as two human beings can be, like eagles, yet doomed to have only a few precious hours together and then be forever parted.

"It was supposed to be a political meeting. Her father had just died, and she claimed to be queen of Allaban, so I had asked for her to be included. Aurolron had refused, saying he would speak for her as husband and as overlord. I had agreed to that. But after our business was over, after the king had left Schagarn and we were supposed to be leaving at first watch, Foan took me aside and said he had made arrangements. I said it did not matter now; he insisted, and I suppose I guessed. There were many guards, you can be sure, but they were watching the aerie and the stables. The two of us slipped away on bicycles to another house, not far off."

Shadow's knuckles were white as he gripped the cider mug, his alcoholic haze vanished like a burned leaf.

"There was no one else there except our host," Karaman said, gazing away into space and time. "No servants around. She gave me her word on the treaty without taking her eyes off Foan. The host tactfully suggested that he and I take a stroll. Soon I said I was weary and wanted to rest before our long journey began. Would he take me back to Schagarn? He did, and when we all arose at three bells, the duke was back also. So I suppose it was my fault. I suppose it happened, having seen the prince. Was I being deliberately nasty to Aurolron, I wonder?"

"Where was this exactly?" Shadow demanded.

"Oh, a lovely spot," Karaman sighed. "One of the old, old castles, fallen into humble straits as a local manor house. Set in a wooded dell with a tiny pond in front of it . . . ivy and gables and wild flowers . . . a story-book couple in a storybook setting. No, it could not have been betrayal. It was love, and surely love can justify itself."

The king's letter had said: *his background is relevant.* The king knew, then, and had been telling the duke that he knew. *I think you owe me this.*

"There is a dove cote and a rose tree in the court-yard?" Shadow asked. "The doves sit on the gables and purr?"

Karaman turned to stare at the tears on Shadow's face. "You know it?"

"Hiando Keep," Shadow said. "I also was conceived there."

And at Allaban there was Potro, who was the young-est of Karaman's many grandchildren, a collection of bones aged around three kilodays, wearing nothing but skimpy shorts and burned almost black by the sun, his hair bleached white and flying loose in a comic parody of his grandfather's. He whirled everywhere around the homestead without pause like a young eagle himself, flashing teeth and filling the air with impudence and laughter.

He was, Karaman said, as good a bird speaker as any, and the very day Shadow arrived, after he had been tended and rested and fed, Karaman led him out to sit on the grass under the trees. Then the old man seemed to snatch Potro out of the sky and sent him over to give Shadow a lesson.

"Right!" Potro said, sitting down cross-legged. "Eight points on a bird's comb, okay?" And he put his hands together and held up a row of skinny fingers, with his thumbs folded down.

"Right."

"You don't happen to play the flute do you?" Potro asked.

"Not that I recall."

"Pity. I'm teaching a flute player, and he finds it easier." The words poured out, as they spilled from the birds themselves. "So each point on the comb can be bent left or right or straight up, right? That's as good as we can do. I mean the birds can do sort of in between, but that's more shade of meaning, if you know what I mean, like being funny or so on. I can read a little of it, but even I can't do it much.

"So our fingers won't bend backward. We have to do straight for left and a little bent for straight up and bent a lot for right. Try that. Gawrn, you're stiff! So eight points for a word, a one-syllable word. This means 'egg.'" And he arranged eight fingers.

Shadow muttered under his breath and let his fingers be adjusted.

"Of course they don't hold it like that—they run it from front to back, and then the next word is starting before they've finished the last one. Back to front for a question. And that's one-syllable words. Now, the word for 'water' has three syllables: this, this, and then this."

"You're too fast for me."

"That's *slow!*" Potro said. "Way slow! I mean, they have to learn to slow down; your NailBiter is too fast for me yet, and even Gramps can hardly get what he says. He'll learn. But when you came over the pass, he'd probably been talking to the wilds before you even saw them. And in a minute or two, he'd have told them who he was and you were, and where you'd come from and where you were going and all about himself back to the egg. They can say more in a minute or two than we can talk in a day— If they want to, of course. They prefer to sing about it. Like they make up great long, long poems, and then they can take a whole day to say what a pretty hill that is, or something. Gabby, they are, but gawrn, can they go when they want to!"

He reached over to Shadow's already cramped hands.

"Take them two at a time. Two fingers straight: that's

Ba. Bend the first one, that's *Be*. Bend it more, that's *Bo*. Now first finger straight and bend the second, that's *Na*. Nine of them: *Ba, Be, Bo, Na, Ne, No, Sa, Se, So*. So you take the eight two at a time makes four—right? —and nine ways to make the two. That word for 'egg' I showed you . . . no, like this . . . that's *SaneNEso*. 'Egg' is *SaneNEso*!"

"Why? I mean, why the *Bo* stuff?"

Potro looked impatient. "Because people remember sounds, not shapes. So Gramps says and he invented this. *SaneNEso* is easier to remember than what you're looking at. So you learn the sounds and then make the shapes, or watch the shapes the birds make and remember the sounds and what they mean. It's easy once you get the hang of it. That water word, remember this? That's *BoboNEsa-beseSEna-sosoNAbo*."

"I don't suppose you could just teach the eagles to read, could you?" Shadow asked.

The twig arms were folded over the wickerwork chest. "You want this lesson or don't you?"

"Yes, please."

"Then don't be silly. B'sides, how would they write back? Now let's hear it: *Ba, Be, Bo, Na, Ne, No, Sa, Se, So*."

"Ba, Be, Bo, Na, Ne, Se . . . Sa . . . ," said Shadow.

"No! *Ba, Be, Bo, Na, Ne, No, Sa, Se, So*."

Five minutes later Potro jumped up. "That's the first lesson. I'll just confuse you if I do more. You learn the sounds and the shapes and we'll start words tomorrow. And work those fingers; they're really bad. Worst I've seen. 'Scuse me."

He glanced up and flickered his hands at the sky, then ran down to the perching wall and scrambled on top of it. A second later a huge feathered shape swooped past him and he was gone. Shadow stifled a cry and then relaxed as he saw the bird soaring away, one foot down with Potro sitting on it, holding on to the leg, his own skinny legs sticking out in front. In a few minutes bird and friend had vanished into the sky.

* * *

And at Allaban most of all there was little wizened
Karaman himself. Retired farmer, he said, and even
more retired priest, but he was father confessor to the
whole country. Everyone came to consult him: the politicians and the priests and the neighbors and the birds. He
had no title and no office, and yet nothing seemed to be
decided without him. His quiet smile was everywhere
and for everyone, calm and understanding. "A quiet,
earthy man," Ukarres had called him, and Ukarres had
known him much better than he had implied.

But let him start talking about the birds and then the
zeal showed. Shadow met it first on his thirteenth day in
Allaban. The two of them and a few others were sitting
on Karaman's porch, drinking cider and planning
Shadow's trip to Ninar Foan. A couple of Karaman's
older grandsons were going to accompany him as trans-
lators, for Shadow had not yet progressed far in bird
talk. Rescuing IceFire was going to be easy, they agreed.
They could stay out of sight in the hills until the eagles
reported that there were no men in the aerie, then just go
and get her—she already knew they were coming.

Delivering Vindax's letter would be trickier. If
Ukarres or Elosa—or even the duke himself—got hold
of it, then it might vanish without trace. Ninomar would
not suppress it, nor would the countess, but they might
be gone already, and obviously accidents could happen
to anyone around Ninar Foan. Shadow would have to
make sure that many people knew about that letter. That
meant attracting attention—and attention meant danger.

It was Karaman himself who suggested that Shadow
stand on the perching wall beside IceFire. That would
impress! And have NailBiter hover in the updraft below,
he said. If Shadow had to leave in a hurry, NailBiter
could catch his sling in midair.

Shadow gulped. Was an eagle capable of that? he
asked.

He provoked an explosion. The quiet old man suddenly became the prophet, words pouring from him as he
stamped up and down the porch. From the expressions

on the others' faces, they had heard it all many times
before, but it was new to Shadow—this was the rhetoric
that had toppled the throne of Allaban.

"Capable? They are as smart as you are, if not
smarter! Stop thinking of them as animals! They are people!

"It is their world, not ours! You have only to look—
they were made for it and we are not. They ruled it and
enjoyed it untrammeled until men came.

"How could they have understood? They saw us
come and start killing their game, their food. At first
there would be little of that, and perhaps at first they did
not mind, for they are generous. But then men started
putting up fences and sowing crops, and there was no
more game there. And men started breeding livestock!
How could the birds have known that those were property? They have no property except their eggs. They
could not have understood that those beasts were not
there for the taking like all others. They cannot hear our
words; men did not see that their combs were speaking.
The fault was ours, for they have no hearing, but we
have sight. But neither understood, and it was war.

"Then men discovered that a hooded bird is helpless.
How? Perhaps that was wisdom from the Holy Ark. Perhaps it was just a lucky chance discovery—lucky for
men.

"They had soared the whole world—an eagle can stay
aloft for days, did you know that? Male and female together, singing of their joy and of beauty. There are many
things you cannot talk about with an eagle: unrequited
love, or interior decorating, or music, or cooking, or
taxes. They think our minds unbearably cluttered. But
try beauty! Try philosophy! Honor...duty...joy...
loyalty...logic! And they have more than a hundred different words for 'wind'—they taste the wind, play in it,
dance in it, use it. They are spirits of the air itself. We
chained them to the ground!

"They use time as we do not. They are at once incredibly faster than we are and incredibly slower. Your Nail-
Biter and his mate probably chose each other within a

few minutes of first sight—and they will still be bonded when your grandchildren are old. They can pass information a hundred times faster than we do, yet they can take days to discuss a single kill. They count to eight— eight points on a comb—and it is their pride to have eight great-grandchildren, neither more nor less. But they have insights into mathematics that we cannot comprehend, into space and time.

"But we hooded them, blinded them! They soared no more. A captive bird lives hooded or blinkered or chained...or doing what a rider tells it. Their captivity is more cruel than we impose on our fellows in dungeons, for they can see and talk with their free brethren and yet may never join them.

"Their cawking is sacred to them, yet we pen male and female together and so force our choice upon them. We feed them drugs to make them breed, for sex is not a drive with them as it is with us—copulation is merely a deliberate act of child making, as we might build a house. They think us insane about mating, yet it is a private thing to them also, and we give them no solitude.

"We treat them as beasts, and they are people, and we made them slaves."

The cracked old voice rose to a shout.

"And our punishment was to be made slaves ourselves!

"Few men could ride the birds. They beat back the wilds and became the protectors. They demanded a price for that protection: food and housing and service.

"Fair enough, perhaps, at first! But gradually they raised that price, and a man on foot is no match for one on a bird, so the skymen came to rule all the rest. The protectors became the leaders, and the leaders the lords. Men always seek to rule one another. Birds do not.

"We encouraged the skymen to enslave the birds, and then they used them to enslave us!

"And it served us damn well right!"

14

"A boy's best friend is his mother."
            —Very ancient proverb

JARKADON left King Shadow and the guards indoors and walked out alone across the terrace to where his mother was sitting. She seemed about half the size he remembered, a black elf under a bell tree, staring at nothing across the terraces and parks. Her hair had been cleansed of dye and was now starkly white, her small face like dried bone.

"Good sky to you, Mother," he remarked, pulling up a chair.

She turned and looked at him for a moment, glancing at the clump of papers he held in his hands. "And to you, Son."

"Still moping? You should at least keep your hands busy—sew, perhaps. Or have someone read to you. This just sitting isn't good for you."

"Perhaps I could take anatomy lessons," she said quietly, and went back to watching the horizon again.

He suppressed irritation and made himself comfortable. "I came to ask you for something."

"Why else? I am allowed no social calls."

"Mother!" he said as patiently as he could. "Pay homage to me as everyone else has and your indisposition can end at once."

She did not answer.

181

He sighed. "I want you to tell me about Schagarn."

That startled her, and her eyes came around quickly. "I was never at Schagarn."

"No, you were at Kollinor. Most of the time."

She frowned and then shook her head. "Your father painted the kingdom with blood to keep Schagarn secret. Ask elsewhere."

He shrugged. "I have news of Vindax."

"What! What news?"

"You will tell me about Schagarn, then?"

Her lip rose in contempt. "Very well. What I can. When did you hear?"

"Two days ago. He is alive."

She covered her face and seemed to pray.

"Apparently. I have a letter supposedly dictated by him, with his signet. So at least his body has been found, and Foan seems to think it is genuine. Here, read it."

"You read it to me," she said.

He read it.

She sat for a long time and then said, "So who did that terrible thing?"

He watched her carefully. "Ninomar still thinks it was an accident; but if it was deliberate, then the duke's daughter, Elosa."

Then she wept while he waited impatiently.

She rubbed her cheeks with the back of her hand. "So now you will abdicate and become regent?"

He did not want to annoy her, but he could not help laughing. "Mother! You know me better than that. Foan is burning feathers on his way here. Worried about rebels—and Schagarn. The news of my dear half brother will not be released until the duke's face is available. Just in case of arguments."

She looked frightened. "If you bastardize your brother, then I suppose you do to me what you did to King Shadow?"

"Quite impossible," he said cheerfully. "You wouldn't last nearly long enough for all those things. He did very well, didn't he? Much tougher than he looked. I enjoyed that." He put a hand on her arm. "Mother! I know I have faults, but I'm not the first king of Rantorra to succeed through violence. Yes, some of my friends get a little out of hand sometimes when we are partying, but you are my mother. Even your naughty son has his standards. You are quite safe, I promise you."

She was not convinced. "Your father wasn't."

"He was going to disown me. We'll talk about that later. First Schagarn. What was it all about?"

She turned and spoke to the distant sky again. "Alvo rescued us from Allaban, and the rebels took over. I was called to court, ordered to marry your father—you know all that. We thought Karaman would attack Rantorra next, and your father was preparing for war. Then Karaman made an offer, a truce. Alvo said he thought that Karaman could be trusted to keep his word. He brought him leftward along the Rand under safe conduct, and your father met with him at Schagarn. They agreed that there would be a truce, to last for your father's lifetime —no penetration past Eagle Dome by either side. That was all."

He wondered if he could trust her. "There is no record of a treaty."

"Of course not. Kings do not treat with rebels."

He thought about that. "Why so much secrecy?"

"Kings do not treat with rebels," she repeated. She was hiding something more.

"And Father had a very selective memory for verbal agreements," he said, "so that would be part of it. But it's not enough. You are right about the blood—there are no witnesses left. And a truce could have been made by letter. Why a meeting?"

"Ask Alvo when he gets here," she said.

"No!" he shouted. She jumped. "I want to know now!" he said.

She sighed. "I suppose you should. The history books are faked, too, about Allaban. You think that the rebels were skymen? You think Karaman was a warrior? He wasn't. He was a priest, a sweet little man. There were no skymen on the other side, only farmers and priests and tradesmen. And eagles."

"You're joking!"

"No," she said. "It wasn't a rebellion; it was a religious crusade, preached by Karaman." She swung around and looked at him fully for the first time. "The eagles are intelligent!"

"Well, yes . . ."

"Not smart! Intelligent. Like people. Karaman had learned their language. Most of the fighting was done by the birds alone, without riders."

Jarkadon started to laugh and then saw that she was serious.

"Have you ever tried flying a whole day on a blinkered bird?" she snapped. "While trying to fend off attack? That was how we escaped—our own mounts were fighting against us. Many fled the palace; very few of us made it to Ninar Foan.'"

Her women had told him that this was one of her good days. She had seemed to be recovering her wits. But this?

She guessed his thoughts and smiled. "Just a mad old woman? But that was why the blood. 'My troopers can fight birds,' your father said, 'and they can fight men, but they cannot fight ideas.' He suppressed the heresy."

"Schagarn?"

"Schagarn most of all," she agreed. "Karaman was a much better rebel than negotiator. He offered the truce as the price of a meeting. If he could convince the king, then the eagles would be freed in Rantorra. Of course he proved his point—I knew it all from Allaban, and so did Alvo. He made the birds do tricks and pass messages, anything your father could ask for. There was no doubt at all."

"But Father was not convinced?"

"So he told Karaman, and the truce had been promised. Karaman went back to Allaban, and the birds stayed in the aeries."

"I should hope so!" Jarkadon said.

"And your father put the far Rand into quarantine, to keep the secret. That is why so few people have traveled between Ramo and Ninar Foan."

"Until Vindax." Jarkadon snickered.

"You have ended the treaty," she said, and smiled at her hands in her lap.

"Shadow ended it! We had a trial—brief, but legal. But you were not at Schagarn."

She did not look at him. "No. I went to Kollinor. I had a great-aunt whom I had never met. Your father went to Schagarn to hunt—it was a good place for a secret meeting."

"He didn't trust you near dear Alvo?"

Color showed in her face. "Perhaps not. There were certainly many troopers around Kollinor."

"So Vindax is alive," he said. He rose and moved his chair around so that he was directly in front of her. Then he leaned back and sat with folded arms until she raised her eyes nervously to meet his. It took quite a while.

"You think I should abdicate?" he asked. "Well, Mother, if you will give me your sacred oath that you never met Alvo after you left Ninar Foan, then I shall accept Vindax as my king. Go ahead."

It should not have been possible for that dry-bone face to go paler, but it did. "You dare question my honor?" she asked pathetically.

He felt an enjoyable sense of triumph. "I don't need to. I checked the aerie records—as I suppose Father did when he at last became suspicious, long, long after. Kollinor is not far from Schagarn, and between them lies Hiando Keep, and one of your ladies was graciously allowed to fly home for third watch each night, for some kissing and cuddling. I suppose the guards grew accustomed to the habit. But on the last night of your stay she flew on WindStriker."

"That proves nothing!"

"Mother, Mother!" he said patiently. "I talked this over with Father, not long before King Shadow killed him. He said I had reminded him of something. That same day he had Sir Whatever-it-is Harl thrown in the dungeons and his wife, too. I suppose he would have put them to death, except that their son was Prince Shadow and his loyalty was needed—until Vindax returned."

He had been thinking that it was all a coincidence. Now he suddenly saw that it was not—Vindax had met Shadow, the Harls' son, in the palace school. The Harl woman was the connection—no real coincidence.

"Had Vindax come back from the Rand, then there would have been a new Prince Shadow and two fewer witnesses. Of course Father had found out eventually about your little escapade, but he hadn't realized until we spoke that Harl was another Schagarn witness also. He had met Foan on the Range, perhaps even Kara-man."

She bent her head. "Yes."

He laughed. "I pulled them out of the cells and explained that their son was now guilty of treason, because of Vindax. A royal pardon loosens tongues like nothing else!"

She met his eye again momentarily. "A sealed pardon?"

"Certainly," he said. Of course there were faults in the wording; the pardon could be repudiated, but that was none of her business.

"So they will be willing witnesses if you decide to put Alvo and me on trial?" she asked, gazing at her own clasped hands.

"Another interesting possibility. But if the likeness is as strong as I hear, then Foan's face at court should be enough." He giggled. "So you went to Hiando Keep and met dear Alvo. Only once...day 1165...but once is enough, and I expect you did it more than once."

Now he had roused some spark in her. "You disgust me more every time I see you," she said. "Yes, we met at Hiando Keep. Yes, we were alone there for many hours. Whatever else I say, you will believe what you will believe. Fill in the details from your own experience."

"I can't guess," he said, grinning. "I prefer my women coy and reluctant, certainly not eager." That made her redden, as he had known it would. "What happened—afterward?"

Darkside was warm compared to her stare.

"The next day he went rightward on the Rand, and I came back to Ramo. And when your father and I were alone together, I asked him what had happened at Schagarn."

"Ah! I want to hear that."

She shook her head. "No, you don't! He said it was terrifying. He said he had won peace for himself only, for his lifetime. But . . ." She closed her eyes. "I think I remember his exact words. He said, 'But it will bring great trouble in future; great trouble for that son you carry, my darling.'"

Jarkadon's mouth opened and then closed.

"I was pregnant!" she shouted at him. "I had told the king. I told Alvo—he would have refused me otherwise. I was carrying Vindax when I went to Kollinor. That was day 1165, if you say so. And Vindax was born on 1374!"

"It is still possible," he mumbled. "He was a very small baby. You could have been mistaken."

"Yes, I could have been mistaken. It was very early. But I never doubted."

"Wishful thinking!" Jarkadon could feel his face burning. "I'm told it is an incredible likeness. Which is more probable: that you missed a thirty, or that remote cousinship could produce that?"

She turned away from him and spoke very calmly. "Neither is likely, but one happened. You make up your own mind—it won't change your plans."

"Vindax is Foan's bastard!" Jarkadon yelled, rising. "I am the rightful heir. Why did you and Father not disown him? Perhaps you weren't sure when he was a child, but later it must have been obvious to both of you!"

She stared up at him coldly. "I never believed. Perhaps your father did—he never said. And by the time the likeness became obvious, so had something else."

He knew he shouldn't, but he asked. "What?"

"That the alternative was unthinkable. And it was too late for me to have a third son."

He turned to go, and she laughed. He stopped in surprise.

"And the trouble Aurolron saw has not come to Vindax!" she said shrilly. "It is coming to you! I know him —he will demand his birthright. Train your birds, King Jarkadon! Sharpen your arrows! Prepare to defend your throne!"

15

"Who has seen the wind?"
—Rhetorical question

PALM trees and rice paddies and sugarcane . . . The hot countryside unfolded gently below Shadow's bare toes. Prepared for the heat at Pharmol, he was wearing only shorts and a loose shirt, and he sat at ease in his sling and mused on what a strange way this was to fly. Now he could not command—he must humbly ask. NailBiter had considered carefully and then consented, but his comb had changed color at once at the question, because he was still a very young eagle and not yet accustomed to being free to choose. And he enjoyed carrying his friend Shadow around and feeling important.

Shadow had changed color also. He was not as dark as Potro, but thirty or forty days in Allaban had browned him, except for the frost scars on his face. He thought he might even be putting on some fat for the first time in his life. That would not worry NailBiter. As Karaman had explained, eagles were not built to be ridden; girths constricted their lungs, and the weight distribution was all wrong. By choice and by instinct the birds carried their kills in their beaks or talons, and they found a human passenger in a sling a much lighter load than a rider on a saddle.

Soon it would again be time for the ordeal of facing

Vindax and telling him how much better he was looking.
The prince would not be deceived.

Off to the right was IceFire, with the tiny form of
Karaman sitting below her beak. It was a great honor to
carry him. Potro was just ahead, sitting on his mount's
foot as usual, without a sling, but he had promised not to
change feet in midair on this trip.

Now the house and outbuildings of Pharmol were
coming up ahead, set in a rare array of open water: paddies and canals and even a reservoir which also served
as a swimming pool. One reason Vindax had been
brought there was to exercise in that pool. Potro's mount
was sweeping in low over it, IceFire following, NailBiter
soaring in high circles, waiting until the little perching
wall was clear.

There was a distant roar from Karaman—Potro had
dismounted in midair, vanishing in a cloud of spray as
the bird soared away. After a heart-stopping moment he
reappeared, paddling to shore. The young idiot could
easily have broken his back, and his grandfather would
have words for him when they met, but Shadow doubted
that they would make much impression on Potro.

NailBiter spread his primaries and landed gently at
IceFire's side on the worn stone wall of the perching.
Then he bent his head, and Shadow's feet touched down
also. Shadow stepped aside, smiling at Karaman, and as
fast as he could he made the carefully rehearsed gestures
which meant "thank you": *SaseSEso noboSObo* ... Nine
of them: "My kill is your kill."

NailBiter's comb flickered almost too quickly to follow, but Shadow caught the meaning: "chick signals."
Baby talk—the bird was poking fun at him. Shadow
laughed and raised his hand. The huge fierce eye met his,
then the great head was lowered and he reached up to
stroke the comb. Then he saw what was coming and
braced himself.

Darkness and hot, rank breath ... Shadow froze as
the enormous beak enclosed his face and a black, slob-
bery tongue ran over his hair—NailBiter was stroking
his human friend's comb. The experience, though nau-

seating, was oddly touching, but he was glad when it stopped.

He rubbed the bird's comb then, wiped his own sticky hair with an arm, and trotted down the steps to join Karaman. He was surprised at the expression on the wrinkled old face.

"What's wrong?"

"It's dangerous," Karaman muttered. "He means well, but you don't taste right. That can trigger a nasty reflex. I've warned him before not to do that—but you can't argue with an eagle."

The sun was gentle, padded by atmosphere, but the wind in their faces was a furnace breath, lip-cracking and harsh, drying sweat before it could even appear. They walked slowly together over to the buildings of Pharmol. The farm was an untidy scattering of unroofed sheds and fenced vegetable patches, clumps of fruit trees and junk piles. Chickens paced stiff-legged, studying the ground, but there was no larger livestock in sight.

Suddenly Shadow realized that he was alone with Karaman, and that was a rarity. "May I ask you a question?"

"Always. But you won't necessarily get an answer."

"About Schagarn," Shadow said. "Why did you agree to such a truce? You had won the battle of Allaban. Why not press on to conquer all of Rantorra?"

"Ah!" Karaman said, strolling head down, studying the ground like a chicken. "Well, you are not the first to ask. Some think that Aurolron outfoxed me."

"I didn't say—"

"No, that's all right. You should know. Quite simply, my young friend, I had no choice. I had no army left."

"No army?" Shadow repeated blankly.

The silver mane nodded. "The eagles had had enough. Fighting is horrible to them—bird against bird. They are not cowards, but war is not part of their thinking—and remember, they have much longer life spans to risk than we do. They drove the monarchy out of Allaban for us, and so freed their captive cousins in the aeries, but the cost was too high for them. They don't count very well, but they could see the bodies. There were many more dead birds than dead men."

Shadow had learned as much as he could about that ancient war, but he had never thought to consider it from the eagles' viewpoint. A skyman with a bow, against birds armed only with their talons—were he a trooper in such a battle, how would he fare? How many eagles would he be able to shoot before they got him? That would depend on how badly outnumbered he was and how well he was able to control his own mount.

And when the man was eventually killed or crippled, then his mount was helpless and died also, falling blind from the sky.

"I hadn't thought of it from their side," he admitted. "How do they feel now?"

"Still the same," Karaman said. "You are a new generation, but they are the same birds. Does your Vindax dream of returning to Ramo at the head of an army of wild eagles? I should have thought you would have known better by this time."

Shadow felt himself blush, though Karaman did not appear to notice. Yes, he had been thinking along those lines, and so was Vindax.

"How about one on one?" he asked. "Man-on-bird against man-and-bird?"

Karaman glanced at him cryptically and then dropped his gaze to the path once more. "The republic has very few troopers, and it has no pigeon-hunting aristocrats any more. Work it out."

Shadow visualized. "I would have an advantage in a sling," he said, "because my bird is more maneuverable, but I couldn't direct him with my hands full, and a sling sways around, so I suppose my archery would be no better. But if he gets me, then my bird escapes."

"If you get him, then you kill his bird also."

"True," Shadow admitted. "And he can shoot my bird, which is an easier target than I am, and I may hit his by accident. It's still no better than even, is it?"

Karaman nodded once more. "And being blind in the

air is deepest hell for an eagle. They can imagine no greater torture, nor any worse way to die."

"So if Aurolron had spurned your truce and moved against the republic..."

"The birds would have stayed out. It would have been the skymen against the peasants again—no contest."

It had been Aurolron who had been outfoxed at Schagarn.

With a deep thunder of wings, NailBiter and IceFire passed overhead and settled on the ridge of the house to watch the coming proceedings.

The meeting place was a semicircle of chairs set out on grass in the shade of the house. Toys were scattered about. Vindax was there already, waiting—he did not like people to see him being carried around. He was talking to two small, naked children idling on swings which hung from a frame in the center of the lawn. They jumped down and fled at the sight of the newcomers.

Shadow put on his cheerful face and made the formal nod that Shadow should give his prince. But this was not the prince he had served—and failed? The old Vindax had gone. The new one was a poor fragment of a man, shrunken and crippled, paralyzed from the waist down, a noseless horror. He had lost all his fingers and thumbs except two stumps, on one of which blazed the gold signet of the crown prince of Rantorra. Gone were the fine clothes of royalty; he wore only the brown homespuns of the peasants who supported him on their charity, and even those looked too big for him. Always Shadow wondered what Elosa would think if she were to see her handiwork—and what thoughts of Elosa burned inside that tragic ruin.

And was Elosa perhaps already floating among the silks and glitter of the court, even now betrothed to the reigning king?

Shadow took the chair on Vindax's right, moving it back slightly as though he were taking his proper place behind, but really so that he need not look too directly into that ravaged face.

"Shadow?" Vindax sighed. "I should not be calling

you that now. Said is your name, but you are the chief and only minister in my government, so you should have a title. Pick a name and I will make you a duke." That was at least an attempt at humor, which was a small improvement.

"I am honored, King," he replied. "But a coronet would not suit me, I think, and I do not feel like Sald Harl anymore. The eagles call me 'The-one-who-came-through-the-dark'—which isn't far off being called a shadow, is it? I think I shall stay with that name until we shed some light on Rantorra."

Karaman, having finished a feeble lecture to an unrepentant Potro, sat on the other side of Vindax. The three of them were looking darkward, across a wide grassy place. The grass that grew in the fixed shade of the house was not the same as the sunlit grass next to it. Beyond the little meadow was the pool, and trees and then fields.

And hills—hills stretching up endlessly, ridge after crumpled ridge, growing bluer and dimmer with distance, as far as the human eye could see into the sky. Beyond that stood the cobalt canopy of space, crenellated along its lower edge by faint icy peaks.

"Those are volcanoes, you know," Karaman remarked, making safely neutral conversation. "It is geothermal heat in this area which melts the ice of the High Rand, feeding springs and making Allaban so fertile." He was knowledgeable on almost any subject after a lifetime of studying the ancient lore. The conversation continued on impersonal topics.

The wind was a gentle torment, hot from its long fall off the High Rand, growing ever hotter as it sped past toward the deserts far below, but soon Shadow could see tiny specks drifting down that unlimited hillside—others coming to the meeting.

It took an hour or more for them all to assemble—farmers and merchants mostly, both women and men. Some of the men were enormous compared to Shadow and Karaman and Vindax, but the eagles could manage them in slings. There were introductions to "Citizen Vindax" and "Citizen Shadow," awkward attempts to shake hands with Vindax's stump, and courteous chat. Then they all settled into the chairs of the arc and waited.

NailBiter and IceFire were preening themselves on the roof; the birds had infinite patience. A few of the arrivals' mounts joined them, while the others returned to the sky. Shadow did not know whether that was a personal choice or whether juniors were not allowed to join in the meeting—the other half of the meeting, high in the air.

Finally the group was assembled.

An eagle swooped in across the reservoir, braked, then landed awkwardly on the flat grass. It stalked forward a few paces and stopped, its great bulk seeming to complete the arc and turn it into a circle.

A full-face view of an eagle was still unnerving to Shadow, a sight he had rarely seen before he came to Allaban. This was an elderly female, brown with a few silver primaries, and on flat ground she stood twice as high as he would have done, glaring slowly around the circle. Her gaze finally settled on Karaman.

High above, not much more than spots in the sky, hung two or three dozen others. Far away beyond human sight there would be others watching, and others beyond them. The talk would be reported all across Allaban.

"Er...who speaks to the High Ones?" the president asked.

"Me!" Potro said eagerly, jumping forward into a circle of disapproving glances.

"All right," Karaman said, indulging him. "Sit here." The skinny form dropped cross-legged to the grass and faced toward the bird.

The president stood up. He was a lanky, bony, middle-aged spice merchant, shabby in his work clothes and smelling strongly of coffee and cinnamon.

"You want to do the talking, Ryl?" he asked hopefully.

Karaman shook his head. He had half twisted in his chair, as though not too much concerned in the affair at all, but he had stayed next to Vindax, which was a hopeful sign, worth many votes if there were to be voting. "You do fine, Jos," he said.

The president shuffled a toe at the ground, finally leaning back against the frame of the children's swing set and sticking his hands in his pockets. "Citizen Vindax," he mumbled. "When you arrived, we said that you were welcome to stay until you got better and then we'd send you back. With no conditions."

Potro's fingers were racing and the eagle's fierce glance was following them, her comb moving as she passed the speech up to the watchers in the sky. Karaman was unobtrusively watching the translation but seemed to be satisfied with it.

"Well, we meant that," the president said. "And that's still fine by us. But the death of . . . of your father . . . has made a bit of a difference. See, we got a letter from Ramo. Seems they still had a bird they took from Allaban, and they've sent this note to us and we've talked it over and it makes things a bit tricky, like."

He explained at length, but Shadow had been told earlier by Karaman. Jarkadon wanted "the pretender Vindax" turned over to him. In return, he would renew the truce his father had made, to last for the duration of his own reign.

"Well, we don't want a war," the president said apologetically.

That was obvious—it would be a rout, although perhaps Jarkadon did not know that.

"But we don't fancy turning you over—under the circumstances."

He dried up for a while, looking around hopefully for volunteers and not finding any. "We thought if you wanted to stay, then maybe the king would settle for a letter from you," he said at last, uncomfortably. "Waiving any claims on his throne."

"And Allaban," someone muttered.

Vindax nodded and waited. Shadow wondered who would support him and feed him. The republic was not very good at raising taxes, even when the government voted them. Who would provide charity for a helpless cripple with no family?

But certainly these politicians would have thought about finance, and eventually the president glanced toward Shadow. "We think we could find a house and a bit of land for you and your friend," he said. "If that's what you want to do."

So Shadow would be peasant for two, would he? And also nurse. The damage to Vindax had been drastic, and nothing worked below his waist; he was not a pleasant patient to tend. Was this divine punishment for a failed bodyguard? A lifetime of exile and horrible drudgery?

"Well!" the president said. "That's what we wanted to suggest. Who speaks for the church?" Again he looked hopefully at Karaman, but again the old man shook his head, and it was a plump, matronly lady who rose. The president sat down quickly. Even this apparent formality of having the speaker stand was observed only so that the eagles could tell which one was talking.

Perhaps Potro was regretting his eagerness; he rubbed his fingers to ease them.

"The church would be much against turning over a refugee!" the woman said fiercely. "We would rather hope to have Citizen Vindax's help in overthrowing this Jarkadon and freeing all the birds in Rantorra, as we should have done eight kilodays ago! Would you agree to that, Citizen? If we can put you back on your throne, would you free the eagles?"

"Not the throne of Allaban!" two or three said together. Potro glanced around angrily.

She started a lecture about moral obligations, and eventually the president suggested that perhaps they should hear from Citizen Vindax.

Vindax raised one of his hand stumps, and the eagle's eyes flashed toward him.

"Explain that I cannot stand, please," he said. His voice had changed tone but not timbre. It was still deep and commanding, but the arrogance had gone.

"I did," Potro said. "I said your legs are broken."

"Then I ask the representative of the church: *Can* you put me on my throne? Is your army capable of it?"

The woman rose again, looking pink. "We can probably persuade a lot of men to help. We would need the government to help us with money and weapons. But you would give up any claim on Allaban, wouldn't you? For yourself and your . . . successors?" She turned much pinker and sat down quickly; she had almost said "heirs."

"Good archers?" Vindax asked.

"They'd need practice," she admitted weakly.

"And the mounts?"

The president jumped up. "Let's hear from the eagles."

Potro's fingers flickered and went still. He translated. "She says that the eagles should be free. It would be an updraft . . . a good thing to free all the eagles. The birds of Allaban mourn their friends who are slaves." He signaled, probably telling her to go more slowly. "But she says that you would kill them, not free them. The men would ride out on them to fight, and they would all die. Many eagles of Allaban would die also in the fighting. That would be a big downdraft."

"Does she understand about law?" the prince asked. "How a royal command works?"

"Gramps?" Potro said urgently.

Karaman chuckled. "Tell her this. The-one-with-broken-legs is the highest man in Rantorra. If he goes back, then all other men will be lower than he and must do what he signals. He could tell them to free their eagles."

"She wants to know why he doesn't," Potro muttered for the benefit of the rest of the company.

"Tell her . . ." Then Karaman decided to tell her himself, and flickered his fingers for a few minutes. "I explained about the brother. It's a hard idea for them."

The eagle was scanning the sky, studying the discussion going on up there. Then she put her menu-inspecting glare back on Potro.

"She says would it be like the last time? Would many-many-many eagles die?"

"Yes," Karaman said.

"The High Ones say that that is a big downdraft to kill many-many-many eagles to free not-so-many eagles," Potro announced.

Vindax seemed to shrink inside his homespuns.

The president stood up. "We talked about this in the government. We can't fight, because we have no mounts. I think we need your decision, Citizen: go or abdicate as we suggested. The eagles won't help."

"Shadow?" Vindax muttered. The gaunt and ruined face swung around to him. The heavy brows were still there, and the dark eyes had sunk back into the skull, pits of agony and despair. "What can I do? Advise me."

"Jarkadon will kill you," Shadow said. Here was the loyalty test, then—he must make the sacrifice and the offer. "Accept the land and stay in exile." *And I must tend that disgusting lump of flesh until eventually its life of pain comes to an end.* "Perhaps one day the kingdom will tire of his excesses and send for you."

Vindax reached out a flipper hand to touch his arm; if there was expression on that mask of scar tissue, then it was compassion. "I will not impose on you, my friend. If I go to Ninar Foan? The duke would not hand me over, I think."

That was a possibility; there would be many servants to care for the cripple, and surely the duke's conscience would be stricken by the sight of this horror his daughter had created. But it meant a once-proud prince throwing himself on the mercy of his disowned father. Where was the arrogance now?

"We do not know that the duke is there," Shadow said. "He may be in Ramo; so may Elosa. And if Jarkadon has her as hostage, then the duke is a dry pond."

Vindax nodded miserably and looked away. "I was just hoping," he mumbled, "that you might work one of those miracles of yours, think of something that no one else had. Some other way."

Shadow shook his head. It was easy enough to display fake brilliance when surrounded by marble-minded aristocrats like Lord Ninomar, but these Allaban farmers were deeply practical souls themselves. Unless the equation would work in reverse...

He was a skyman, a trooper, a soldier. Was there something that he should be seeing that they might have missed? He pondered and then realized that everyone was waiting for him, watching him. Yes, perhaps there was something.

"I cannot restore your health," he said. "Within the limits of the practical, though, what do you *want*?"

The deep-buried eyes flamed with a fury as fierce as that of the eagles. "Justice!" said Vindax.

"That's all?" Shadow asked.

The eyes searched his. "What else could there be?"

Karaman was peering curiously at Shadow. So were the others. Shadow stood up, thinking of Potro's arrival at Pharmol.

"Can the birds understand experiment?" he said. "I would have to try something, and I'm not sure it would work."

"No, they can't!" the old man snapped, as though he felt responsible for this failing in his beloved eagles. "They're not *handy* like us, and their world is unchanging." He signaled. "I've told her you think there may be an updraft but you won't know until you go to look."

Shadow knew that NailBiter's beak could reach almost any part of him except his head, but there was one movement he could not recall seeing in all his years of skyman training. "Ask her if she can put her head back like this," he said, looking straight up at the sky. Then he looked back at the eagle and recognized the flicker. "No, not chick signals. I'm serious."

"Hey, good!" the busy-fingered Potro muttered, approving of his pupil.

The eagle bent its head back briefly in imitation and then glared down at Shadow again.

"Now—could she fly like that for a while? Could she land, maybe even just on the flat—but could she?"

The humans seemed just as irritated and puzzled as the bird. Potro scowled and started to signal.

"She says it could be done. Sometimes it would cause

an accident, but it could be done usually. And why are you asking?"

"They're inquisitive devils, Shadow," Karaman whispered. "You've got them all twiddling up there."

"I have another question," Shadow said, mentally crossing his fingers. "Sometimes eagles will carry their kill in their talons. So they could carry rocks—if they dropped them, could they make the rocks land where they wanted them to?"

"Holy Ark!" Karaman was staring at Shadow in stupefaction. "Sure they could! They don't think geometry, they live it. Why did I never see that?"

Because he was not a fighter.

"She says, 'cast,'" Potro announced in a puzzled voice. "What's cast got to do with it, Gramps?"

Karaman chuckled, and he signaled to the eagle. "I've asked her to show us on that," he said, pointing to the children's swing set in the center of the circle.

"That could be dangerous!" Shadow said uneasily, glancing around the group.

"What the hell is 'cast'?" the spice merchant demanded.

For a few moments no one spoke. Then Potro explained in a patient, superior tone, "Cast is what they throw up, the bits they can't digest in their crops. It's hard balls of nails and teeth and pebbles and stuff."

NailBiter had stopped his preening. He and the six or so other eagles on the roof ridge were watching the sky, and so was Shadow, waiting for one of those tiny specks to start a dive, but nothing was happening. Perhaps the birds were having one of the songfests he had heard about and would make their choice in a kiloday or two.

Then a clap of thunder showered the spectators with splinters and hoof fragments and a few sheep teeth—one of the swings had gone, leaving two wildly dancing ropes, each attached to half a plank. There were loud screams and belated raisings of hands in front of faces. Potro's shrill soprano shouted, "Gawrn!"

"Holy Ark!" Karaman muttered.

"Holy Ark yourself!" Shadow yelled. "From that height?"

"I told you—they are spirits of the air!" Karaman insisted. "They know the air as we know the land."

"She asks if that would kill a man," Potro said.

"Yes!" Shadow said. "If he was sitting up, they could smash his head in with that. Even lying down, it would break his back. In fact, it would hurt the bird—it was harder than we would need."

Karaman caught the next message. "She wants to know what the other chick talk was. They understand now that they don't need to carry archers."

Shadow suppressed uneasiness—he had given the eagles a new weapon, something they had never had in their ancient war against mankind. They had never seen that they could use missiles as men did, any more than it would occur to men to kick at the birds. Whose side was he on? Fortunately his other idea needed human hands, so men could still retain some control . . .

"I'm not sure," he confessed cautiously. "But I think it would work."

"Hooks?" a voice said. The speaker was a small, dark, crinkled man who looked like a farmer.

"Yes!" Shadow said. "We kill the rider and the reins go slack, blinkering the bird. If one of us flies in close with a long hook, then we could catch the reins and drop the hook, see? The bird holds its head back, like we saw, and the weight of the hook will hold the reins back—"

"It doesn't work," the farmer snapped. "We tried something like that. You forgotten, Ryl?"

"Why not?" Shadow demanded, suddenly deflated.

The older man counted on his fingers. "First, there are a dozen other troopers shooting at you, lad. Second, it's almost impossible to get two birds that close in the air because they get in each other's wind. Third, there isn't time. A blind bird without human guidance panics and just drops," he finished triumphantly.

"He's right, Shadow." Karaman sighed. "We did try something like that. It worked in rehearsal a couple of times, but not in practice. You use your ears to balance, did you know that? The birds have none. They need their eyes. Sorry, sonny. Nice try."

Shadow sank back into his seat angrily.

There had to be a way!

"I do not wish to impose on your charity," Vindax said to the president. "I believe that I could write to . . . to the duke of Foan and he would send money. Then I could buy a suitable place and hire servants."

Shadow stopped listening. He was a skyman—was he anything else? Was there any other way of looking at the problem which the farmers and merchants could not see, which Karaman had not seen when he led the rebellion? Karaman was a priest, a student of the ancient ways— wise but not trained to think of new things. He was emphatically not a fighter. He was a bird fanatic, of course, and had taught Shadow something of how the birds thought, although their way of looking at the world was so different from men's that it was almost incomprehensible.

Up on the roof, NailBiter had inspected and approved every feather and was now standing on one leg, licking the talons of the other with that same tongue he had used to wash Shadow's hair. NailBiter thought that Shadow was his friend—the man who had unhooded him in the hellish dark of Dead Man's Pass and so freed him. So he thought. But it had been Karaman who had freed Nail-Biter. Shadow would not have known. He would have acquired another hood at the first chance he got and gone back to business as usual with a captive mount, a beast of burden.

Not a friend. How could a man be friends with an eagle? The affair in the pass had been an accident, caused by exhaustion, by carelessness, and by the wind.

"You can't trust Jarkadon," Vindax was insisting.

The president wanted that letter of abdication, and the sword was sliding slowly from the scabbard.

The wind?

"Wait!" Shadow shouted, leaping to his feet in excitement. "Maybe there is a way!"

"Now what?" a man growled, standing between Shadow and the president.

"We *can* free the eagles!" Shadow tried to pass, but the man stared down at him without moving away.

"Playtime is over, sonny," the president said quietly. "This is grown-ups' business."

Shadow felt blood rush to his throat, and his fists clenched. A tradesman speaking to the son of a baronet? An elected king speaking to a homeless exile?

"Go ahead, lad," the spice merchant said, eyes glinting. He spoke not as a king or a tradesman, but as a big man speaking to a smaller one.

Shadow spun on his heel and stalked out of the circle, face and soul burning. In Rantorra he was a commoner among nobles, and in Allaban he was a runt. There never was justice, he thought bitterly. He was nothing. All he had was his skymanship, and he should have gone to Piatorra while he had the chance. Free the eagles? He was the last one who should want that.

In his blind anger he almost tripped over a heap of old fence posts, broken farm tools, and rusted bicycles. Flailing arms to regain balance, he put up a flock of chickens, which rushed flapping and squawking in all directions. The flapping became a continuous roll of thunder and was joined by screams and huge shadows leaping over the grass as an eagle came slithering down the roof to sprawl onto the grass, wings wide, narrowly missing Vindax. Then two more filled the air, wings beating madly and loudly. The human screams were redoubled, and the meeting exploded into flight. Eagle Speaker reared tall and spread her wings, a living curtain shutting off the lagoon, her comb blurring in a silent shout. Feathers and dust filled the air. More giant birds went lurching noisily away, fighting for height... chickens shrilled madly among legs...

What the hell?

Up on the roof NailBiter had squared off with a young brown wild, both rearing as high as they could, wings thrashing, combs inflamed, beaks locked and breast straining against breast in a battle quite silent except for the drumming of wings and talons scraping on wood. Other birds were dropping from the sky, coming to restore order. Then IceFire dislodged the last of the other wilds, turned toward the duel, and took the brown from behind, leaping bodily on his back, and all three overbalanced and started to slide. The fight was forgotten in more thunder and clouds of dust . . .

It was a subdued but angry meeting which eventually reassembled. NailBiter and IceFire had the roof to themselves and were unrepentantly preening each other. The wild eagle, Shadow now learned, had remarked that The-one-who-came-through-the-dark had obviously been eating batmeat. NailBiter had taken action which might seem reasonable to a man but was not correct eagle behavior. Karaman looked more shaken than anyone.

"I must have taught him bad habits," Shadow said, regarding NailBiter affectionately. He found the episode amusing. *Big mutt!*

Karaman shook his head. "Or driven him crazy. First he spared you in Dead Man's Pass, now he's going around picking fights like a human being. It isn't allowed, Shadow!"

"What do you mean, 'isn't allowed'?"

"The High Ones have banished them," Karaman said. "NailBiter and IceFire. As soon as they've taken us home, they have to leave Allaban." He nodded at Shadow's astonishment. "Yes, they even had a trial already, after their fashion."

The president called the meeting to order. Shadow strutted over to him, turned his back, and addressed Vindax.

"King," he said loudly, "I can give you your justice—I can put you on your throne. But I would need the help of the republic, so you must waive claim to Allaban. I would need the help of the eagles, so you must swear to free all the birds in Rantorra. Are you willing to pay the price?"

The mask regarded him steadily, unreadably.

"Yes," Vindax said. "I agree to those terms."

Shadow swung around and looked up at the president.

"I shall need an army. It won't matter if they're not very good—there won't be much fighting, but I must have men to seize the palace. Will you permit King Vindax to raise a force? With the help of the church, of course. He will need money, but you will gain security. You will never need to fear attack from Rantorra, ever."

The spice merchant folded his arms. "How are you planning to work this miracle?" he asked, but his manner was cautious; money had been mentioned, and he was wary now of this puny youth whose displeasure had so aroused the eagles.

Shadow grinned. He turned to Karaman, who had been translating for Eagle Speaker. "The birds can't keep a secret, can they? Anything we tell them here will be all over Allaban and then the Rand?"

The circle of eyes was skeptical and impatient, but Karaman was giving Shadow a stare of shrewd appraisal. "They can't keep a secret," he said. "And I wouldn't keep that one. Think before you speak."

"Come with me!" Shadow snapped. He almost dragged Karaman from his chair and led him off to the side, out of the shade and into the sunshine beside the pile of grindstones and cartwheels and old bicycles.

And then he explained the obvious: The eagles could free themselves.

"God the Pilot!" the old man exclaimed. "You sure? It doesn't make sense!"

Shadow was aware that he was grinning like a monkey, and he couldn't help it. "What's the last time you ate with your feet?" he asked.

Yes, he was sure this would work—and how simple it was! It wasn't a case of thinking from a different viewpoint. It was a case of putting it all together—what Karaman had taught him of the birds and what he knew as a skyman and what had happened in Dead Man's Pass. And NailBiter cleaning his talons.

Karaman shook his head in wonderment. "You certain?"

"Yes! How many skymen did you have on your side in the war?"

The old man sniffed. "About two, more or less. I just can't believe it could be so easy!"

"That's the problem," Shadow said. "If the word gets out, then Jarkadon could block it just as easily. We'll have to go like a stooping eagle, hit them so fast that they don't know and have no time to take countermeasures."

Karaman was still skeptical. "Why has it never been done?"

"Who cares? It'll work," Shadow said, "won't it?"

"Yes, I think so," the old man said, and took hold of his arm. "But do you know what you're letting loose, lad?"

Shadow hesitated. "Yes."

A pair of sad old eyes regarded him from a face as brown and wrinkled as the Rand. "Do you? Life is not the same after, you know. And why? Why are you doing this?"

Why? "To free the eagles? Is that not what you have always wanted?" Shadow asked.

The silver mane waved in a nod. "Me, yes. But you? And I wanted to make a republic, as the First Ones had. You are putting another king on the throne."

"Vindax will be a good king!" Shadow protested. "I always thought so, and now he has seen poverty as no king of Rantorra ever has."

Karaman turned and stared at the group of watchers, at the back of Vindax's head. He sighed. "You can't turn a straight furrow with a bent plow, lad."

"Perhaps not!" Shadow snapped. "But good things can grow in crooked furrows!"

The old man studied him in silence and then sighed. "Only if the soil is fertile. All right, if you're sure. Come along." He led the way back into the circle.

"Yes, it will work," he announced. Astonishment swept the ring of faces. He started to sign to Eagle Speaker, translating as he went. "The-one-who-came-through-the-dark has shown me an updraft, and I follow him. He can free the eagles, if the eagles will do as he says. Not-many eagles will die and many-many-many

eagles will be freed. But he cannot signal the way now—
if he hatches the egg too soon, then the dark ones may
kill the chick."

Flicker. Pause. Flicker.

Karaman nodded. "She says they will follow you if I
vouch for you. As long as you do not start killing many-
many eagles."

"We want peace, though," Shadow said. "Will the
eagles be merciful? We do not want many-many-many
men killed, either. When a slave bird is freed, will it turn
on its rider?"

Fingers flickered; comb replied.

"She says 'what would you do?'" Karaman asked
grimly.

Revenge?

"The High Ones will ask the slaves to be merciful?"
Shadow asked. "The birds of Allaban and the men live
together without war. That's what we need in Rantorra,
too."

There was more flickering, then a pause for discussion in the sky. It was a long pause by bird standards.
Was a big argument going on? Finally the birds replied.

"She says they will try," Karaman said. "They can't
sign contracts, Shadow—that's they best they can do."

"Right!" Shadow said. He turned and grinned at Vindax. "What size crown do you take, King?"

Teeth were bared in the inhuman face. "You will give
me my revenge?" Vindax said.

Not justice?

"Yes!" Shadow said as confidently as he could.

NailBiter was rocking with excitement. Shadow
would have to negotiate that sentence of banishment.

"What do we do about this letter from Ramo?" the
president demanded.

"Stuff it!" Shadow snapped. "They can't be sure
you've even received it. I know Jarkadon! He's probably
far more scared of you than you are of him."

The spice merchant looked doubtful.

"We're going to depose him anyway," Shadow said.

"And I also know the Royal Guard. They're scattered all over the Range. They're great at evicting old ladies who can't pay taxes, but they can't put more than three hundred decent fighters in the air."

Vindax raised his eyebrows but did not speak.

16

"Rapture is a state of mind."
—Anon.

THE Range was everything Elosa had expected and a thousand times more. Its fertility amazed her after the barren lands of the Rand: vineyards and orchards and brilliant greenery. The slopes were crowded with hamlets and little towns; there were roads with traffic on them, and the distant birds in the sky were mounts being ridden, not dangerous wilds to avoid.

But then, Ramo was a thousand times more again—she could hardly believe the size of the city floating endlessly below her, and when the palace itself came into view, she wondered if it was real. Surely it would have stretched from Ninar Foan to Vinok. She saw marble porticoes set amid flowers, palm trees and fountains, roofs of every hue, courtyards and lawns, cupolas and balconies and ornamental lakes . . . the place was huge! And it was beautiful beyond imagining—paradise.

The palace aerie alone was larger than her father's castle, with ten layers of roosting. *Ten!* And her guides took her to none of those but to yet another perch close to the ground, reserved for the arrival of honored guests. She was hardly out of the saddle before a groom had flown her mount away to be cared for.

Her father was waiting, greatly handsome but hardly

recognizable in splendid court dress. She rushed into his arms, and they hugged.

"Father!"

"Fledgling!"

Yes, she had had a wonderful flight and it was all marvelous and the fairy-tale palace was amazing and she was ecstatically happy to be here.

His hug was warm, but his face was strained. She looked again and saw that he had aged. There were worry lines there that she did not remember and gray on the temples, and he had certainly lost a lot of weight. She inquired anxiously how he was, and he said he was fine and now she must meet her welcoming party.

They were a dozen or more—a couple of men but mostly ladies, some young, some old—and her head started to spin madly with the effort of trying to remember so many names. Yet the first face of all was familiar—the very beautiful woman she had been told was called Feysa, the spurious lady's maid who had been Shadow's mistress on the journey. Her name was not really Feysa, and she was a marchioness, no less.

The whirling dream sensation grew stronger and stronger. She was swept out to a landau with two white horses and driven off before she had remembered that she ought to thank those who had brought her so far. Feysa was beside her and her father behind, so she could not speak to him, but in any case she was too entranced by all the sights of the palace as the carriage jingled along to have said much to anyone. The extent of it overwhelmed her—the beauty, the crowds of gorgeously dressed people, the innumerable servants who seemed to spring out of nowhere as soon as anything was needed, the stupendous staircase of onyx and marble, the tapestries and the ankle-deep rugs, the enormous silk-draped bedroom that she was told was to be hers, with its adjoining bathroom. There were gold taps on a tub large enough to drown an eagle.

Her father had disappeared, and obviously Feysa—Marchioness who?—had taken her in charge. Women who were to be her maids, all dressed in finer clothes than she had ever owned, were curtsying to her. They bathed her, and she was too dream-struck to be embarrassed at all. They dried her in towels of lamb's wool and massaged her and rubbed her with scented oils. They dressed her in silk underclothes. They measured her for dresses, and they coiffed her hair and varnished her nails and painted her face . . .

And suddenly she was standing before a mirror, admiring a lady who had a vague facial resemblance to herself but whose gown and jewels and elegant coiffure were totally strange. The gown! Ocher silk, it was open down the front almost to her navel, yet tight enough to show off her admirably fashionable flat chest. The maids had politely raved about her figure and her complexion. From her hips the gown sprang out in a great wide crinoline of foamy lace. She sparkled with jewels.

"There," Feysa said. "I think that will do to begin with. How do you feel?"

"Stunned," Elosa said.

The marchioness was very beautiful and very gracious, and obviously in charge. She smiled. "Wait till tomorrow—you have twenty-two gowns to try on after breakfast."

Elosa gasped. Feysa laughed and brought in the duke to inspect. He was very complimentary, although she noticed again the deep lines of anxiety.

"Perhaps I may have a word with my most beautiful daughter?" he said with a warm smile at Feysa.

He was asking permission? No, that was ridiculous.

The Feysa lady hesitated. "Make it quick," she replied in a whisper. She made a fast nod toward the balcony and turned to shout at all the maids to get the place in order.

The duke led Elosa out to the balcony.

"A little fast advice, fledgling," he said. "No, face the rail while we talk. Don't trust anyone . . ."

Really! She felt her face start to burn under the paint.

"Father, I may be inexperienced, but I am not a child!" No silky-tongued courtier was going to take advantage of *her*. Kings must marry virgins—and she already suspected that she might be the only virgin in the whole court. She was going to stay that way, certainly.

Now her father went red. He placed a hand over hers where it rested on the balustrade. "I did not mean that, fledgling. I am sure you will be sensible. But this is a court—everyone is conspiring against everyone else, all the time. Try to keep out of it. Be polite and gracious and noncommittal. The marchioness will be giving you guidance, but don't trust her, either. We are invited to dine with the king in just a few minutes."

The king! Her legs started to shake.

Her father nodded unhappily. "I did try to explain that you had come a long way and needed a day or so to adjust to palace life, but the king wants to meet you." His voice became quieter yet and more urgent. "Remember, he is God here. His smallest wish is absolute law. His slightest whim! You understand?"

She nodded, frightened. "Father, is something wrong?"

"Of course not."

His eyes said that there was.

"We should be moving, Your Grace," Feysa's voice said. It was so close to her back that Elosa jumped.

Dining with the king, not-Feysa explained as they strolled in ladylike procession through the palace, did not involve eating. The king ate, and the others atched. There would be nobles serving him, of course, lords with the hereditary right to pour the royal wine, for example. The king would invite only two, or at the most three, persons to sit and actually eat with him—that was a tremendous honor—but the several dozen other guests would stand. Later the king would withdraw and they could have a hurried meal before joining him in whatever entertainment was planned for afterward. Today there was to be a masque.

Elosa did not think she was very hungry, anyway.

"One word of advice," the marchioness muttered between vivacious greetings to passing friends. "Don't

make jokes. Not yet. When you know your way around,
maybe. He likes humor . . . to a point."

"I don't feel very humorous," Elosa said.

She got a frown. "Be cheerful, though! Smile all the
time. Enjoy yourself." Feysa dropped her voice to a
whisper and covered her mouth with her fan. "One
young man two nights ago topped one of the king's jests.
The king had him taken out and flogged like a serf—
Good sky to you, my lord!—and he is a viscount."

Elosa did not feel humorous at all.

The reception court was magnificent in its golds and
colors and gleaming furniture. The courtiers waiting
around were veritable peacocks. She was presented to
this one and that one by Feysa or by her father, and they
circulated and scintillated, and the dream sensation came
pouring back like the hot wind. Either the rugs were
even softer and thicker than they looked or her elegant
shoes were not touching them at all.

All her life she had waited for this—her arrival at
court. It was vastly more magnificent than she had ever
imagined.

Then the great doors opened. The king entered with a
small entourage of three older men, two of his own age,
and four girls, all of them looking younger than Elosa
and even more splendidly bejeweled and bedecked. The
king began to circulate, greeting his guests.

Dazzling in mauve and gold, he was about the height
she had expected but broader and more muscular, with
very fair hair hanging loose to his shoulders. His fingers
glittered with treasure. Much handsomer than—she tried
to remember Vindax and saw the face of Tuy Rorin.

Jarkadon had bright blue eyes, she saw as she was
presented and curtsied. Very bright and very blue.

"It has been too long!" the king said. "We have been
eager to meet you—and had we known what beauty we
were missing, we should have been much, much more
impatient."

He was charming

In a moment or two, Elosa began to realize that she
was being greatly honored. The royal procession around

the room had stopped at her. He was ignoring the rest of the company. Charming—that was the only possible word. His blue eyes and his attentive smile charmed her as he gave forth a stream of compliments about herself and her long journey and her faithful father and loyal family and on and on . . .

Then she was sitting at his side and dinner was being served. The king and she were the only ones eating. Her father was there in the circle of onlookers around the table, and he smiled when she caught his eye and the conversation flickered to and fro. She thought she was managing to make sense. She made no jokes. She smiled.

The marchioness had not mentioned the possibility of only one companion. Two or three, she had said. So this was very special, and she was getting some dark looks from the younger women.

The king sent back the wine and demanded a better. The talk turned to wine. The king remarked on the excellent vintage produced by someone's estate, and the owner hastily offered to have several hogsheads sent at once and to fly a few bottles in daily until the carts could arrive.

"I must say, Majesty," the duke remarked, "that almost any wine on the Range is better than the thin swill we produce at Ninar Foan." *Warning: The wine is strong.*

Elosa agreed that she had never tasted . . .

Her head was starting to ache.

They were on the eighth or ninth course, and the food kept coming.

Jarkadon was nibbling at some strange-looking meat. "You know what this is?" he inquired.

No, she could not guess.

"By law and ancient tradition," he said proudly, "it is a dish reserved for the king alone. Our father never cared for it, but we had the tradition revived. Taste some."

He offered her a mouthful from his fork. It was highly spiced and rather tough. No, she still could not guess.

"Eagle comb!" he smiled. "Here, we shall share it with you." He dumped all of it on her plate.

"Doesn't it hurt the eagle?" she asked, feeling sick.

"Oh, they're useless for anything afterward," the king said. "Usually go mad. That's why it is so rare."

She set to work on the horrible stuff.

"Talking of eagles," the king said, "our cousin of Foan, you breed silvers, we understand."

Her father said modestly that he had some silvers.

"Our father was a great fancier," Jarkadon said, leaning back. Having given most of his dish to Elosa, he had plenty of time to speak, and she had to gobble so as not to keep him waiting. "We could never see the point in breeding birds—I mean, the damned birds get all the fun, don't they?"

With much laughter the company agreed.

"The royal breeding aeries," the king said. "You know them?"

The duke said that he had not had the pleasure of visiting those.

"They are not far off. Our father never flew in his later years, so they are an easy horse ride; a few minutes by bird. Vast! Huge! They are bleeding the exchequer dry! There must be some economies we could make there, mmm?"

The subject was tossed around, and everyone agreed that economies could be found.

"Foan!" Obviously the king had had a Good Idea. "You look into it for us. Go over there and poke around. See what can be cut. I mean improved. Give us your comments and suggestions. You're a knowledgeable bird breeder."

Her father's face was quite expressionless. "I shall be honored to do so for Your Majesty."

"Good," the king said with a smile. "Now?"

The duke bowed to the king and to Elosa, then turned and walked away.

"Eat up, my darling," Jarkadon said. "It's time for dessert."

My darling? Elosa started gulping even faster.

She was being tested! The unfair rush from eagle to royal table, the crude heaping of her plate, the dismissal of her father—they were tests of her nerve. To be queen she must have poise and grace, so Jarkadon was testing to see if she could be rattled. Obviously she had impressed him physically—the gleam in his eyes said that. Now she must impress him with her personality. When she was queen, she would sit by him at table every day.

She decided to risk a joke and show him. Her father was just going out the door.

"I thought I was the only one who could order him around like that, sire," she said.

The sapphire eyes lit up with amusement. "It is nice to be king," he said.

And nice to be queen, too?

"I am sure Your Majesty does it very well."

He switched his gaze to the onlookers. "I *do* do it well!" he said. "I'm irresistible!"

The company laughed loudly once more. She wasn't sure she understood that one, but she laughed too.

"How old are you?" he asked.

She gagged, then swallowed. "I am exactly two hundred days younger than Your Majesty."

"Terrible!" the king cried. "Old age is upon you!"

There was more laughter.

"But then, you have a birthday coming in a few days?" he said. "Your seventh, too! We must find a suitable gift for the occasion."

Elosa mumbled with her mouth full.

"Meanwhile," Jarkadon said, leaning toward her, "here is a small advance on your birthday gift." He held up a brooch for her to see—two eagles, rubies set in gold. It was large and beautiful and obviously worth a fortune.

She choked down the last horrible lump of comb and made appropriate thanking sounds. She knew that the rings he wore were there to be used as gratuities, but the brooch was worth many rings and was a woman's ornament. He must carry pockets full of things like that around also.

"Allow me," he said. "A little premature, perhaps,

but we can correct that...Oh! I am sorry, did I prick you? That was careless. Here, let me try again." This time he slipped fingers inside the front of her dress to make sure that the pin did not prick her, touching her nipple as he did so.

She thanked him again. He seemed amused. She sensed something odd, looked across at the guests, and saw glances being exchanged. There was something more to that little episode than the brooch itself. Another honor?

The meal ended, and the king withdrew. Elosa found herself in yet another luxurious courtyard with him and three men of about his age and half a dozen girls, all of them younger than she. Some looked hardly older than four kilos, yet all were dressed like grand ladies. She noticed that they all wore two-eagle brooches identical to the one she had been given. So those were obviously a sign of royal friendship and probably a great honor, especially when he had just met her. She must ask Feysa as soon as possible. Feysa did not have one.

There was King Shadow, too, of course, in matching gold and mauve and a black baldric. He was a surly-looking young man with an irritating habit of sniffing.

The king's attention was still for her alone. "Now, what trifle can we find to amuse you, my dear Elosa," he said, "while we wait for the rabble to eat? Cockfighting? Do you have cockfighting at Ninar Foan?"

They didn't, and the king conceded that it was technically illegal—but what was the use of being king if you had to obey all the silly rules like everyone else? So they spent an hour watching the bloody business of cockfighting. A couple of the girls seemed to be nauseated by it, but Elosa joined in the cheering and was adamantly not rattled at all. The king was an avid spectator.

Then they rejoined the rest of the party to view the masque. Elosa knew that she should be exhausted, but she was soaring, buoyed up by the excitement as though she were riding an invisible eagle. She was making a

good impression—that was certain. He could not keep
his eyes off her.

The masque enthralled her. She had never seen professional acting and singing; she gloried in the music and
the costumes and the acting. The king sat her beside him
in the front row, with the rest of the dinner guests around
and behind, and the artists were right at her toes—a
very intimate command performance. The king's hand
settled on her arm, and she thrilled at his touch.

He began to stroke her skin with his fingertips.

A boy soprano was singing a glorious aria, high as the
Rose Mountains.

"You don't get much of this stuff at Ninar Foan, I
suppose?" the king asked loudly.

The boy's voice cracked on a note, and the musicians
missed a beat.

He was trying to rattle her again. To whisper back
would be a criticism.

"No, nothing more exciting there than bird breeding,
Majesty," she replied in the same tone, and he bellowed
with laughter.

He was stroking her arm with his nails now, very
gently, but the constant scrape was beginning to hurt.

"We usually get much better talent," he said, still
loudly.

She said that she was no judge but was enjoying it.

The other guests remained silent while the performers
struggled along, now obviously terrified. The king kept
up his conversation and his insidious gentle scraping.
She responded as naturally as she could, deliberately not
moving her arm or even looking at it, although the pain
was intense now and was making her eyes prickle.

The players were dancing a gavotte. The king had
stopped scraping and put his arm around her. Her heart
started beating faster than the gavotte.

The gavotte ended; jugglers and comedians sprang
into action.

Jarkadon's hand slipped lower, and his fingers
reached around to fondle the silk over her breast. She
moved away, dislodging them.

The king yawned and stood up. Instantly the performance stopped, and everyone else rose also.

"We are a trifle fatigued," he said. He pulled off a ring and presented it to the leading lady. "Please continue for our guests. A charming performance! No, the rest of you, do stay. Lady Elosa, we welcome you to our court and we hope to see *much* more of you in the near future." He kissed her hand as she curtsied.

The king walked out with Shadow behind him. The door closed. Everyone sat down—except that Feysa had appeared from nowhere and had hold of Elosa's elbow. "Come!" she said.

"But . . . I was enjoying . . ."

Elosa was led firmly from the hall.

17

"You can't teach an old bird new tricks."
—Skyman proverb

THE eagles came to Ninar Foan.

How many? Shadow had no idea. He was the leader of an army whose size he could not guess. There were three hundred men in it, young farmhands mostly, eager and excited at the novelty. Many could shoot a fair arrow, but few could handle a sword as well as they could a sickle, and the rest would be almost as dangerous to their companions as they would ever be to an enemy. A surprising number, though, knew bird speech and an ever more surprising number of birds seemed to have learned the halting, tortoise-slow gestures required to speak to mankind.

He had organized the men into six companies and put the best commanders he could find in charge. It was all very hasty and makeshift—and it was a bluff. The birds were the army, and the only real weapon he had was the idea which had come to him when he saw NailBiter cleaning his toes. Now he must test it, and if it did not work, the great war would be over without a bow being bent.

Here on the Rand he would have died in the flimsy clothes of Pharmol. Soaring high over the bright, bare mountains, he shivered even inside the fleece-lined flying suit which Ukarres had given him. Close at Nail-Biter's side floated IceFire, and the three of them

seemed to have the whole vault of the sky to themselves.
The naked sun glared angrily through the thin air over
the distant plain.

Yet if he peered hard in any direction, he could see
eagles, some from Allaban and also local wilds gathering
to watch the outcome. He had not understood in his days
as a skyman that the eagles were never alone, that the
constant and seemingly meaningless rippling of their
combs was conversation. He had the world to himself,
yet he had a vast and uncountable audience also.

IceFire signaled: "There are one-comb-and-four
eagles in the aerie. One has left and is coming." Shadow
acknowledged.

As he had expected, a messenger had been dispatched
from Ninar Foan as soon as Shadow's army appeared in
the sky. That was why he had bypassed the castle and
positioned himself along the path to Vinok, and soon he
would see this solitary courier racing to warn the men of
Rantorra that the invasion had started.

One-comb-and-four? A human mind had counted and
sent the word—there were only twelve eagles left. Then
it was certain that the duke and his household were
gone, and a fair guess that they were in Ramo. That
should make the coming battle easier.

"It is my father that comes," IceFire signed.

IceStriker, he remembered—a huge silver, as big as
NailBiter. The cautious duke would have left his best
silvers at home in case Jarkadon took a fancy to them.

Shadow was unarmed, but around his neck hung a
priceless farewell gift from Karaman, a pair of binoculars
from the Holy Ark. With those he could see far better
than with his own eyes, although still poorly compared
to the birds. Hopefully he raised them and peered toward
Ninar Foan. He saw nothing but wildly swaying rock and
scrubby hills, and put the glasses down again before he
became nauseated. This sling riding was much less stable
than straddling a bird; good archery would be impossible. It was also chilly work, for he could not stretch out
along his mount's back to seek shelter from the wind.

Then he saw the lone flier, floating down in a long

glide toward an obvious thermal, and he signaled IceFire
to intercept. She passed the word to NailBiter, and the
two veered in unison.

"Speak to your father. Tell him that we come to free
him and he must not resist his rider. He is to do what the
man wants until you tell him."

IceFire's comb flickered the message. Shadow just
caught the start of it—"This one flies behind Friend-of-
eagles . . ."—but the rest was much too fast for him.

About ten minutes later they drew close, as the lone
rider circled for height and Shadow came gliding in at
about the same elevation. He tried the binoculars again.

He almost dropped them in surprise, seeing Vindax,
the hooked nose below goggles. Impossible! It had to be
the duke himself—but surely he would never flee his
own castle. No, it was the young groom, Tuy Rorin, the
duke's other bastard. Rorin was a good skyman, too; he
was handling his bird beautifully. He had seen Shadow
and was waiting with bow in hand. Shadow held out his
arms to show that he bore no weapon, then signaled Ice-
Fire—and so NailBiter—to approach as close as possible but to look out for the bow.

"Rorin!"

Back came a faint reply. "Shadow?"

The air grew warmer as he entered the thermal. Then
the birds were level, facing one another across the invisible column of wind and apparently almost motionless,
rising and falling slightly with respect to one another,
although all were steadily gaining height.

"Turn back!" Shadow called.

The reply was an obscene gesture.

"You will die!" Shadow yelled. "I can free your bird.
Turn back, lad, and live!"

This time the obscenity was verbal, and Shadow was
not surprised. Why should Rorin believe him? He hardly
believed himself. Rorin was studying the terrain, planning the next hop of his journey.

"Your last chance! Turn back or die!"

Shadow was ignored, so he started the war.

He signaled to IceFire. "Tell your father that it is a downdraft to hurt the man. I ask him to spare the man."

IceFire's reply was too fast for him, which perhaps was deliberate. Perhaps her father was using bird obscenities.

"Tell your father to do three things. First he must raise one talon and scrape along under his beak. He will break the strap which holds the front of the helmet. Then he must dive, and the wind will blow it away from his eyes. Lastly, he must keep on diving until he lands."

"That is forbidden!" IceFire replied.

Forbidden? Shadow was nonplussed. Forbidden by whom? In all his plans he had not expected argument from the eagles. Forbidden? *NosoNEne* ... he needed young Potro! *NosoNEne* ... forbidden ... off limits ... inadvisable!

"Forbidden by whom?" he asked.

"When I was a chick, my father himself told me."

Rorin banked IceStriker and dived away steeply.

"Please!" Shadow begged. "Tell him to try!"

IceFire's comb reddened angrily, but she sent the message, then passed the reply. "He says it is forbidden. He cannot land on one foot."

The straps were thin leather. The stitching holding the buckles was only thread. Shadow thought of those mighty talons and beaks carrying goats—carrying him. There was far more muscle there than was needed ...

You can't argue with an eagle.

IceStriker and his rider were dwindling in the distance. Shadow felt panic. "Tell him Friend-of-eagles says it will work. Tell him ... if I lead badly, then NailBiter will drop me ... *Tell him!*"

He caught IceFire's ferocious glare and thought that perhaps, just this once, that expression represented her true feelings. She passed the message.

His suicidal offer was accepted, as he had known it would be. The eagles were literal. The eagles were also fast. The signal, IceStriker's reaction, and NailBiter's surge of excitement seemed to be simultaneous. Rorin hardly had time to scream as his mount bucked and dived. The reins went slack, and the helmet flipped inside out and flapped back toward him, useless. The great raptor beak flashed around momentarily, for just long enough to bite off his head.

Then the whole world whirled and swayed, and Shadow yelled in terror and grabbed his harness straps as NailBiter did a dance of joy. For a moment he thought the bird would drop the sling in his excitement and the victorious general would fall to his death, following IceStriker as he plunged earthward, still trailing a long plume of blood. IceFire was tumbling around like a new-flown chick. Far beyond human sight in all directions the watchers would have seen, and perhaps they also pranced and gamboled in the sky. The secret was out: The eagles could free themselves.

When NailBiter calmed down and Shadow's stomach returned, he signaled again. "Tell your father that we shall send a man to take the body off his back, but the man is a friend and must not be harmed."

IceStriker was already lost to Shadow's sight against the bright hills below, but the reply came at once. "My father will not hurt the man you send. His kill is your kill, One-who-came-through-the-dark."

"Return to the castle," Shadow ordered. He asked for the rescuer to be sent but was told that he was already on his way—his eagle would know where to go.

Then IceFire relayed another message. "My father has landed safely. He has bitten through the saddle straps but cannot reach the one around his neck. Send an eagle to do that. He does not need a man."

Shadow acknowledged sadly. He had seen that possibility and had been waiting to discover if the birds were smart enough to work it out. Obviously they were. He had hoped to keep some part for men to play in this, but they were not needed. Yet the birds in the aeries were still hostage, and it would not be difficult for Jarkadon to have all the bird helmets fitted with chains instead of straps.

"Speak to the High Ones. I have hatched the egg as I promised. They must send word to all slaves that the army is coming. The slaves must wait. Any slave who does this thing before we arrive will warn the men, and the men will kill the chick. The slaves must wait."

Who were the High Ones? He did not know. Perhaps two or three, perhaps hundreds, but they spoke always with one voice, through whichever bird was nearest, who in this case was IceFire.

"You have hatched a fine chick, One-who-came-through-the-dark. The eagles will follow."

The point was critical. The birds could not keep a secret—certainly not news like this. It would flash from comb to comb along the Rand with the speed of sight, from wild to aerie and wild to wild. The courier bringing news of Jarkadon's accession had taken thirteen days to reach Ninar Foan, and that had been good time. An unladen bird could do it in two. How long would it be until this message reached the birds in the capital? Probably only hours. The race was on.

Shadow was surprised by the swarm of birds over Ninar Foan—there were at least two unladen for each one carrying a man. So he must have a thousand eagles at his command. He was going to seize a whole country with three hundred men and a thousand birds? He was crazy.

The castle was battened down for siege. Eleven birds sat on the sunward side of the aerie, all hooded and still. Whoever was in charge had not ventured a sortie against the impossible odds. Shadow had made his orders plain: The army was to wait for him to return. Had his strategy not worked, then the battle would not have needed to be fought, for it would have been useless.

NailBiter landed on the pyramid roof of the aerie itself, and Shadow slid carefully down the old weathered timbers toward the dark side. As he had expected, the wood was dried and ancient, exactly like that of the Vinok aerie, where the troopers had ripped out a few boards to cook a meal.

He made himself comfortable on the awkward slope, just back from the edge. Below him was the terrace and the deserted perching wall, flanked by a thin litter of mute pellets. He had jumped from that wall once . . . He shivered again at the memory. He was well above the roof of the castle, safely out of bow shot, but NailBiter was exposed and a tempting target if anyone thought of it, so Shadow had to hurry.

His arrival would have been heard by those below him.

"Who's in charge down there?" he shouted.

"God save King Jarkadon!" The voice belonged to Vak Vonimor.

"It's Shadow."

"I saw you. Come and get us, bird lover."

"Vak, I owe you a debt," Shadow said without hope. "I don't want more bloodshed. Rorin is dead—there will be no message passed and no help coming. Give up the castle. Proclaim the true king and we'll go away and leave you alone."

"Go lay an egg!" the voice below him shouted. "You're bluffing. Come and get us."

No doubt the man assumed he was in a strong position. He would have archers, standing on a solid floor. The attackers had to come in against the light, in unstable slings which would seem ludicrous to an old skyman like Vonimor. Even if Shadow's men were to land on the roof and chop holes in it, they would still black out the light when they tried to shoot through those holes. If he set fire to the roof, he would kill the birds, which were on the downwind side. So Vonimor would be as confident as Rorin had been.

"All right!" Shadow yelled. "When you're ready to give up, release the eagles."

He clambered back up the slope to NailBiter, who was shivering with excitement. As they dived away from the aerie, a couple of arrows flew unpleasantly close.

The army melted away to clear the air. Shadow signaled for a comb of rocks, then soared on a thermal in the distance and waited, watching.

The first two went through the planks, making small holes but undoubtedly scaring the hell out of the defenders below as they shattered against the floor. The third rock struck a corner beam, and the whole roof shuddered.

Then the final five struck simultaneously, and the ancient timbers on the darkward side collapsed, crumpling and folding and taking much of the barred wall with them.

The hoods started coming off—and the battle of Ninar Foan was over.

Shadow did not cheer. Never had there been a peace treaty in the Old Times struggle between man and bird—it had merely decayed into guerrilla warfare as the eagles abandoned the middle slopes and retreated to places where men could not follow. The killing had become random terror, when a wild saw a chance to take an unarmed man or the skymen a wild. There had never been a peace, and now the full fury of war was about to erupt again.

Never before had the eagles captured an aerie. But this time they had a skyman on their side.

A traitor.

Bong!

More like a prisoner than a victorious general, Shadow marched along a corridor with three swordsmen in front of him and another three behind. Each one of them was a head taller than he was, and most were twice as wide; he did not trust the hospitality of Ninar Foan.

Bong!

Instinctively he was keeping time. Every third step of his left foot coincided with a stroke from the great bell as it echoed mournfully through the stones and the passages, drifting out over castle and town, wafted away in the wind toward the Great Salt Plain.

Bong!

"This one, I think," he said. The door was opened, the room inspected before he could enter.

It was well furnished yet cluttered with a lifetime of personal effects: paintings, shelves covered with souvenirs, inlaid wooden chests, a dozen trophy heads decorating the walls. The drapes were partly drawn. The air was stuffy and stank of death.

Bong!

Leaving his guard by the door, he advanced to the big bed and wondered if he was too late. The tiny mummy face was yellow, and the good eye closed; the dead eye was half-open and blank as usual.

Bong!

Then the eye opened slightly. "Why don't you turn that damned thing off and let a man die in peace?" the old voice wheezed.

Shadow reached down and took one of the limp hands. It was cold as the High Rand. "I am sorry you are unwell, Sir Ukarres."

There was a pause while the eye studied him. "I am sorry you are well."

Bong!

"I have a score to settle," Shadow said. "You tried to kill me. You sent me to Dead Man's Pass, but you did not tell me that it had never been done from this side."

The old man stared at him contemptuously. "There had to be a first. But go ahead—settle."

Shadow shrugged.

"Pah!" Ukarres sneered. "You wouldn't settle anyway."

"Probably not," Shadow agreed, and smiled. "Now the king will be proclaimed, and then we shall leave and not disturb you further."

Ukarres licked his lips and gestured toward a table. Shadow reached for the beaker of water and held him up while he took a sip. In contrast to his hands, his body burned, but the water seemed to revive him a little. The funereal tolling had ended.

Ukarres coughed feebly and sank back. "So you have liberated twelve eagles? How many left to go?"

Shadow sat on the edge of the bed. "No idea. The king alone has thousands."

"Vonimor is a fool," Ukarres wheezed. "You would not have had it so easy had I been there. Yes, the aerie, maybe; but not the castle itself."

"It was only the birds we wanted," Shadow said. "We could have just bypassed the castle and gone on."

Ukarres frowned. "And when Jarkadon comes, he will burn and pillage because we surrendered to Vindax. Such is war. Well, I shall not be here."

"Jarkadon will not come," Shadow said. "The duke will not be returning either. You may never hear from the capital again, Ukarres."

"Bah!" the old man said mildly. "Karaman may win battles, but he will lose in the end. How is my old friend?"

That was better. "He is well, purring over a new great-grandson. He stayed in Allaban. But his health seems excellent."

"I am glad," Ukarres said with surprising grace. "And your prince—or king?"

"He was less lucky than you," Shadow said grimly. "He will not be visiting this place." Vindax had gone on ahead days before, strapped in a litter and well guarded by men and eagles. He would stop only at isolated farms, but would needs make slow time because of his weakness. He could traverse the sparsely populated Rand without other men knowing. Birds, yes; men, no.

Ukarres did not speak, so Shadow said, "And Elosa? She has gone to court, I hear."

"The duke forbade her to go with him, and we kept her shackled, almost. But the king's orders became more demanding." The eye glinted. "The last one was specific: Alvo would hang by his thumbs if the child did not go. Elosa was ecstatic, of course. She will be there by now."

"Why?" Shadow mused. "What does Jarkadon want with her? To thank her, do you suppose?"

Ukarres flicked his faint eyebrows in a sort of shrug. "A hostage for the duke's good behavior if he sends him back, perhaps."

That made sense. The gaunt duchess had refused to discuss her husband or daughter. She would be down at the gate now, attending the proclamation of Vindax VII.

Ukarres closed his eye as though the conversation were ended. Shadow waited. After a minute the old skyman's curiosity got the better of him, and the eye opened again.

"You have taught the birds to throw rocks—that is a dangerous innovation, lad. What if the wilds copy them?"

"They are wilds! Karaman was right, and you have known it for years. You were keeping slaves, not beasts of burden."

"So?"

"No repentance?" Shadow asked sadly.

Anger brought back some life to the shriveled corpse. "None! It is the eagles that make it possible. Do you think I would rather be a sheepherder in a hovel, or a skyman living in a castle with servants and comfort? How is it in Allaban? Did Ryl make his paradise?"

"They have a republic. All men are equal."

Ukarres snorted. "If you believe that, then I have some young lunks here to wager against you, pipsqueak. Arm wrestling? Boxing? All men equal? Feathers!"

"They have no masters—put it that way." In truth, Shadow had found Allaban very strange.

Ukarres was about to make some angry retort but was seized by a fit of coughing and then needed more water. He sank back weakly. "They eat lettuce, I suppose. Did you have much steak when you were there?"

"I stayed with Karaman," Shadow confessed. "The eagles are constantly offering him kills. But you are right, I admit—most men in Allaban see little meat."

"I knew that would be the way of it," Ukarres said with some satisfaction. "Who would tend livestock if he were not allowed to defend it against the birds? And what of us? There is not much grows up here except sheep and goats. The children are going to starve in Ninar Foan, boy, while your precious birds eat the meat."

Shadow squirmed uneasily. The Range was fertile and could support its human population easily on its crops. The Rand, admittedly, was not. "There will be few birds around here for a while. You had better make your plans quickly."

"I have only one plan now," Ukarres said. "And that is to die as soon as I can. But with luck the fighting will kill off most of the birds. We got plenty of them in Allaban."

"I must go," Shadow said. "The proclamations will have been read—Vindax as king and no fighting against eagles, no more slave birds, elect a local mayor. I must be on my way."

"Why the hurry?" Ukarres demanded, his warrior's curiosity aroused in spite of himself. "Tell me what you think you can do."

Shadow hid a smile. "We are going leftward along the Rand as fast as we can, and that will be very fast. Every aerie will be emptied as this one was. I have shown the way; a few men left at each castle or town can handle it and then hurry on to catch up. Ramo will not know what is happening before we are upon them.

"I stopped the messenger Vak sent," he added sadly. "It was young Rorin. He was the only casualty, apart from Vonimor's broken ribs."

"No warnings?" Ukarres mused. "What of the singles? Jarkadon has good advisers—probably the duke, of course. He has scattered singles all along the Rand. Communications have never been better in my lifetime. You can't stop the Ramo singles going back."

"That's good!" Shadow said. "As long as they carry no messages. Jarkadon will be able to map our progress. There are two things he can do—and I want him to do the wrong one."

"So they will be waiting for you," Ukarres said. He closed his eye as though imagining the battle. "And you offer terms: Put Vindax on the throne and you won't release the rest of the birds. The Rand will be lost, of course, but the Range safe. I don't think you'll get very far with that ploy." He looked up with a satisfied smile.

"You're wrong," Shadow said, content to discover that Ukarres had worked it out as he had expected him to. "What they must not know, and what you don't know, is *how* we are doing it."

He stayed quiet until Ukarres demanded, "Well? How *are* you doing it?"

Shadow told him, and his shock was obvious.

"It isn't possible!" he whispered.

"It is! Karaman went back to the old books. He discovered that the First Ones blunted the birds' talons. They used metal helmets—the birds could not remove those. When the war was won, men started using the birds for hunting and left their talons alone. He isn't sure. But over the ages the equipment has been perfected and made lighter, and the eagles never thought to try again. They were too smart! They thought they knew better." Eagles did not experiment—their thinking was even more rigid than Ninomar's.

The old cynical smile briefly flickered on the pillow. "And over the ages we bred larger birds and smaller men! Do I detect an irony there?"

"Possibly." Shadow smiled also. "It was just something very obvious that no one had seen. The birds never preen their own heads—they do each other's. But I knew that NailBiter could reach his beak with a talon, and I knew that the helmet had only the two straps and certainly the neck strap alone could not hold it firm in a strong wind."

A helmet had to be a flimsy, pliable thing, for it had to slide up under the hood and fit around the comb and beak. So a helmet was only two pads of leather, joined by two straps at the top and fastened by two buckles below.

Ukarres was staring in horror. "You cannot stop this thing, then? It is already too late?"

"Yes," Shadow said. "The days of the skymen are over. The eagles will be freed, and they will take good care that no one ever enslaves another, by any means."

Ukarres gave him a skeptical glare, then his gaze wandered away to the far distance. It was a while before he spoke.

"The keeper of the Rand is the last of the skymen," he said quietly. "Did you get that lecture from Karaman?"

"No. I thought I was a skyman."

"No." Ukarres sighed. "You were a trooper, and the troopers are tax collectors. The real skymen were rulers. Once all the local lords ruled their own fiefs and defended the men against the eagles. But they were always quarreling and having little wars. The kings gradually pulled them all into Ramo and made courtiers out of them. Taught them revelry instead of rebellion, finery instead of fighting, madrigals instead of mayhem."

"They are parasites!" Shadow said.

"Yes, they are now," Ukarres agreed. "Only the keeper of the Rand remained. He is the last of the skymen. And the kings did all the ruling and became tyrants. That's what Karaman says."

"I think I agree with that," Shadow said. "Perhaps you do?"

"Perhaps a little. Why did you come to see me?"

"I . . . to say good-bye."

The creaky voice rose in fury. "Wanted to talk to a skyman, didn't you? Not many in Allaban! Tired of farmers and priests?"

That might well be true; Shadow had not thought of it.

"And you wanted my approval!" Ukarres said angrily. "You wanted to confess to me what you've done and see if I approve. Well, I don't. You've swallowed Ryl's rubbish about being nice to those killer flying monsters, and you've betrayed your own kind. You've freed the birds and taught them to throw rocks, and now they're going to rule us, instead of the other way around."

"Most of the folk in Allaban seem to be friendly with the birds," Shadow protested. "They have a feathered friend or two who drops in and gives them a leg of mutton once in a while."

"For what? Just for chat? You're saying that the birds are amused by the humans?"

"Well . . ."

"That's it, isn't it? Entertainment! Curiosities? In Allaban the humans are pets now?"

Shadow rose. "I would rather be a pet for a bird than

a slave to Jarkadon. Karaman is right: We were wrong to enslave the birds, and we paid for it. I hope you recover, Sir Ukarres."

"Shut the door and let me die in peace," the old man said, and closed his single eye.

18

"An eagle never forgets."
—Skyman proverb

BETWEEN the Rand and the Range lay a gap which the skymen called the "Big Jump." It was not especially deep—a drover road crossed it, snaking over the great monoliths, the cinder cones, and the jagged fault blocks like a snail track through a garbage tip, spanning chasms on ramshackle bridges and seeking always the highest ground. The herds and the ox carts crawled painfully along there, the men gasping in the heat and thick air, and they had another name for it.

To the skymen, though, it was the Big Jump, and its width was always a challenge. The sunward crossing— from Rand to Range—was the easier, aided by the cold wind. For both mounts and wilds the technique was the same: Climb in the strong thermal which poured upward from a great sun-blasted cliff below Krant, and then glide. Ridden birds had a steeper angle of glide than wilds or spares, but in most cases they could all arrive safely at the little mountain called Rakarr, which marked the start of the Range.

Against the darkward face of Rakarr, of course, the cold wind rose in an updraft, and skill was needed there: The rider had to gain altitude to be able to circle the peak and reach the thermal above the sunward face. After that his road to the Range was open, an easy line of thermals to Ramo and beyond, all the way to the end. But with too little altitude he would not reach the thermal, while too much would sweep him up into the turbulence of rain and storm that lay on the darkward side of every mountain in the Range. It was those clouds which kept the Range fertile, their precious rainfall seeping through the volcanic rock to emerge as springs on the sunward side, but they could be death for a bird and its rider.

The darkward crossing from Range to Rand was harder, at least for the skymen. The wilds merely rode a convenient thermal up into the hot wind and let it carry them, and they were not even restricted to using the Big Jump—they could cross at wider places. But the men could not go that high, so they had to fight the cold wind all the way, and many a rider ran out of air before he reached the thermal at Krant. Then he would be swept back and down and suffocated in the desert, unless he was lucky enough to achieve a landing near the drover road and could hitch an ignominious ride for himself and his mount on an ox cart.

So the Big Jump was the main obstacle between the Rand and Ramo, and it was there, obviously, that the battle must be fought. When Lord Ninomar had been put in charge of the Guard, he had seen that point at once.

He had his promotion: full Marshal Lord Ninomar now. Of his two superiors, one was senile—well over thirty—and the other had rashly complained about the king's treatment of his granddaughter and had not yet recovered his health.

"We don't think much of you," the king had told Ninomar, blue-blue eyes glittering in a way very reminiscent of his father's, "but we think even less of the next three in line. So you will be in command—and your adjutant will be Colonel Rolsok."

That had been a hard dose to swallow, but when the king said swallow, one gulped. Rolsok was a baby-faced stripling, a close friend of the king's and rumored to be one of his orgy partners, although it was difficult to believe from the look of him that he was old enough to know what it was all about. Before Jarkadon's accession he had been a mere ensign, but he came from a fine family, with good skyman connections; his brother was the courier who had brought the news of the king's accession to Ninar Foan.

So it was Shadow all over again, with Ninomar approving what his nominal subordinate said. Like Shadow, Rolsok knew what he was doing, but he was a gentleman and much more tactful. He couched his suggestions in phrases such as "Have you considered, my lord..." or "His lordship has decided..." and things were magically done.

Edicts went out and every man who could fly and bend a bow was conscripted: retired troopers, country gentlemen, junior aristocrats...everyone. They drained into the palace from the whole length of the Range. Their mounts filled the aerie and the breeding aeries and then started lining the balcony rails. Logistics became a nightmare: food and shackles and equipment and weapons...

The rebels were moving with astonishing speed. Fortunately they had overlooked the singles' compulsion to return to their mates. Day by day the solitary birds returned and another mark was made on the map.

There were no messages either with the singles or by courier. That strange silence bothered Ninomar more than anything. The rebels' archers must be superb.

And their speed was unbelievable.

"Sastinon!" the king snarled at one of the daily conferences. "The bird from Sastinon returned only eight days after the two from Ninar Foan? Could you move an army from Ninar to Sastinon in eight days, Marshal?"

That was faster than a royal courier traveled. Ninomar was about to say that of course he couldn't, when young Colonel Rolsok coughed.

"His lordship was just pointing out to me, Your Majesty, that it takes a single two or three days from Ninar Foan to Ramo, but about one day from Sastinon. So the rebels must have taken *nine* days, not eight."

"Oh?" the king said. "Astute of you, Lord Ninomar; we had missed that." He smiled at Colonel Rolsok.

"Perhaps Your Majesty would like to hear his lordship's plans for Podrilt?" the adjutant suggested, returning the smile.

"We should be delighted," the king said.

Ninomar had no plans for Podrilt, so he told Rolsok to go ahead.

"Just a suggestion of his lordship's, sire," the youngster said, "subject to your approval, of course. If you will look at the the map..." He counted off the distances—a force sent now from Ramo should reach Podrilt just before the rebels did. "He thought about two hundred men, Majesty—and all riding singles. A reconnaissance in force? Perhaps delay them a little?"

Ninomar did not think much of the idea. There was a serious danger that such a force would destroy the rebellion all by itself, leaving no glory for anyone else. It meant dividing forces, and the manual warned against doing that; while if the rebels were much stronger than expected, it meant a loss of two hundred good men.

"And another point," Rolsok said smoothly. "The rebels must be stopped at the Big Jump, as his lordship has repeatedly pointed out. But it will take us at least eight hours to reach there from here. You will note from the map that the rebels will need about half a day to travel from Podrilt to Krant, on the far side. So word of an encounter at Podrilt would be our signal to launch."

Smart young fellow, Rolsok.

The departure of two hundred was hardly noticeable; still the skymen kept coming and the problems grew worse. They were being billeted on earls now, with dukes' houses next on the list. Human food was becoming short and bird fodder so scarce that even horses were sacrificed. Ninomar began to worry that the rebels would halt their progress at Krant and let the royal army starve itself to death. There were over twelve thousand men on the rolls already, and that seemed absurd—Allaban could never have raised more than a thousand.

Exactly ten days after the singles from Ninar Foan had sounded the alarm in Ramo, he was roughly shaken awake in the middle of third watch by Rolsok, who was looking very shaken himself.

"Singles from Podrilt!" Rolsok snapped, his voice perceptibly higher than usual.

"How many?" Ninomar demanded, sitting up.

The boyish face was pale and beaded with sweat. "Thirty-three when I was told," he said, "and still coming."

"How do they do that?" the king demanded for the third or fourth time. He had called the council into session; he had summoned all the senior officers of the Guard. They were still stumbling into the cabinet, hair awry, rumpled and bleary-eyed—the chancellor and the chamberlain, the earl marshal, and even some unusual choices like the royal breeder.

For the third or fourth time, the king received no answer. Well over half the singles were back now, with more coming all the time. Most of them bore dried blood on their tails or wings. None was injured in any way.

Many of them had borne a message tied to a leg—and no sane eagle allowed anything as flimsy as paper to remain tied to its leg very long. The messages were all identical: "When you are ready to surrender, release the birds in the aerie and wait in the Great Courtyard for orders. Vindax R." One such note might have been suppressed, but there were too many of them—everyone had seen one, or heard the words.

Jarkadon stopped his pacing, went back to his desk, then sat and glared around. Most of the men standing before him were elderly, but all had flown at some time. If any group in Rantorra knew eagles, it should be this.

"Well?" the king demanded. "I ask again: How do you kill a rider without killing his mount? Was every man crazy enough to go into battle with his reins tied? How do they do it? Foan told me about the battles he had in Allaban, and the rebels couldn't do it then. How are they doing it now?"

There was silence.

Ninomar did not know, and such problems were not for him. If Jarkadon or Rolsok could not solve them, then he never would. But the mention of Foan was interesting—Foan ought to be here. In truth, he ought to be in charge, but he was known to be still under house arrest at the breeding aeries, and if the rumors about his daughter were true, then he was not going to be returning to court very soon. Jarkadon was creating his own problems—but that was a treasonable thought.

A courier marched in unannounced and bowed to the king. "One hundred and eighty, sire," he said. He turned and left without waiting for a reply.

"Twenty to come," Jarkadon said sourly. "Anyone want to bet against that?"

"Majesty," Rolsok said quietly. "We should launch the army."

He received a glare from his royal friend which obviously startled him.

"Not until we know what they are going to be fighting," the king said, almost snarling the words.

Rolsok looked appealingly at Ninomar, who stayed silent. No one had ever called him a coward, but one hundred and eighty out of two hundred? He could not doubt that those men were all dead.

"Majesty?" creaked the elderly voice of Chief Air Marshal Quortior, nominal head of the Guard. "I think I agree with the colonel. Once the rebels cross the Big Jump, they will be very hard to track down."

"They could pillage and loot and hide among the hills," the earl marshal suggested.

"If they ever take possession of the thermals around the palace, they would have us under siege," the chamberlain muttered.

"Then our numbers would be useless," the chancellor added.

It was amateur soldier time, obviously. The noncombatants wanted the rebels kept well away from Ramo.

"If they do to the army what they did at Podrilt, then we shall have no one left to guard the palace," the king snapped. "And no eagles. In the aeries they at least are safe."

"They will starve within five days," Rolsok said. "And so will we."

Jarkadon drummed his fingers on the desk and chewed his lower lip. The decision must be his. He had not had much experience at the harder side of kingship. If he made the wrong choice, Ninomar realized, then he might not get much more.

"I want to know what they did to those men!" the king growled.

"They were killed by eagles," Rolsok said. "There is too much blood for arrows."

Jarkadon nodded. "So?"

"So—an eagle must attack from above. The rebels must lose altitude crossing the Big Jump. That is the only place where we can be certain of taking their air."

The king snarled again. Then he seemed to reach a decision. He turned to Ninomar.

"You're commanding officer! What do you want to do?"

That was more like it! It was time for the experts to step in—and the astonishment on Rolsok's face was most gratifying. Ninomar considered the problem with professional care. He had almost fourteen thousand men ready to go, incredibly, but that was a grave responsibility—it was not fair to lead them into a battle against an unknown enemy.

"I should like to take counsel with the keeper of the Rand, sire, as he—"

"No!" Jarkadon snapped.

No help there! Suppose he took the army to Rakarr and the rebels did not come? How long could he keep his men in the air? Where would they perch, and what would men and birds eat?

Ninomar straightened his shoulders. "I am of the same opinion as Your Majesty. Keep the birds in the aeries."

"Then I was obviously wrong," the king said. "Launch the army."

Rakarr was a very small mountain, small enough that
men on the top of it could breathe. Leaning into the
wind, Ninomar stood there and surveyed his forces, and
in spite of his tension and deathly weariness, he felt
pride. No general had ever commanded so large an
army: 14,248 men was the official count. A few of the
militia might have found urgent business elsewhere, of
course, but the absence of cowards need not be regret-
ted.

Say fourteen thousand. To hold such a force in military formation was impossible. The air to sunward was
full of wheeling birds and cursing riders, a great column
of specks curving high into the sky with its base close
above the fields and terraces on the sunward side of Rakarr. Those in the best part of the thermal could hold
altitude, but the crowding was continually forcing men to
the edges, where they had to sink and try to fight their
way back in again. Near the base the turbulence of the
cold air coming around from darkward was stirring the
nearer specks in and out and up and down in a pattern
that was visually pleasing but was certainly hell for the
riders. At the top of the thermal, where it curved out far
above the next peak, the birds were barely visible at all.
The men there would be going through another sort of
hell just trying to breathe, and once in a while he would
see one plunge suddenly, heading down to safety—or to
death if the rider did not recover consciousness in
time.

It was a damned nuisance that thermals curved, for
Ninomar's proper post as commander was at the top of
his army. Indeed, he had never doubted that that was
where he would wait for the attack—until Rolsok had
tactfully pointed out that from there he would be unable
to see the enemy, unable to know when to signal, and
probably unable to signal in any case.

Rolsok was a smart young fellow; Ninomar would
have to see that he got a medal for something, afterward.

Cleverly, though, Ninomar had found a way around
the problem. He had set up his headquarters on Rakarr

itself, on one of the many jagged pinnacles that topped it. Here he stood with Rolsok and a small group of aides and, of course, their hooded and tethered mounts. He had ordered tents, too, but time, transportation, and wind had frustrated that idea. Sunward his army waited. The tiny rocky space was flanked on either side by rushing streams of mist pouring through narrow gaps in the fanged ridge to vanish when they saw the sun. Above him stood empty sky, and darkward he could look down on the surging clouds that blanketed the windward side of the peak. Beyond that he had a clear view of the Big Jump and across it to the Rand and Krant and the enemy.

They were coming—or so some of the sharper-eyed youngsters insisted. Ninomar could see nothing himself. Rolsok was certain that there were birds in the thermal over Krant. Half an hour should do it.

Ninomar sent a messenger to the palace.

He stamped his feet, slapped his arms to keep warm, and wished his eyes were not watering so much. He thought he ought to be making light conversation with his companions, acting the confident leader, but he couldn't think of anything to say.

"See any more, Adjutant?" he demanded.

"Not yet, my lord." Rolsok rubbed his eyes. "I suppose it could just be smoke from a brushfire? Or else there must be a hell of a lot of them." He sounded very uneasy.

Ninomar thought of a cheerful subject at last. "Don't look for riders," he said. "The men of Allaban sit in slings like bundles of laundry and let the birds carry them."

There were expressions of polite incredulity all round.

"Oh, it's true! The duke of Foan fought them years ago, and he tells me they were doing it then. I've seen one of their suits with a sling attachment." It was comforting to be able to sound so experienced. "Of course it calls for very good bird training—we must grant them that. But I shouldn't like it. What if the damned fowl sneezed, ha?"

There was appreciative laughter.

"It must make for difficult archery, too, my lord."

"Very," Ninomar agreed. "Never fear—we're going to fill the Big Jump with dead rebels today. The cowboys will be able to walk their herds across on the bodies."

When did he order the attack? The rebels had no options: They would lose altitude in the glide, so they had to enter the updraft below the cloud. Ninomar had no options, either, in truth. His force had to dive out of the sunward thermal and pass directly over his head and down into the Big Jump. It was a problem in calculating speeds. He must not let the rebels into the updraft, so the battle would be fought over the nearer end of the gap itself. There were going to be many men forced to ditch their birds then, and he should have thought to organize recovery teams. But it was too late for that.

His force would be traveling much faster, so the right moment would be about when he could see the rebel birds as clearly as his own. It was simple.

Then Rolsok spoke in a whisper that was somehow worse than a shout. "Ark of God!"

There they were.

At first Ninomar thought there was something wrong with his eyes. Or some sort of freak dust storm?

He turned and looked at his own army. Then he looked back into the Big Jump.

If he had fourteen thousand, then there must be thirty or forty thousand on the other side. He started to shake. It was cold up on this damned peak.

Small wonder that the two hundred had not returned from Podrilt.

They were still coming? The dust cloud was growing thicker. He had not known that there were that many birds in the world.

He could not guess how many there were. Sixty thousand? Eighty? Many, many times more than he had.

"It's a bluff!" he snapped. "There can't be that many men—just a few thousand. The rest are all wilds."

But wilds would attack a man on birdback, and they

were a lot more agile and hard to hit. "The wilds will attack the rebels, too!" he shouted.

"Then why don't they?" Rolsok whispered.

The wilds were escorting the men in slings. Was that why the rebels used slings—because they did not annoy the wilds? How did the rebels get the wilds to follow them, anyway?

Now his eyes could resolve the great cloud of birds into dots, and he could see how those bearing slings had sunk to the lower edge, but they were still higher than he would have expected. And there were yet more dust specks behind. In the name of God, where had they all come from?

He straightened. It was time—if it was not too late.

"Attack!"

Every man jumped from his paralysis. Mirrors were ripped from bindings and turned sunward; to the waiting army, the top of Rakarr must have flickered suddenly in dancing pinpoints of light. And the birds of the Royal Guard began their glide.

Those in the lower part of the column had still to gain altitude, so they continued to circle. To Ninomar, the rest seemed to dwindle in size as they turned head-on.

The higher birds had farther to come, but their dive was steeper, so they would be coming faster. He had not thought of that: Two-thirds of his force was going to pass directly over his head at very much the same moment, and there would be impossible crowding in that tiny patch of sky. Damn, but there had been no time to plan all this properly!

He looked back into the Big Jump. The first ranks were close enough to be obviously eagles, but the dust cloud behind was still growing thicker—they were still coming, a bee swarm of eagles. Two hundred thousand? Four? He could not even guess—the odds were hopeless. Where had they all come from?

The others around him were thinking the same. "If every man gets a bird with every arrow. . ." a voice said.

There were still not enough arrows in the army.

"Stop that!" Ninomar shouted.

If those unridden birds were going to fight and were not merely camouflage, then Marshal Lord Ninomar was going to lose this battle.

It would be no battle—it would be a massacre.

The sun was darkened. He looked up, and the royal army was there, birds filling the sky, a forest of birds, thousands, some so low that he wanted to duck, packed in the air, hurtling darkward—men yelling and cursing as their neighbors crowded in on them. Here and there he saw some very near misses.

His heart swelled with pride at the sight of his gallant host, this royal army, his army: the skymen, the lords of the air!

Brave lads! Many of you will die today, he thought, and I am sending you into a very unfair fight. But you will do your duty, and I have done my best for you. Now you must do yours for His Majesty.

A solid cloud of eagles poured overhead, all diving at great speed into the wind.

Then something very odd happened.

Every bird raised its feet and ducked its head in a move he had never seen before—*every* bird.

Simultaneously.

Fourteen thousand men screamed in unison.

And the sky was full of blood.

19

IF the palace at Ramo was the most luxurious dwelling place for men in the world, then the royal breeding aeries nearby were the eagles' equivalent. Aurolron had spared no expense or trouble to build and equip and staff them. In spite of his cynicism and his lack of interest, the duke of Foan had been impressed. Even had he truly been expected to inspect, comment, and improve, he could have added nothing to what had already been done and was being done. His banishment had been for other reasons entirely, and he knew that he could do nothing but submit. Rage would be useless.

So the duke threw the breeder out of his luxurious quarters and moved in. He ordered a large supply of good wine, hired three or four limber girls, and proceeded to spend most of his time in bed, drunk or wenching or brooding.

On the first day he received a brief note from the marchioness: The king was very pleased with Elosa, but she was fatigued after her long journey and the doctors had suggested a few days' bed rest. The duke burned the note and called for the next girl.

Days dragged. He had no friends at court, had not shared in the gossip, had been a pariah, his very face evidence of treason. Only loneliness had been his com-

panion since he had left Ninar Foan, and only his sur-
roundings had changed now. Were it not for his rank he
would be in the dungeons, and at least his present
quarters were better than that.

He endured. Mostly he mulled over his own mistakes,
and there seemed to have been many.

Firstly, of course, he should have married Mayala—a
passion like that comes but once in a life, and never in
most. But dukes and princesses required royal permission to marry. Aurolron had refused it and summoned
her. Foan could have resisted, but that would have
placed him between rebels on one side and an outraged
liege on the other—it would have been rebellion itself,
with the state already threatened. So he had submitted.
Had that been loyalty or cowardice?

He had made possible the truce between the king and
Karaman. He had always believed that truce to have
been a triumph. Now he suspected that it had been a
second error.

He should never have married Fannimola. She was a
link which had brought him lands, but little lust and less
love. At that point in his dirge he usually called for a girl.

Elosa? In his darker spells, he counted four when he
got to Elosa. A diamond shines most brightly on black
velvet; even a hard man needs a soft place, a gentleness,
somewhere in his life. He had lost it in Mayala. He had
not found it in Fannimola or on the bleak and rocky
uplands of his fief. He had made Elosa the tenderness at
the core of his being, pandered to every whim—and
somehow he had taken all the softness away from her,
removing the black velvet and leaving only another diamond, hard and sharp and cold. Elosa, my fledgling!

Another bottle.

And Hiando Keep? More than an error—a madness.
But she had sworn that she was pregnant, and the child
had been born at the right time. When the proclamation
of the heir had reached Ninar Foan, he had done his
calculations and then worried no more, remembering
only those few hours they had spent together as being
the zenith of his mortal passage. Oh, Mayala!

But then Fannimola had gone visiting at court. She had always been a grim-faced bitch, but that was nothing compared to what she was like when she had returned. Put the heir apparent next to the scullery brat Rorin, she had said, and only the age difference would let you tell them apart. Explain that to the king and to the people, Your Grace.

Traffic between Ninar Foan and Ramo had become very rare thereafter.

How many errors was that? Five? Usually he was too drunk or drained to count by then.

Vindax's visit? That had been a disastrous error, but not his.

He had withheld the king's letter from Vindax before the hunt and the accident. In hindsight that had been an error but also an honest attempt to do a kindness. It probably would not have made any difference. He could ignore that one.

Five, then, until the sixth. A man should learn and grow and do better, but his mistakes seemed to have become progressively worse.

His sixth error had been his decision in the aerie, when the upstart serf Shadow had called on him to choose between Vindax and Jarkadon. He had been defending Elosa, true. He had ignored Aurolron's verdict, true. But what man of honor could move to place his own by-blow on another man's throne? That had been his reason, had it not? Honor?

Another bottle or another girl, whichever was closer to hand and mouth.

That sixth error had been the worst—ten minutes with Jarkadon had shown him that. As premier noble, having the senior prince alive again, Foan could have turned the wind and put Vindax on the throne. Instead he had abandoned the kingdom to a sadistic despot, an obviously unstable juvenile who dispensed floggings at random and cavorted with underage girls.

Jarkadon probably thought he could seduce Elosa, but her father was certain she would refuse him. The king would be disappointed there.

* * *

After ten days or so of frustration and debauchery, the duke sobered and checked the date. He humbled himself to pen a groveling letter to the king, begging that he might visit the palace for his daughter's coming of age. The reply came again from the marchioness: The king was planning a surprise party for Elosa's birthday; it would be an intimate little affair, reserved for a few friends of about her own age. He was not invited.

He was pleased to hear that she was making friends. He sent her his best wishes by letter but received no reply.

The next day he discovered two things. First, that there were guards at the doors, refusing him both passage and explanation; second, that the aeries were rapidly filling with new birds. His apartment had a good view, and he watched them streaming in at all hours.

It was not hard to guess what was happening, although there had not been a general muster of the skymen in many reigns. He waited hopefully for a summons to help—anything would be better than inaction—but it did not come, and he went back to the girls and the bottles in despair.

He awakened in the middle of the third watch when something passed between his window and the sun. He looked out and saw the eagles rising like smoke—the smoke of a funeral pyre?

The rebels were coming then, certainly. Vindax maybe. Unsure which side he wanted to cheer for, the duke went back to bed with two bottles and no girl.

When he awoke, there was a strange silence. He could see only a handful of birds in the aeries, and the roads were empty. The guards had gone from his door. He shaved and washed and dressed and found some food for himself—there were no servants, even.

Then he walked to the nearest of the aeries. He had a choice of birds—ancient or gravid types, not fit for battle—but finding a saddle and helmet took much longer than did his ensuing flight to the palace.

He was challenged, of course, but when he showed that he was unarmed, he was waved through. He could see only five guards over the whole palace, so evidently Jarkadon believed in betting everything on one roll.

The duke flew in to perch on the lowest level of the great aerie.

He made it with two minutes to spare.

There were no grooms in sight. While he was hooding his bird to undress it, he saw the great transformation take place. He saw the guards' eagles snap their bindings and dive. He saw the guards die. He saw the birds land on the grass below and bite off the harnesses.

He had known the truth about the eagles long before Schagarn, ever since Ukarres had escaped over Dead Man's Pass with news of the rebellion and the plight of the nobles trapped in the palace in Allaban. He knew that the birds' communication was almost instantaneous, and he guessed the truth at once.

What he had just seen happen to five guards had certainly just happened also to the royal army. The rebels had won without losing a man or a bird—Karaman's rapport with the eagles would have been enough, with that trick.

But it would have taken a skyman to think of that one, an unusually alert skyman.

When he had fired that arrow at Shadow, he had missed. That had been the seventh error, and the worst of all.

He went in search of Elosa and could not find her. The palace was rapidly degenerating into madness. There might have been a dozen eagles around when he left the aerie; very soon after, there were a hundred. In another hour, the sky was black with them.

The whole maze of balconies, terraces, gardens, and courtyards was open to the air and now open to the birds. The siege was solid; no man could reach a gate alive. The few covered passages and hallways could hardly contain the frenzied crowds milling through them. The troopers had all gone to battle. The duke knew that none would return.

So there were no guards, no fighters. Many of the enclosed rooms and halls had huge, high windows leading from the courts outside; a few ravening monsters came straight through glass and woodwork, snapping gigantic beaks like scissors. Those died on swords eventually, and the other uncounted thousands outside seemed content to wait before trying such suicidal attacks. Men and women fled to cellars and cupboards and servants' quarters, while the vengeance of the ages descended on the palace of Ramo.

Rocks fell.

The roofs had been built to withstand nothing heavier than sunlight. Some shots went through floors as well, to the levels below. The cannonade echoed continuously, rattling the whole palace complex. More death. More terror.

And the projectiles were not merely rocks. Anything an eagle could find and could lift was used: benches and wheelbarrows and grindstones, small statues from the gardens, chimney pots and butter churns, all falling from an incredible height; even a few headless bodies, which were the worst of all, exploding on impact, but those soon stopped coming, as though an order had been given.

He had to fight his way through service passages and cellars, but eventually he found the government: an ice-white boy cowering at a desk in a big egg-shaped room, surrounded by a dozen or so old men, all shaking and most looking ready to die of fear. From the smell of them, several had lost control of their bodily functions. The lord chancellor, the archbishop, the lord chamberlain, supreme air marshall, ministers of this and that . . .

Foan pushed through them and walked around to stand beside Jarkadon. He folded his arms and waited, and no one spoke.

So he said, "God save King Vindax."

They mumbled it back at him.

He took hold of Jarkadon's hair and twisted his head around. "How were you told to surrender?"

The mad-wide blue eyes stared up at him, and Jarkadon started to scream obscenities. The duke silenced him with a slap.

"I am quite prepared to torture it out of you myself," he said. "What is the signal?"

"We all saw the letters," King Shadow said, and told him.

The duke of Foan found his way through cellars and shattered hallways to the aerie. He climbed up three levels before he found any birds. There were six—and six men of Allaban also, with drawn bows aimed at him as he reached the top of the stairs.

"Want something?" their leader asked. He sounded young, he sounded like a peasant, and his tone was contemptuous. Both he and his men were indistinct against the light shining through the bars behind them, but they were slouching, and their arms trembled as they held the bowstrings. They must be exhausted if they had come from Ninar Foan in eleven days or so.

"I came to release the eagles, as King Vindax commanded."

"You're too late." The man spat at the floor.

It had come to this? "I wish to surrender the palace."

"Who are you?" the man asked, but then he did order his men to lower their weapons.

Foan told him who he was.

"Right!" the peasant said. He raised his hands and signaled to the birds watching on their perch. A few moments passed, then the noise of destruction died away. The rocks had stopped.

"The boss'll be here shortly," the peasant said to the duke. "Go and wait in the courtyard. Move!"

The single throne on a dais at one end of the Great Courtyard faced a vast emptiness; the walls were encrusted with balconies where in happier times the lesser folk would have gathered to watch the important ceremonies below. Here there had been no bombardment or invasion, and that was an awesome tribute to the control that someone held over this horde of wildlife.

The duke walked out and stood in front of the throne and waited, feeling very conscious of the crowded sky above him and his own vulnerability. He had to wait a long time, but then a single bronze circled down and settled on the lip of a balcony at the far end. It lifted one foot and turned to face him. One of his own silvers swooped over and perched on the top of the wall nearby, higher up.

He knew the bronze, and he knew the small male figure sitting in the sling it carried. He thought he would give up everything he had ever owned to have his bow in hand—but he would not have dared to use it.

He started to walk forward.

Shadow stayed in his sling, feet dangling over a long drop.

As soon as Foan was within earshot, Shadow called, "Not you."

The duke shrugged and turned to go, then stopped. In spite of the war and the siege and the death, his own mind was full of thoughts of Elosa—and the kid up there was human, too.

"Shadow? Jarkadon did release your parents. I checked when I arrived."

Shadow looked down at him for a while without expression. He was very pale, as though exhausted or in shock. "I had thought my father would have been in the army."

"I don't know what may have happened recently," Foan said, "because I've been kept away, but when I checked, they were at home under house arrest. So perhaps not."

Shadow nodded. "I flew by Hiando Keep, and their eagles told me they were there. It's too late to make friends, Keeper."

The duke spun on his heel and walked away. He eventually found the lord chamberlain. He dragged him back to the court and then along it until they stood together at

the end, staring up at the kid high above them. Shadow
had moved from the sling to a bench on the balcony and
gone to sleep—they had to shout to waken him.

"I have a proclamation here, from the king," Shadow
called down to them. "You can fill in whatever name you
want; it grants power of regency until the king arrives.
Probably tomorrow."

He tossed down a roll. The duke picked it up and held
it while the lord chamberlain and he read it together.

Proclaim Vindax VII as King of Rantorra.
Proclaim _____ temporary regent.
No one to leave the palace.
The following to be held in chains, awaiting the
king's pleasure:
the usurper Jarkadon,
the duke of Foan,
Elosa, his daughter.

Shadow climbed over the wall as the bronze took hold
of his sling once more. "Got any questions?" he called
down.

"No," the lord chamberlain said.

"I have!" the duke of Foan shouted. "How do you
feel?"

The big bird launched, flapped wildly to gain altitude
as it flew the length of the courtyard, and narrowly
cleared the far wall beside the high mirror. Then it was
gone. IceFire followed.

But the question remained behind, unanswered.

20

"Birds of a feather flock together."
—Very old proverb

So it would end where it had begun. Shadow stood at the side of the throne and stared out at the assembled courtiers of Rantorra. One by one the senior nobles were coming forward to kneel and do homage to Vindax.

They had managed very well, those courtiers. The palace was a devastation, its interiors littered with fallen beams and smashed artwork, with plaster, with fragments of plows and cartwheels and chunks of rock. Throughout the grounds bodies still lay in heaps, especially near the gates. Yet somehow the nobility had rounded up its servants and its finery and dressed itself again in grandeur. The coiffures glittered with jewels, and the brocades and silks and laces shone in a thousand hues from doublets and plumes and sashes. They had painted the face of a corpse.

The balconies were deserted. High in the vault of the sky floated the eagle army, faint as gnats, waiting with endless patience. A single bird sat on the far wall, behind the courtiers: IceFire. She was chatting with the watchers overhead and once in a while would pass a message to Shadow.

Sweat trickled down his ribs and face. His legs trembled with the effort of standing, and he wanted to crawl off to bed for a hectoday. Even NailBiter had been ex-

hausted by that journey, that great sweep along the
Rand, flying three watches out of three, with Shadow
sleeping in the air, grabbing food when he got the chance
as towns and castles fell and the eagles flocked to his
banner. His plan had worked, worked too well: Jarkadon
had fallen into the trap and emptied his aeries.

The inside of Shadow's head was ringing like a tolling
bell in an empty church, echoing back and forth, and the
peals were the words of Karaman: *Do you know what
you're letting loose, lad?*

No, he had not known.

Where it had begun . . . yet it was not the same. Two
hectodays ago that nervous Sald Harl had worried about
his coat of arms, how he looked, how to behave. Now
Shadow still wore his battered flying suit with its cum-
bersome sling—his getaway suit, he called it to himself,
grimly aware that he might need a fast getaway very
soon. In the vertical blaze of sunlight around the throne
he sweltered, and certainly he stank. He had not been
out of that garment since he had left Allaban, and he had
unfastened the front of it as far as he decently could. He
did not care. Nor, seemingly, did the courtiers. No eye
met his. They were not admitting his existence—long
might that last.

There was a new archbishop, holding out the sacred
text as each noble repeated the words of the oath.

The portly duke of Aginna, Sald's old neighbor from
the robing room, came stumping forward to do homage.
Like all those who had preceded him, he looked at
Shadow not at all, and very little at the human wreckage
now occupying the proud throne of Rantorra.

Vindax had survived his journey well. He seemed to
burn with some fierce internal forge. How long could
such a cripple live? How long would he be allowed to
live?

"Explain," IceFire signaled, "why this *BobaSAsa-
neneNOna*?"

If only he were not so weary . . . How to translate *Bo-
baSAsa-neneNOna*? A dance? Three-dimensional ballet?
A romp?

"They are showing," he signed back, "that The-one-with-broken-legs is higher than they are."

No wonder the eagles thought that the human race was mad.

The courtiers had changed. Women outnumbered men by three to two. There were almost no young men. This was a joyous occasion, the throning of a new king. Mourning was not allowed, else that swarm of fireflies would be an army of ants. Husbands, sons, brothers, friends—fourteen thousand had died in the bloodstorm over Rakarr, and unknown hundreds in the bombardment of the palace.

The homage ended, and the last man retired, bowing. Vindax sat for a moment and gazed with satisfaction over the Great Courtyard. He wore royal blue, taken from his brother's wardrobes, and a gold circle shone on his dark hair, but he had made no effort to disguise his injuries. His fingerless hands rested in full view on the arms of the throne, and every senior peer had been required to kiss one of those stumps. The noseless face . . . he was an ape playing king.

The bell in Shadow's echoing head was knelling the words of Eagle Speaker: "She says what would you do?" It had been a reflex. He had been warned. Again and again he had pleaded with the High Ones, but they had been powerless. They could stop the slaughter afterward —once the birds had been released, there had been no more killing, but whenever one had been freed in flight, it had turned on its rider. Perhaps even Karaman had not realized how hotly burned the resentment of a ridden eagle, the gnawing of lifelong ignominy.

"And now," Vindax said, "we must distribute reward. And punishment."

The court took a deep breath.

There had been no way to turn back. Had Shadow faltered, then the eagles would have done it by themselves. He had believed that he could do it better and faster and therefore, he had hoped, with less bloodshed in the end. And so his juggernaut had thundered along the Rand, gathering freed slaves and wilds by the thousands as it came.

"Sald Harl, known as Shadow!"

Shadow yanked his mind back to the present. He stepped to the front of the throne and knelt. Vindax studied him for a moment.

"Know, my people," the king proclaimed, "that in all Rantorra, only one man remained true." Unfair! What chance had the others had of demonstrating loyalty? "Only Shadow was loyal. He made this justice possible; single-handedly he overthrew the usurper." Better that fact not be made public. "We shall reward him as greatly as lies within our power, and he shall have our favor forever."

There was a silence. Then Vindax growled, and Shadow looked up in surprise. "We forgot to think up a suitable title, my friend! I am not used to this king stuff. Duke? No, perhaps we can make you a prince. King of Arms?"

The old man whom Shadow remembered from the dressing room of so long ago came limping forward; he bowed and waited.

Duke of Hiando? Prince Sald? Shadow's skin crawled. It was all a sham now. There were no slaves and no skymen, either. No one could hold a dukedom—today a man's land ran the length of his bowshot. The court itself was about to fade like a puff of dust. To become a noble would be a mockery.

"We can appoint a prince, can we not, King of Arms?" the king asked.

If the old man was disgusted at the thought, it did not show on his craggy features. "Your Majesty is the fount of honor; you may confer any title. Not, I fancy, a royal prince, although you could certainly decree an equivalent precedence."

"Pick a name, Sald," Vindax said.

"Sire . . ." Shadow said, then hesitated. He wanted two things only from Vindax, and a title was not one of them.

The heavy brows scowled. "Well?"

"Shadow," said Shadow.

Surprise showed on the king's face, then a frown, then a royal smile. "Why not? So be it! We name you Prince Shadow and grant you precedence after ourself and our royal mother. We deed you the royal estates of Kragsnar and Schagarn as your fief, to you and your heirs forever. Record it, King of Arms. Arise, Prince Shadow!"

Courtly honors were already history, so it didn't matter. Shadow muttered thanks and stayed where he was.

"I crave a boon, Majesty."

He wanted two things only: a proclamation to free the eagles—and release. The thought of escape to Hiando Keep was a great ache, a haunting, an irresistible yearning.

Vindax scowled. "Later! First the punishment."

Reluctantly and uneasily, Shadow rose and stepped back to the side of the throne.

Now the courtiers saw him; he was the object of dozens of furious glares. They were angry not about the title or the land, probably, but the precedence. Fools!

Vindax leaned back and rubbed his palms. "We shall proceed to justice! Earl Marshal? Bring in the prisoner, Foan."

Shadow cringed and wished he could think of any excuse in the world to leave. He had promised Vindax his revenge, and now it must be delivered. Had he killed so many just for that?

On a chair of state at the side of the dais sat the dowager queen, Mayala: a wraith, a legend. She alone had dressed in black, a plain robe which covered her totally except for hands and head. She wore no jewels or ornaments. Her hair was tied starkly back, partly hidden by a black mantilla, and her face was the same shade of white. She had been the first to pay homage; since then she had sat like a figure of ice, seeming not even to blink, staring over the heads of the crowd. Strangely, a trace of her former beauty showed again. No, it was not quite beauty, but the fading of fear had returned her grace and dignity. Now she slowly turned her face to study the horror on the throne.

The first man in the procession was the executioner, brawny, raven-hooded, bare-chested, carrying a knife and a rapidly cooling branding iron as symbols of his art. Guards followed, and within them the duke of Foan. He had been decked in sackcloth, his hair filled with mud, and he could barely walk under the weight of chains. Thus by law one accused of high treason was required to come to judgment. When he had shuffled to the front of the throne, he was forced down on his knees.

Vindax smiled.

There was no more expression on the duke's face than there was on the queen's, but Shadow was shocked at the sight of him. Yesterday in this same courtyard he had been nobility in defeat; now there was only defeat. How had they stamped on him so quickly?

The queen was studying him, but he had not looked at her.

"Executioner," Vindax said. "Review for us the punishment prescribed for traitors."

Shadow closed his mind to the litany of horrors. The courtiers rippled silently. Rank had its privileges, and freedom from that sort of systematic public demolition was supposedly one of them. And Foan was the premier noble.

The executioner fell silent.

"Barbaric!" Vindax said. "But if that is the law ... We shall see about changing it—someday." The courtiers squirmed in unison. Foan's expression did not change.

High on the wall an eagle spread its wings and then folded them again—IceFire was trying to attract Shadow's attention.

"One-who-came-through-the-dark, there are many-many-many people going through the gates, all bearing kills."

This whole monstrous performance was a charade. The troopers who enforced the law were all dead; when the food ran out, the palace would starve. The servants knew, obviously, and as soon as the king had lifted his blockade, they had loaded up and started to move. While the court hierarchy was standing here watching the king gloat, the understructure of the government, the cooks and the cleaners and the gardeners and the footmen, were heading for safety as fast as their feet would go with whatever their hands could carry. Shadow could think of no reason to stop them. As soon as these bemused aristocrats discovered the truth, they were going to become a mob of ordinary people. Possibly a maddened, out-for-blood mob. He still had his flying army at his beck, so the sooner they made the change, the better. He moved fingers unobtrusively at his waist to acknowledge.

Had Vindax realized that his power rested entirely on Shadow?

Now the executioner had finished; the king licked his lips and addressed the prisoner.

"You are charged with high treason in that, knowing me to be alive, you continued to support the usurper. How do you plead?"

"Guilty," Foan said, and was cuffed by a guard for failing to add the proper form of address.

Vindax looked disappointed. "Do you wish to beg for mercy?" he asked hopefully.

Foan merely shook his head and was struck by the guard on the other side.

This, Shadow reminded himself, was the king's father. But how could a man not beg for mercy when faced with such torments?

"Well, it wouldn't do any good, anyway," Vindax said. "We find you guilty. We sentence you to loss of all titles, ranks, honors, and lands, and then to death as ordained by law. We shall start the first session shortly, I think, as the court is already assembled. Move him over there . . ."

He waved a flipper, and the guards dragged the prisoner off to one side. He fell when they released him, and was unable to rise because of his chains.

The bell in Shadow's empty head tolled again: *You can't turn a straight furrow with a bent plow, lad.* Karaman had seen in Vindax what Shadow had not. Shadow had not dared to dream of a republic, only a better kingdom, and again Karaman had been wiser. *If the soil is fertile.*

"Bring in the prisoner, Elosa Foan," the king said.

The earl marshal dropped to his knees.

"She is dead, sire."

"No!" Vindax roared. "Who killed her? I'll have him flayed. When? How?"

The earl marshal had turned gray with terror. "She took her own life, Your Majesty, some eight days ago."

Obviously the duke had not known that the previous day.

Vindax pounded both arms of the throne without producing any sound. "I wanted her to see what she had done! Why?" He turned his head to look at the prostrate form of the former duke. "Bring him back here!"

The duke was dragged over and lifted to his knees before the throne once more.

"Tell me what happened!" the king ordered.

"Take off these damn chains first!" the duke shouted, and was instantly prostrate again.

There was silence. One of the guards drew back a foot to kick, and Vindax yelled at him to stop. He had already sentenced the man to the worst death he could find; he had no threats left.

"Remove his chains," he growled.

With much clattering, Foan was released. He climbed stiffly to his feet beside the heap of shackles and rubbed his wrists. The last of the skymen, Ukarres had called him. He should be a tragic figure, Shadow thought. Nobility in defeat again, the young hero of Allaban grown gracefully to elder statesman—but the duke of Foan was a flawed hero. Always he had found solutions which served his own purpose or that of his daughter. His motives had never flown quite true. If this was the last of the skymen, then it was time to close the book on them.

"Now talk, traitor!" the king said.

From somewhere that filthy, half-naked figure drew a

pathetic dignity. "I know only what I learned in your jail, boy."

Boy? Son? If Foan confessed to adultery with the queen . . . but he would not do that.

Again the guard raised a fist, and again the king stopped him.

"Which is?"

"That your brother did it. He invited her as guest . . ." The duke's voice began to rise. ". . . and pretended to welcome her. Then he beat her into submission, savagely, brutally. He raped her!"

"Good!" Vindax said, mollified. "What else?"

Foan spoke with contempt. "When she had recovered from the beating, he held a party for her birthday. She did not know what his parties involved. Afterward she was carried back to her quarters. Before the medics arrived, she somehow managed to drag herself over to the window—" His voice cracked, and he fell silent.

"Pity!" Vindax said. "I did not approve of the Lions when they abused innocent victims, but in her case I only regret that they did not leave her for my professionals. Still, they were very inventive amateurs."

Now the duke's face was incandescent with fury; hatred hung in the air like a stink. Yet who should presume to judge Vindax? He would never more know life without pain. He had owned the world: youth, power, health—who could lose all that and not desire revenge?

The courtiers were as silent as a field of rocks.

Vindax had dealt with his father and sister. "Bring in the prisoner Jarkadon!" the king snapped.

The earl marshal prostrated himself.

Foan laughed.

Vindax flushed around the scars on his face.

"You thought that mongrel could survive in a jail in this place?" the duke asked. "I had the cell directly across the passage. Noisy prisons you keep, King Vindax!"

"Who?" the king hissed.

"All sorts of people. Brothers and fathers, I suppose." Contemptuously the duke added, "You'll be pleased to hear that he took a whole watch to die. But indulge yourself: Send for the remains and pass them around."

Vindax almost overbalanced as he turned his head. "Shadow! You promised me my revenge! They have cheated me!"

Now the courtiers were beginning to rustle and stir. Shadow could feel danger rising like vomit, and he was shaking with fatigue and revulsion.

"Cut off that one's head and be done with it, sire," he said. If he did not get Vindax safely out of this place, and quickly, there was going to be more bloodshed.

"No!" the king snarled. He glared at his prisoner. "He will have to suffer enough for three."

Shadow thought: I am not Shadow, Vindax is. Ever since his conception he has been a shadow on the throne of Rantorra, growing and spreading . . . but that was only fatigue scrambling his mind.

"*There is another traitor!*" said a new voice. The queen had risen, and now her tiny form walked slowly across the front of the throne and stood beside the duke. "I plead guilty to high treason also."

The whole court seemed to recoil one step, and Vindax grabbed vainly at the arms of his throne to hold himself steady.

"Silence!" he said.

"I will not be silent!" she shouted, and for so frail a figure she was astonishingly loud. "It was not King Shadow who killed your father, it was Jarkadon. I had to watch that poor man die—I perjured myself at his trial, and that itself is treason!"

Vindax's sigh of relief was quite audible.

"Jarkadon is beyond our reach," he said. "And I don't give a damn about King Shadow. Go and sit down, Mother!"

She put her arm around Foan, who seemed to recoil slightly from her touch.

Once Karaman had seen these two as the ideal romantic couple. Now they were a haggard old pair, and yet Shadow could find little pity for them. He could see nothing noble in their tragedy. They had caused all this trouble by not being honest with themselves and with their children.

"I plead guilty to high treason!" the queen repeated stubbornly. "I shall suffer under the same law as this man does."

Threat? Blackmail?

"By God, if you defy me, then you shall!" the king roared.

Father, sister, brother—now mother?

The queen spoke again, but clearly she was intent on saving Foan, and to speak of Hiando Keep would drag him down with her.

"Then there is another traitor!" she shouted, and raised an arm to point at Shadow. "He is a traitor to his own race! He has freed the eagles!"

There was a pause.

"Some of the eagles," Vindax said.

"Sire!" Shadow protested.

"The queen is right!" the duke shouted. "Without eagles, how can you rule? How will you keep order or collect taxes? How will the nobles receive their rents?"

"Well, Prince?" the king asked.

Everyone was waiting.

Then Shadow realized that they were waiting for him.

"Horses," he said.

Over the rising tumult from the audience the duke shouted, "Nothing tastier than a young foal to an eagle! No more horses . . . How will you cross from one peak to another? On bicycles?"

It was true. Many of the gaps were impassable to men on foot. The First Ones had not settled all of the Range. Shadow had not thought of that—but certainly Karaman had. He had not said so. Would that have held Shadow back from his purpose?

Vindax raised a stump, and the noise died away.

"Well, Prince Shadow?" he said again.

Shadow stepped forward. "You agreed to free the eagles, Your Majesty!"

Vindax hesitated. "We need them! Before we issue that proclamation, we must make a contract with them,

Shadow. They need not be slaves, but we must have mounts."

Betrayal! Shadow was too shocked to speak, too exhausted to think.

The company murmured.

"You can't make a deal with the eagles!" Foan shouted. "You have nothing they want!"

Shadow raised his hands.

"*Seize him!*" the king commanded.

Two burly guards appeared instantly at Shadow's side, gripping his arms so tightly that his feet almost left the ground, keeping him from putting his hands together to signal. They must have been forewarned. He squirmed helplessly.

The courtiers fell totally silent. Now they knew the stakes.

"Shadow, my friend," Vindax said sadly. "Prince Shadow? I owe you everything, but without the birds I have nothing. You must make me a treaty with the eagles."

Could he? True, he had nothing to offer that they would want, but they were loyal. As utterly loyal to their friends as they were to their mates, Karaman said. He, Shadow, was a hero to them now. He could impose on that friendship perhaps. For his sake they might agree to supply transportation.

Yet that would be a corruption of friendship, a breach of trust, a usurpation.

Why should he?

Whose side was he on?

Prince or commoner?

He struggled to drive a brain choked with a sludge of fatigue and shattered loyalties. He tried to see this as the birds would see it, in their strangely inhuman thinking—and suddenly he knew what they were seeing at the moment.

"Majesty!" he shouted. "Release me! The eagles—"

It was too late. To a sound like the smashing of melons, Sald's arms were wrenched almost from their sockets, pulling him back and throwing him to the ground.

Half stunned, dazed, he lay for a moment, watching the wheeling specks in the bright sky, dimly aware of mass screaming echoing from walls as the crowds fled to the doors. Gradually the noise died away and there was peaceful silence.

He wanted to stay there forever.

Then he realized that he was lying between two twitching bodies and that his face had been spattered with something wet. He put a hand to his face; it came away red. The bodies had no heads. Shuddering and nauseated, he clambered to his feet. He was alone in the Great Courtyard. Two cast balls?

No, three. The back of the throne was dripping with blood and brains above the huddled corpse of King Vindax.

Shadow was too weary to weep.

"Good-bye, my prince," he said. "Fate dealt you a mean hand."

He paused, almost as though there should be an answer.

After a moment he added, "You must have known! You knew that there could be no kingdom without the eagles. You let me smash it so your brother could not have it. Then you wanted me to put it all back together for you!"

He choked back an angry sob, and the silence returned. He glanced around that great empty solitude and looked back at the corpse.

"You always wanted too much, Prince. You wanted to be a good king of Rantorra. That is not a possibility. It never was."

He turned and walked away, and the courtyard was empty.

Sald dragged his feet along corridors still cluttered with debris and came at last to a balcony. Blinking in the sunlight, he could see one distant gate. People were streaming through it, many carrying bundles on their heads. He raised his hands and signed to the sky.

There were two bodies still lying there, and one had a golden chain around its neck. He helped himself to it: salary arrears.

Momentarily the sun darkened as NailBiter landed on the balustrade and fixed his unchanging remorseless glare on Sald.

Had the eagles been able to look at people in any other way, he thought, then they might have been accepted as sentient right from the First Times. He could read the comb, though, and he saw the excitement.

"The High Ones speak," NailBiter said. "You have a new name. You are The-one-who-led-us-out-of-the-dark. Also you are Friend-of-eagles." That was Karaman's title, too. Yet "friend" was a poor translation—it meant much more to an eagle.

"Thank the High Ones for me," Sald signed wearily. Honors? He had had his fill of honors. The gold chain would be useful.

"Your nest and your mate and your chicks will be guarded and cherished," NailBiter said almost too fast to read. He rocked slightly.

"Have you also been given an honor?" Sald asked.

NailBiter's comb darkened. "I have a new name, too. I am Friend-of-Friend-of-eagles. But all kills are your kill."

"Tell the High Ones that the greatest kill they can give me is that there be no fighting between men and eagles. We shall have to free the aeries of the Range as we did those of the Rand—The-one-with-broken-legs was not going to help, and the others here will not." But there could not be many birds left now to free.

The message was passed.

"And," Sald signaled, "I am proud to be a friend of Friend-of-Friend-of-eagles."

NailBiter's head cocked slightly to one side, which indicated laughter. "I am proud," he signed, "to be a friend of a friend of Friend-of-Friend-of-eagles."

With his juvenile humor he would keep the game going until it reached eight and he lost count.

Sald cut it off. "Me, also."

"We go now?" NailBiter asked.

"Yes," Sald said, his weariness settling over him like all the ice on the High Road. "Let us go to the nest of my parents. You know the way."

"I know it. You will remain there for many-many kills?"

"Yes." There was nowhere else to go. He could send out his army from there to deal with the other aeries. The eagles would protect Hiando Keep if the neighbors and the countryside sought revenge, and surely his parents and his sisters would welcome him, traitor though he was. There was no one else he could trust except the birds. *He who ever trusts a bird . . .*

But NailBiter was still chatty. "There is a good aerie at the nest of your parents."

Oh, so that was it.

"My mate is making an egg."

Sald felt his face smile, and it was an unfamiliar sensation. *Big mutt!*

"My parents and I shall soar very high if you and your mate make your nest there. Let us go and see about it. I may have a quiet time while we fly." He would sleep the whole way; his eyelids were drooping already.

He walked over and turned his back, and the great beak picked up the sling. He was lifted over the balustrade and then up into the sky. As they circled once over the palace, he saw that fighting had broken out already in the Great Courtyard, rival factions struggling for the throne. What good would it do them?

Higher and higher he floated in the hot thermal. Now the palace was a mere scribble on its rocky spur, its inhabitants shrunk from sight. He could imagine that it was deserted, given over to wind and sun, fallen already into ruin as it would soon be in truth: a historical curiosity, a disused relic of the fallen kingdom of Rantorra where nothing moved except the shadows of birds.

IceFire had appeared alongside, and they were floating up over the tops of sunlit hills. There, too, was change. A few hours earlier Sald had seen the peasants at their work; now they were standing in groups and talking. The word would spread.

Republic? Democracy? He did not think so, although doubtless Karaman would send his missionaries. Every peak would be a kingdom to itself, many tyrannies instead of one, wars and battles. The big men would rule now.

His eyes were blurring with fatigue, but when he raised his face to the sunlit hills, he saw that he had an escort: tens of thousands. And perhaps he did not feel so bad.

All the heavens were full of eagles, flying free.

GLOSSARY

AIR: The composition of the atmosphere is not known, but it probably contains less oxygen and more carbon dioxide than standard (terrestrial) atmosphere. This is normal for planets without oceans or with plant life restricted to small areas.

BICYCLE: One of the great inventions of the human mind. Almost no culture has ever regressed far enough to lose the bicycle.

BIRD: Usually an eagle, but also used for a whole family of flying creatures similar to terrestrial birds.

CAWKING TIME: Pairing or mating time (falconry term).

COLD WIND: The steady surface wind flowing from dark pole to hot pole. The temperature is relative: Where the flow falls off the Rand (*qv*), the drop causes adiabatic warming.

COVER: A flier positioned above and behind another as protection from attack by wilds.

DAY: An artificial human division of time, apparently close to a terrestrial day in length. The world is gravitationally locked on its primary, rotating once in a year. The presence of life and of crustal differentiation (see *Rand*) suggests that at one time the world had oceans. Possibly, therefore, it did rotate, even if very slowly, and meteor impact or, more probably, tidal drag stopped this rotation in remote times; an alternative explanation would be that the sun had a binary companion now lost or too far cooled to be effective in warming the Darkside.

EAGLE: The dominant life form of the world, resembling a terrestrial eagle, but of greater size and intelligence and having an eight-pointed comb.

FEAK: To clean a beak by rubbing it on the perch (falconry term).

GOAT: A rock-dwelling mammal. Like many other species of plant and animal named in the text, the goat may be either a terrestrial import or a local form of similar appearance. Human settlers anywhere tend to use familiar names whenever possible: for example, the North American "buffalo."

HIGH RAND: Probably mountains standing high on the continental crust, and very high above the oceanic crust of the plains. (See *Rand*.)

HOT WIND: The high-altitude return of air from hot pole to dark pole. Note that the descent of this air over the dark pole warms it: The coldest part of the world is just darkward from the terminator, where water is precipitated. (See *Ice*.)

ICE: Almost all the free water of the world is locked up in vast ice sheets on the dark hemisphere. Geothermal heat keeps the base of the ice plastic; slow flowage and local continental drift move enough of this ice to the terminator to provide a very minor circulation of water in local areas of the world, as in Rantorra, and thus permit life to continue.

MUTES: Bird droppings (falconry term).

PLAINS: Flat, low-lying area of oceanic crust, equivalent to the abyssal plains of Earth. Atmospheric pressure is too great for humans. (See *Air*.) On the dark hemisphere, of course, the plains are buried in ice.

RAND: In terrestrial terms, the continental slope. On Earth the slopes are smoothed by a cover of sediment; on this world they retain their block-faulted ruggedness. Vertical relief is obviously extreme, perhaps even greater than on Earth, where it can reach several miles: for example, between the Andes mountains and the floor of the Pacific. The continental surfaces lie above breathable atmosphere for mankind, partly because air has replaced water within the ocean basins, but perhaps also because of a less favorable atmospheric composition than the terrestrial standard. (See *Air*.)

RANGE: In terrestrial terms, a volcanic island arc marking the edge of a crustal plate, such as the Aleutians or Antilles. In the absence of oceans, the whole ridge is exposed.

RED AIR: Skyman term for conditions of very high pressure at low elevations. Carbon dioxide or nitrogen poisoning is indicated. (See *Air*.)

SHEAR ZONE: The interface between the cold wind flowing sunward and the overlying hot wind returning; a zone of great turbulence and electrical activity.

SINGLE: A paired bird separated from its mate, to which it will attempt to return.

SPARE: A paired bird accompanying its mate without a rider and hence able to carry small loads.

STOOP: To dive in attack (falconry term).

TAKING (HIS) AIR: To be above (him) (falconry term).

TERMINATOR: The boundary between light and dark hemispheres. Life is impossible elsewhere on the planet, and human life also requires favorable elevations.

THERMAL: A plume of relatively warm air ascending from a sun-warmed surface. The prevailing (cold) wind bends the column sunward.

THIRD WATCH: The final watch of the day, reserved for sleeping.

TWO BELLS: Start of the third watch.

UPDRAFT: A skyman term for wind moving upward over a surface elevation, but at times also including thermals (*qv*).

WATCH: One-third of a day, or eight hours, signaled in major population areas by a bell.

WILD: An undomesticated eagle.

WORLD: The world of the story is never named in the text and has not been identified with any known inhabited planet, although much effort has been spent in searching for it. It was apparently settled in the First Diaspora. The tale of Shadow has been found in many forms in early literature throughout the Galaxy and must therefore date from early in the Second Diaspora, when settled planets were first reestablishing interstellar communication. Its wide distribution suggests that it enjoyed much popularity at that time, perhaps due to a morbid fascination with the problem of cultural regression, which was a very real risk for settlers of inhospitable worlds. The earliest known version is found in the Sirian Sector in a very primitive inflected language descended from one of the many Indo-European tongues of Earth.

ABOUT THE AUTHOR

DAVE DUNCAN was born in Scotland in 1933 and educated at Dundee High School and the University of St. Andrews. He moved to Western Canada in 1955 and has lived in Calgary ever since. He is married, with three grown-up children.

When a career in petroleum geology began to pall after thirty years, he turned his hand to writing, thinking it would make an interesting hobby. Less than two years later, he had sold two novels and switched to writing full time.